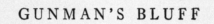

GUNMAN'S BLUFF

GUNMAN'S BLUFF

BY

EDGAR WALLACE

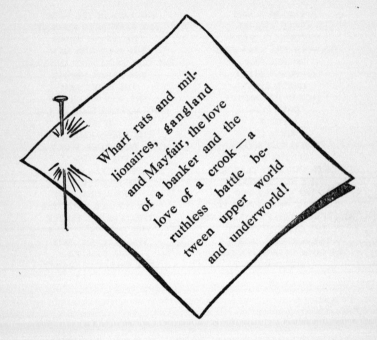

Wharf rats and millionaires, gangland and Mayfair, the love of a banker and the love of a crook—a ruthless battle between upper world and underworld!

PUBLISHED FOR

THE CRIME CLUB, INC.

BY DOUBLEDAY, DORAN & COMPANY, INC.

GARDEN CITY, NEW YORK, 1929

GUNMAN'S BLUFF

CHAPTER I

"BUT you *are* going to marry him, Peggy?"

There was an agitation in the voice of Rex Leferre that almost startled his sister: it certainly diverted for the moment the resentment that was growing toward her unpunctual fiancé.

"What makes you say that?" she asked. "Does it mean that I am breaking off my engagement because Luke is a bad host and has kept us waiting ten minutes?"

They were in the palm court of the Carlton, and the remainder of the guests, mercifully occupied with their cocktails and gossip, were apparently unaware of Luke's bad manners.

She stood apart with the young man who was her only relation, and no stranger seeing them would imagine them to be brother and sister. Rex was red haired, weak chinned, a fretful young man with a nervous trick of adjusting his dress tie every few minutes.

Margaret Leferre had the carriage and poise of the great lady. She was fair skinned, faultless of feature, gray eyed—a model of cold dignity. She had never succumbed to the fashion in short hair: her own was braided about her head so that she seemed to be wearing a coronet of dull gold.

"I don't know." Rex was nibbling at his nails; he could not be cured of this ugly habit. "Only Luke is a good fellow—in a way. Rather a tightwad."

"What is a tightwad?" she asked, her steady eyes on him.

"Well—I mean—he's not terribly generous with his own money. He gives tips and things, but somehow I've never been able to get into the market in time to benefit. My own fault, of course."

He tried to avoid her gaze, but she was the stronger character.

"Have you been borrowing money again?" she asked, and he wriggled uncomfortably.

"No—what rot! Only Danty and I had a scheme . . ."

She looked round at that moment. Somehow she knew that the dark-eyed Danton Morell was watching them. Danton was rather a dear and she had come to rely upon him. He seemed to sense her trouble now, and detaching himself from the group of which he was a silent member, made his way toward her.

"Oh, shut up, Peggy. Don't talk to Morell about it. If you're going to make a scene . . ."

With a shrug he turned and left her as Danty came up.

Danty, that splendid man of the world, was amused at her fears. He was on the borderline of forty, a handsome, entertaining bachelor, and she had come to know him through Rex.

"No, I don't think he has been borrowing. Rex is an improvident devil who will be broke for the next ten years. Then he will settle down and be terribly successful. Your young man is rather late."

She knew instinctively that he did not like Luke Maddison; she had always known this. Luke, she told herself, was rather a prig in his way. He was "county"—was related to or friendly with almost every great family in England. Only once had he spoken disparagingly of Danton.

"Where did *he* spring from? I've never heard of him before," he asked.

She might have told him that Danton had spent the greater part of his life in the Argentine, but she had stiffened at the disparagement of her brother's friend—and hers. And then Luke had made it worse.

"He's a rum bird. I shouldn't be surprised if he was one of those light-fingered fellows who are known to the police—if one only made inquiries."

"You had better make inquiries," she said icily.

This was before she had taken the plunge and had sent an ecstatic Luke Maddison to his house walking on air.

As she listened to Danton she was looking absently at the solitaire diamond ring which was the outward and visible sign of her engagement.

". . . Rex is volatile and a bit unstable—sometimes there is nothing too bad he can say about Maddison. Sometimes nothing too good. Hullo, here's our blessed host!"

Luke Maddison came through the vestibule with long strides. He paused to strip his overcoat and take off his silk hat, which he almost threw at an attendant, and took one step toward the door. As he did so his foot slipped sideways on the marble floor and he would have fallen unpleasantly but for the hand that suddenly gripped his arm.

The man who held him must have been unusually strong, for he literally, and in the most effortless fashion, lifted Luke Maddison bodily and placed him on his feet. Luke turned with a half smile of dismay and found himself looking into a hard, lined face, the colour of teak; into two unsmiling eyes, expressionless.

"Thank you—awfully!"

The stranger nodded.

"It might have been a very nasty fall. I'm greatly obliged to you!"

"Not at all," said the unknown.

He was in evening kit, a perfectly fitted man; you saw the ghost of an efficient valet behind him. Maddison saw lines in the face which were not entirely nature's handiwork. He could not know that the two scars which disfigured the right cheek of his helper were souvenirs of an encounter with the late Lew Selinski of New York City. Lew used a knife when he was annoyed and he had been very annoyed with the well-dressed man when he had left his mark upon his enemy's face.

"I am glad I was here. Fortunately, I always wait in the lobby when I am expecting people to dinner. Good-night."

He half turned away as though he objected to the attention he had called to himself, and Luke went in to his party full of apologies.

Two lives touched at the Carlton that January night —touched and went looping away one from the other, to touch again in a moment of crisis. Rough roads they were: a bitter, heart-aching road for one, a methodical hell for the less favoured, to be tramped with that cynical smile with which "Gunner" Haynes met every misfortune.

Luke Maddison saw life like that—a bewildering mass of crossing and parallel paths. If he fell into error it was in believing that his own was the straight-as-a-ruler highway to which and from which all other paths inclined or diverged.

Eight generations of gentlemen bankers, all gently bred and belonging to the class which produces statesmen and commanders by divine right of appointment, were responsible for his wealth and his six feet of good-looking humanity. He was fair, blue eyed, straight of back, in his happier moments irresponsible. He was extravagant, a free spender of money and an idealist, which means that he was spendthrift of the material which keeps men in the City solid and comfortable. Something of a gambler, he took chances at which his more conservative friends might shudder. Yet, as somebody said, "With half a million of gilt-edged securities on deposit, who could not gamble to a ten per cent. margin?"

Gunner Haynes, whose strong arm had saved him from a fractured wrist or worse, had no collateral worth speaking about. His principal assets were an immaculate dress suit, a cultured voice, and perfect manners, which more than overcame the handicap represented by his lean, dark, sinister face. He lived God knew where, but was to be seen at such of the best hotels as did not know him for an expert jewel thief.

They called him "Gunner" because of certain happenings in New York City. It was said, but never proved, that he was the man who bumped off Lew Selinski, that notorious gang leader, and shot his way through Lew's gunmen to the safety represented by a cattle boat which sailed from the Hudson River an hour after the police reserves answered a riot call.

Nobody had ever seen him with a pistol in England; but the detectives who arrested him a year after his return to his native land fully expected gun play and came armed.

When he came up for trial, nobody came near him: not his pretty wife or his best friend Larry Vinman. Larry was a prince of confidence men, young, good-looking, plausible.

There might be excellent reason why Larry should not wish to draw attention to himself by appearing in court; no reason why Millie should not write or do something. She had a thousand pounds in hard cash; a good lawyer could have been briefed; but when the Gunner sent for her, she had left the lodging they had occupied.

He never saw her again. A few months before his release from prison he heard that she had died in a workhouse infirmary.

The Gunner's smile when he heard this was a grim one. He always smiled when he was hurt—and as he smiled now, his heart was one great throbbing wound.

So he came from prison, and in due course to the Carlton Hotel, where Mr. Luke Maddison was celebrating his engagement. Of Luke he knew nothing—what had brought him there was a jewel box which a rich American lady kept in the hotel safe all day and in her bedroom between 9 P. M. and 1 A. M. Gunner Haynes had taken a room on the same floor.

"I really am at your feet and prostrate," said Luke, not for the first time in the course of the dinner. "The truth is, my car hit a taxicab sideways—it was the cabby's fault—and up came an officious Robert and must take down all particulars very laboriously in his little book! Why don't they teach policemen to write shorthand?"

"My dear, it doesn't matter—really."

Margaret's voice was a little weary. Everything and everybody was going wrong to-night. Even Danty was distressed about something and was not his usual self. Luke was late; he had made an acrobatic entrance, performing wild gyrations in the arms of a strange gentleman. What had upset Danty? She had seen his face turn a sickly white when Luke came in. Rex was grumpy and silent, scarcely speaking to Lady Revellson on his left. And Luke had insisted on sitting next to her, after she had arranged the table, with the result that everybody at the table was in his or her wrong place.

"If that fellow hadn't been on the spot I should certainly have broken something—I couldn't possibly have saved myself. It has been trying to snow and I must have got some caked on the sole of my shoe—I walked the last hundred yards or so. The car was caught in a traffic jam in Piccadilly Circus. . . ."

"What was he like—in appearance?"

Danton's voice sounded a little hoarse, as though he were speaking from a dry throat.

"Who—the man who held me up?" And when the other nodded Luke went on: "A dark-looking fellow— I thought he might be a German—two scars across his right cheek—the sort of wound that duelling students love to acquire. I remember when I was at school in Bonn . . ."

Danton was not listening now. Two scars across the right cheek! Then he had not been mistaken. The question was, had the Gunner recognized him? It was seven years since they had met—Danton had been clean shaven and rather towheaded in those days. Millie Haynes used to call him "the gold-hair boy" in the days of her fascination. He had grown a moustache and darkened his hair down since then—he no longer filled the police description of Larry Vinman. He made the change long after he had thrown over Millie and left her to drift to a workhouse infirmary. It had been rendered necessary by the success of a trick which had left an Australian

squatter poorer by eight thousand pounds, and the sub-
sequent activities of Scotland Yard's confidence squad.

Gunner Haynes! He breathed a little faster. Down
his back ran a cold shiver of apprehension. Suppose he
had recognized his old friend; suppose he packed a gun,
suppose he was waiting out there in the lobby . . .

Danty wiped his moist forehead, caught the eye of
his hostess, and, with an appealing glance for permission, left his seat.

"Just remember I had to telephone," he mumbled as
he passed her.

He went down the broad steps into the palm court.
The Gunner was not there. He crossed the court into the
lobby—empty. There were two lobbies, one in Haymarket, the other in Pall Mall. They were connected
by a passage, and down this he went silently.

As he came to the second vestibule he saw his man
and drew back. Gunner was stepping into the elevator
and his back was half turned to the watcher.

It was he; there was no question of it. Gunner
Haynes! The lift door closed on him. Danton looked
around. He recognized the quiet-looking gentleman
who was lounging by the revolving door.

"You're the hotel detective, aren't you?" he asked.

(When Danty Morell was plain Larry Vinman he
knew most hotel detectives by sight and could guess the
others.)

"Yes, sir—anything wrong?"

"Who was that man?"

The detective told him. It was one of the assumed

names that the Gunner invariably used, and the heart of Mr. Morell leaped.

"Like hell he is! Number 986 is his room, eh? He's Gunner Haynes and he's after jewellery. Get Scotland Yard—they'll check him up in a second. But my name doesn't come into this, do you understand?"

He left the man busy at the telephone exchange and went back to the party, exulting.

It was too good a secret to be kept. Moreover, he loved an audience; he had the table's breathless attention for five minutes.

"He's got a room here, mumber 986. I know the fellow rather well—I was very friendly with the district attorney in New York and he showed me his portrait. One of the most dangerous men in New York—a gunman. I hope there is no trouble. I recognized him as soon as I saw him, but I had to go out and make sure."

"What have you done?"

Luke's face was troubled. He was on the soft side, as Danty knew.

"Naturally I put the hotel detective on his track— I left him 'phoning the Yard."

Luke Maddison fetched a long sigh.

"Poor devil!" he said.

Margaret shook her head at Danty helplessly.

"You've spoiled Luke's evening," she said, and her fiancé winced at the mild sarcasm.

"Not a bit, only—will you excuse me?"

He was gone before the astonished girl could protest.

"How like Luke—and how everything fits into the scheme of this wretched evening!" she said.

"Where has he gone?" Danty was momentarily alarmed.

She shrugged milky shoulders.

"What does one do? Bail him out? Give him money for his breakfast—something horribly philanthropic," she said.

Luke went straight to the second vestibule and into the elevator.

"Where is number 986?" he asked, as the lift went up.

The attendant stopped the lift on the fourth floor and pointed to the door. For a second only did Luke Maddison hesitate, the door handle in his grasp, and then he turned and walked into the room.

The occupant of the room was standing by the window, his back to the visitor.

"Well, sir?"

He did not look round, and Luke realized that he was being viewed through the medium of a mirror which was fixed on a bureau in an angle of the wall.

Luke closed the door behind him.

"If you're Gunner Haynes, I advise you to clear out," he said in a low voice. "If you're not, I owe you an apology."

Haynes swung round at the mention of his name.

"Oh!" he said. A pause, and then: "I am greatly obliged to you."

"Have you any money?"

Another pause.

"Yes—I have all the money I want. Thank you."

The Gunner was smiling, his underlip pouted. Something had amused him in his secretive way.

"Thank you—I think I understand. I wasn't quite sure if it was Larry. After big pickings, eh?"

All this was Greek to Maddison. He saw the Gunner pick up an overcoat from the footrail of the bed, and then the door was thrown open and a big man strode in, followed by two others. There was authority in his voice.

"Hullo, Gunner!"

The Gunner nodded.

" 'Lo, Sparrow—you carry your age very well!"

The big man chuckled.

"Don't I?" His hands passed quickly round the hips of his prisoner. "Got a gat?" he asked, in the friendliest way.

"No, sir." The Gunner was still smiling. "The legend that I carry a lethal weapon dies very hard. My condition of disarmament would earn three hearty cheers from the League of Nations."

The big detective snapped handcuffs on his quarry; then he looked shrewdly at Luke.

"This man hasn't anything belonging to you, Mr. Maddison?" he asked.

Luke was staggered to discover that he was known.

"No—I am sorry to say," he said.

"Mr. Maddison—I'll remember that name," said

the Gunner, and gave a friendly nod to Luke as they hustled him from the room.

"Poor devil!" said Luke Maddison for the second time that night, and went back to his party.

This time Margaret Leferre did not accept his apologies, and when he told her where he had been, her face grew as white as Danty Morell's.

It was fully three weeks before that little rift was closed.

CHAPTER II

THE storm that swept on London found at least two people unprepared. Luke Maddison was cheery. He had been formally forgiven—the marriage was to be quiet, and only a few guests were to be invited. He had only a few minutes before arranged his train reservations—no secretary should perform that sacred duty!

His heart would have sung a gay song even if every thick flake of snow burned as it touched his face. The flower girl shifted the strap of her basket from one shoulder to another and gazed with dismay upon the tumbling white fog that descended upon St. James's Street, blotting out every landmark. You could not see from one side of the street to the other. Almost instantly the ground was thick where the white flakes lay. But for their asthmatic engines one would not have known that such things as motor busses were passing.

Snow covered the violets in her basket, soaked into the thin shawl about her shoulders, and even when she sought shelter in the doorway of a bank, followed her in gusty showers.

Two men brushed past her into the bank. She offered a bunch of flowers automatically. The younger of the two did not notice her; the middle-aged man with the trim moustache gave her a quick, appraising glance and stopped.

"Hullo, honey—busy?"

She did not reply. He hesitated a moment, and then the door swung open and the impatient voice of the young man called him inside.

At that moment Luke Maddison came striding down the street, swinging a light cane. He wore no overcoat and his shoulders already carried a white blanketting.

Out of the corner of his eye he saw the girl shivering in the doorway, checked his stride and came up to her.

"My dear, you look cold! My heart keeps me terribly warm—and if you think I am making love to you, I'm not! I want a flower, and you shall have a present, and then you and I will drift away and we shall be dead to one another—born and dead in this freezy moment! Buy a wreath!"

He took a banknote out of his pocket and dangled it before her eyes laughingly. And then he had a slight shock.

She was pretty—which flower girls, outside of musical comedy, are not; her figure was frail, her skin flawless.

Yet she was poorly dressed; bore in her person all the evidence of penury.

"Here's a better one."

He put the note in his pocket and produced another, scribbled a line or two on the back of it.

"That's the name and address of my company—if,

when you try to change it, the police say that it is stolen, refer them to me."

She did not answer, but looked from the note in her cold hands to its giver. It was for a hundred pounds! When she looked up he was gone.

The swing doors of the bank opened again and the two men came out. She crumpled the note in her hand, dismayed, exhilarated, and, in one respect, disappointed. It was then she saw the young man's face. It was deathly pale and he was breathing quickly—this was noticeable, for the weather was cold.

"By God, that was a horrible coincidence, Danty— suppose he'd come in——"

"Shut up, you fool!"

The elder of the two shot a glance at the flower girl. She was arranging her violets.

"But if he had—— He said he was going out of town before the settlement."

He was trembling violently: the flower girl might have seen that if she were observant. Danty's dark eyes roved the streets for a taxi; they rested momentarily on the flower girl. She was pretty, but at the moment her face was vacant. More interested in her flowers than in unintelligible scraps of conversation, he supposed.

"Now see here, Rex, there's nothing to worry about. You could easily explain that Margaret . . ."

His voice sank to an indistinguishable mutter of sound. The girl heard the word "settlement" used several times, and "carry over" and "account." Also "Margaret" was mentioned twice, and "Luke."

". . . fix it, don't worry!" Danty patted the other on the back. She decided that she did not like "Danty." "Here's a cab!"

The younger man signalled and sprinted out to the taxi. The other went at a more leisurely pace. He dropped something onto her flowers—a visiting card.

"Come along about nine and have a drink," he murmured.

She took the card before his eyes, glanced at the name and deliberately tore it up.

He was rather annoyed when he joined his companion.

"Mr. Danton Morell, 907 Half Moon Street," she read. It was a name to remember.

And then she saw a huge figure loom out of the mist of swirling flakes, and instinctively knew that he was going to speak to her. Why she should think this she did not know—he might very well be going into the bank.

He was big in every way. Until he ranged alongside her, his height did not seem extraordinary. Till his length was gauged, the breadth of his shoulders was not remarkable. He stood six feet four in his stockinged feet. His face was dark and broad and unattractive; he had a short, bull neck and a deep, rich, husky voice.

He walked slowly, almost lethargically, through the snow, his hands behind him, his hard felt hat on the back of his head, the ragged cigar, that was burning unevenly, gripped in his teeth.

The flower girl thought he was going to turn into

the bank after all : instead, he stood squarely before her and looked down at her. The expression in those slits of eyes was blank. He might have his attention entirely absorbed by her; he might be trying to remember something.

And then he spoke huskily.

"You're no child of the poor!"

There was something so friendly, so good-humoured in his voice, that she laughed.

"Nor a wrongdoer either," she said demurely, and his big face folded into a delighted smile.

"You're nearly the first that ever gave me the right answer," he said. "Now I'll ask you another : Where in the City of London is that text carved in stone ?"

The flower girl was almost scornful.

"Why, over the entrance of the Old Bailey—'Protect the Children of the Poor and Punish the Wrongdoer.' "

He nodded.

"You've won a butter cooler, but you can have your pick of the board. Keepin' to the general knowledge paper, who and what am I ? For the correct answer you get a pint of peanuts and free admission to the Zoo."

She looked at him with a certain demure solemnity that delighted him.

"You are Detective Inspector Horace Bird—you are called 'The Sparrow.' "

He doubled forward and his face went purple with silent laughter.

"You're free of the fair! Now let me do a little bit of classy detective work, like the well-known Mr. What's-his-name of Baker Street. Your name is Mary Bolford, you're a reporter on the staff of the *Daily Post-Herald,* and you're doing a stunt called 'A day in the life of a flower girl.' Don't deny it! Your editor pointed you out an hour ago an' asked me to keep an eye on you. How's that for deduction? Come and have some tea and I'll tell you the story of my life."

He shifted his cigar to the offside of his face, lifted the strap of the basket from her shoulder, and together they tramped through the slush down St. James's Street. Even in the midst of their own discomforts, pedestrians turned their heads to look back after the enormous man with a basket of violets under his arm.

"I bet you'll suffer for this," he rumbled. "Wet through—no? I hope you are wearing warm undies. Why are undies indelicate and sable coats ladylike? Ask me. It's one of the mysteries. Good-afternoon, Tom." He stopped a man who was trying to pass him quickly, his head bent as though to avoid the drift of wind-borne snow.

"Good-mornin', Mr. Bird—cold, isn't it?"

"It's colder waitin' outside the staff entrance of Hoyce & Drake, Tom. Pretty girl, eh, Tom? I'll bet your wife wouldn't think so. Don't do it, Tom, or I'll come along and blind you! So-long!"

"Horrific!" she murmured as the man hurried away.

"I have to be," he said complacently. "It's the only

language they understand. What's that word again—
horrific? That's a good one. Go straight in, Miss Bolford."

They turned into the tea shop and Mary Bolford
smelt the warmth and hot-cakeness of the place and
sighed luxuriously.

"Order anything you like up to fourpence," said the
Sparrow. "I've only just had lunch, so you'll excuse me
if I stop at the tenth mince pie."

He seemed to pay no attention to the rest of the
people in the long tea room, and yet——

"That feller over there in the corner is Sam Larber,
the con man. Times are bad and suckers are scarce.
There ought to be a cold weather fund for confidence
men. It takes sunshine to bring out human foolishness.
That girl who's with him is Lisa Keane—*she's* no Sister
of Mercy! See that red-haired young feller who's hidin'
behind the newspaper? I got him nine months at the
London Sessions for knockin' off motor cars—'knockin'
off' means 'pinchin' '—excuse my French."

"What do you think of this?"

She unfolded a piece of crinkly paper and spread it
on the marble top of the tea table.

"I don't think of hundred-pound notes—I dream of
'em," he said, and added, in his inconsequential way:
"That's because he's goin' to be married. I saw him
holdin' it up before your eyes and thought he was tryin'
to create a good impression. I was a bit hurt. Mr.
Maddison never struck me as bein' a vamp. And then
I suddenly knew what it was all about."

She might be a reporter, but she was feminine.

"Whom is he marrying?" she asked.

"A lady. That was her bother who was talkin' to another gentleman in the doorway. Danty!—*he's* no lady! What Rex loses on the swings he borrows from the roundabouts. The bookmakers have an insurance on his life—they hate the idea of anything happenin' to their annuity. And when he goes into the City all the sharks file their teeth. He's easy money—somebody else's money. Is that libel or slander?"

"Both—if I printed it," she smiled.

The waitress came—she drank the hot tea gratefully. Mr. Bird sat munching cakes with great earnestness. A big plate of confectionery steadily vanished.

"I'm a big man and have to keep my spirits up," he explained. "Mince pies are a kind of dope to me. After I've had a dozen I get sort of intoxicated and all my troubles disappear. After I've had twenty I go mad and tear up the pavement."

Mercifully he stopped at the seventh.

"What am I to do with this hundred pounds?" she asked. "I feel that I have obtained money by false pretenses!"

"I saw a couple of good evenin' dresses at Cecilia et Cie's," he said. "It's a Modes et Robes shop in Bond Street—and if you ask me why 'Modes et Robes' I'll say 'desist.' There was one dress with spangles on it— wear that an' you'd get a reputation for fastness that'd get you the first prize at Brooklands——"

"Who is Danty?"

She was in a new world; had been in it exactly a quarter of an hour. She went on quickly:

"I know his name—Danton Morell: he gave me his card."

Mr. Bird nodded.

"He would: he's that kind of philanthropist. 'Call round any evenin' when the servants have gone to the pictures.' Danty is clever. I'm one of the few people who know how clever he is. Some day I'll take a stick to him and he'll be in the market for a new head."

And then he began to talk about people—the shifting population of the West End. The men and women who came and went; the mild old gentleman who had a suite at the Cercle Hotel all the year round but spent his time travelling to and from New York playing cards with the light hearted and gullible. Of strange men who did nothing for a living and had no visible means of support yet stayed at the best hotels. He called them "the once-a-year men."

"They go after one coup and that keeps 'em. They're the highest paid tale tellers in the world. Kiplin' and what's-his-name Shaw? They never get the price that's paid to these fellers."

"I suppose you are always getting new experiences?" she said.

Mr. Bird sighed.

"I think I know all that is to be known about the dirty ways of crooks," he said.

But he was wrong.

That night he was called to number 342, Brook

Street. Assisted by the white-faced Mr. Danton Morell, he burst open the door of a bedroom, and there he found Rex Leferre, dead by his own hand. He lay on the floor, a revolver by his side: the quick-eyed Danty saw the note scribbled in pencil on small sheets of paper torn from a telephone message block, and his hand closed over the paper. An hour later Margaret Leferre, pale and lovely in her silken negligee, read the message the detective had not seen.

Margaret darling, I have lost. For months I have been gambling. To-day I took a desperate step on the advice of Luke Maddison. He has led me to ruin—money is his god. I beg of you not to trust him. He has led me from one act of folly to another. God bless you.

REX.

She read the pitiful message again and again. Luke Maddison: the man she was to marry in a week!

CHAPTER III

FOR two days Margaret Leferre moved in a world of hideous unreality. Strange people interviewed her: a tall, big-framed man, who was strangely sympathetic in his heavy way, a bank manager who talked wildly and incomprehensibly until Danty appeared and whisked him off.

One thunderous fact hammered night and day at her weary brain—Rex was dead by his own hand, and the man she was to marry, the man who, frantic with anxiety, was calling three times a day and being refused admission to her, was the cause. Money was his god!

It was hard to adjust her views of him, harder still to comprehend the callous brutality that had sent a young soul wandering into the eternal night.

This engagement of hers had been a thing of natural growth: the families had been friends for years; she had known Luke Maddison since she was a child. There had been no sudden meeting, no violent kindling of a consuming flame—she hardly remembered the time she did not like him, and could not place her finger upon the month and the year when liking was love.

This was the real calamity of her situation if only she could realize it. She remembered now all that Ronnie

24

had said of him—he was a "tightwad." She had always thought Luke was generous to a point of imbecility. But that was the facet he presented to her—men knew better. She set her teeth and brought herself to asking a question of Danty, who had come strangely near to her in these ugly days. Danty shrugged his shoulders.

"I am afraid it is a fact—Maddison thinks too much about money. I saw him the other day, and the only thing he said about Rex was how lucky for everybody it was that Rex was insured."

(Here he spoke the truth, for Luke had referred to the insurance as a protection against the girl being saddled with her brother's debts.)

"He is fanatical on the point. Naturally he doesn't appear that way to you. You are his second obsession." He saw her wince and went on quickly: "That is a horrible thing to say, but it is true—except that I am not so sure that at the moment you aren't the first."

It was after this that her cold hatred of the man whose name she was to bear began to take definite shape. She could not know how much this almost insane resentment owed its growth to the ingenuity of her new counsellor.

Danty was clever—diabolically ingenious. He thought quickly, planned quickly, acted as he planned. The idea came to him on the night of Rex's death. It seemed too fantastic for accomplishment. He allowed the whirling nebula of it to retain its shapelessness until he had sounded her. If she loved Maddison in the proper way, she would take a view charitable to his intentions; she would indorse, however half-heartedly, the conventional mercy of a coroner's jury and put Rex's letter in the category of his minor derangements. This would have dissolved the nebula of Mr. Morell's plan to nothingness. But he found Margaret in a mood to believe the worst, receptive, indeed eager. And then the nebula solidified into form.

"Money is his god," was his text; he worked harder on that theme than he had ever worked in the days when he lived on the credulity of chance-found strangers. All the tricks of his profession, all the eloquent persuasions which can be best exercised by innuendo rather than bald statement, all the craft of suggestion—they were exercised.

"At the moment, I should imagine he is so keen to marry you that he would sacrifice every penny he has. I honestly believe that if you asked him to assign you his fortune—as of course you could in your antenuptial contract; I mean, it is frequently done—he would sign without hesitation. He would hate it afterwards, and I dare say the honeymoon wouldn't be over before he induced you to reassign every penny to him. I often wonder what some of these overgenerous lovers would feel like if their wives refused to be so accommodating."

She stared past him through the window. She was lovely; it was not the bold loveliness of Millie Haynes, who died in an infirmary, but something so delicate and unblemished that it caught his breath. He allowed his eyes to rove the field of her physical perfections. He was gambling on her strength of character—on Luke Maddison's weakness. There was something of the weakling in Luke or he was greatly mistaken—and Mr. Danton Morell was seldom wrong in his appraisement of men.

"It is almost incredible," she said slowly. "If I thought . . ."

The nebula had not only solidified, it was shaped.

"About money being Maddison's god?" His tone was one of surprise: he was almost hurt that his characteristic of her fiancé was not as patent to her as to himself. "Good Lord! I could give you a dozen proofs."

He supplied, not a dozen, but sufficient. Danty's inventive power needed the least stimulation.

"I know a man in Norfolk, one of Maddison's best friends. Maddison was landed with a block of shares in an oil field that had practically run dry. One night he asked this fellow to dinner, and before the night was over had transferred nearly a hundred thousand perfectly worthless shares to a man who trusted him as—well, as you trust him! Another case—and this was common property in the City—was a man who . . ."

The second lie came as glibly as the first. It was all very crude and on a balanced mind must have produced no effect but scornful unbelief. A week before, had he dared presume upon the mushroom friendship, he would have found himself on the wrong side of the door. But Rex lay shrouded in a mortuary chamber and a coroner's officer was already gathering twelve good men and true to pass judgment on the mind that had willed a revolver to explode.

Danty saw the red lips grow straighter.

He had a servant who was a sometime confederate. Pi Coles had been a card sharper until Providence smote his hands with rheumatoid. He was an undersized little man, completely bald, with a face wrinkled with pain and age. To him Danty confided most of his thoughts —but obliquely, for he never mentioned names.

"It's queer, Pi, how the mugs fall for any good story! Do you remember when you and I were on the same landing in Strangways Jail? Doesn't seem eight years ago, and here am I in society, giving advice to people with hundreds of thousands—people who know the top-notchers!"

"You always was a gentleman, Larry—I've never known you when you didn't dress for dinner," said the sycophantic Pi.

"Not so much of the 'Larry,' " warned Mr. Morell.

He could sit in his comfortable room and muse on the favours which fate had shown to him. His position was not altogether unique—had not a famous confidence man once been the guest of an Illustrious Foreign Personage and been presented at one of the few European courts as a friend of Royalty?

It was the third day following the tragedy. The twelve good men and true were to be assembled that afternoon. It was not the happiest day in Danty's life. A message came to him the night before from Luke Maddison, and there was something peremptory, almost unfriendly, in the summons; and what it was all about Danty knew too well, only he had hoped that his presence at the bank one snowy afternoon had been unobserved by the cashier.

Luke had his office in Pall Mall, an out-of-the-way place for a man engaged in financial transactions; but Maddison's Bank had owned the site on which the modern building stood for two hundred years, and that modest room overlooking Waterloo Place had been the "master office" from those far-off days when they overlooked a country vista.

Luke had been at his office since eight o'clock, an hour before the arrival of the staff, and here his bearded manager found him, sitting at his table, his head in his hands, his personal letters unopened.

Maddison looked up with a start as the manager entered.

"Hullo!" he said awkwardly. "Is there anything wrong?"

There were many things wrong from the point of view of Mr. Stiles, that shrewd man of affairs. He laid a small sheaf of papers on the table and detailed the contents of the documents briefly.

"Here are four or five transactions that ought to be closed to-day, Mr. Maddison. I am rather worried about them. The Gulanga Oil accounts should be settled. We made a very considerable loss there."

Luke nodded impatiently.

"Settle it," he said. "No message from—from Miss Leferre?"

It was a stupid question to ask, for he had a private

'phone and he knew that any message that came from Margaret would be put through to him direct.

The manager shook his head gloomily.

"A bad business, sir. I have not spoken to you about it because I realize how badly you must be feeling. The Northern and Southern have been on the 'phone again this morning about that check—you remember they queried the signature yesterday?"

"Yes, yes." Luke's usually gentle voice was harsh. "Tell the manager it is all right."

"I told him yesterday, as a matter of fact." Mr. Stiles was inclined to linger on a subject which was hateful to the other. In desperation Luke reverted to the question of the Gulanga Oil Concession, and for once Mr. Stiles's father interest in the business irritated him.

"Of course, sir, I know that Maddison's is as sound as a bell of brass, but there is no getting away from the fact that we have been making rather heavy losses during the past six months, and I am afraid I shall have to call upon your reserves. Personally," he went on, oblivious of Luke's growing resentment, "I have always believed we made a mistake in not selling out to a joint stock concern. In private banking businesses the personal security plays too big a part for my liking——"

Mercifully the house 'phone rang at that moment. Luke snatched up the receiver and listened with a frown.

"Yes, show him in, please." And, as he replaced the receiver: "I am seeing Mr. Morell and I do not wish to be interrupted," he said.

Mr. Stiles made a little grimace. He had been all his

life in the firm of Maddison & Sons, and he did not feel called upon to disguise his dislike of the caller.

"There is something about that fellow that I dislike very much, Mr. Maddison. I hope we are not going to carry his account?"

Luke shook his head and nodded toward the door.

Mr. Danton Morell came into an atmosphere which he, sensitive in such matters, realized was charged with hostility. Nevertheless he was his smiling self, and laid his carefully brushed silk hat upon the table. Luke did not fail to notice that he wore a mourning tie, and that, for some reason, was a further strain upon his jangled nerves.

"Sit down, will you?" His manner and voice were brusque. "You were a friend of poor Rex's?"

Danty inclined his head sorrowfully.

"Yes, I was completely in his confidence," he said. "I think I told you the day following his unfortunate——"

Luke cut short the recollection.

"Were you so much in his confidence that you accompanied him to the Northern and Southern Bank three days ago when he cashed a check for eighteen thousand five hundred pounds?"

Danty opened his eyes wide in well-simulated surprise.

"Why, of course," he said. "Rex had made very heavy losses in the City, and I advised him to see you. I understood you gave him a check for that amount——"

"Did he tell you that?" Luke's blue eyes did not leave the man's face.

"Certainly. Why, what was wrong? I saw the check myself."

There was an uncomfortable pause, and then:

"Did you see him sign it?" asked Luke deliberately. Danty's gaze did not falter.

"I am afraid I do not understand you," he said evenly. "I saw him endorse it——"

"My name was forged to it. I did not give Rex a check for that amount. I have been making inquiries. I find that he was heavily involved in a derelict West African gold-mining syndicate, most of the shares of which you bought for a song less than a year ago. He has been buying these shares on margin and they have been steadily dropping in value. On the day he paid you eighteen thousand five hundred pounds there came another demand for a larger amount."

Danty's heart sank though he gave no visible evidence of his perturbation. This man knew more than he had dreamed could be known. Here was a crisis in Mr. Morell's affairs which might easily lead him to ruin and undo all those fine schemes of his.

"I do not exactly know what you are suggesting," he said. "My interest in the company is a very slight one, and I was horrified when I learned that Rex had been gambling in the shares. I give you the fullest permission to make any investigation you wish."

Luke opened the drawer of his desk and took out a check. From where he sat Danty thought the signature was a tolerably good forgery. He had thought so when Rex had brought the check to him. It is the simplest thing in the world to forge a name, and so far as he had been able to judge there were no flaws in Rex Leferre's essay in that dangerous game.

"You realize what is wrong with this check?" asked Luke.

The other shook his head.

"Are you suggesting that I knew the check was forged?" he asked.

Before he could reply there was a tap at the door and Luke looked up angrily.

"Come in," he said.

It was the apologetic manager.

"I am sorry to interrupt you, Mr. Maddison, but will you see Mr. Bird of Scotland Yard?"

In spite of his self-possession Danty half rose from his seat. The Sparrow was the last man in the world he wanted to meet that morning.

CHAPTER IV

LUKE thought for a minute.

"Just a moment."

He rose and opened the door leading to the corridor.

"I shall want to see you again about this check, Mr. Morell," he said.

"Why not see me now?"

It was a challenge, but Luke Maddison could sense its insincerity.

"Mr. Bird has come to see me on quite another matter," he said. "In due course we will interview him together."

He closed the door on his visitor as the Sparrow was shown in through the other door. Mr. Bird came heavily into the room and favoured every corner with a long scrutiny. He seemed disappointed—as though he expected to find something or somebody who was not present.

"Havin' a visitor, Mr. Maddison? I thought I saw somebody come in whilst I was waiting in the street outside."

Luke nodded curtly.

"Mr. Danton Morell," he said. "Do you know him?"

34

The Sparrow smiled.

"As one knows the Lord Mayor—from a distance. I'm humble. You never find me bargin' in on society. I've had one dress suit seventeen years an' wear it twice a year—once for the Police Dinner and once to give the moths a cold."

"Do you know anything about him?"

The Sparrow's wide smile grew wider.

"His name an' address—an' that's as much as any policeman wants to know about anybody. Bad business, this young Leferre case, Mr. Maddison. You don't want to appear in it, I suppose?"

Luke looked at him, startled.

"I? How on earth do I come into it?"

Mr. Bird coughed.

"Well, you do and you don't," he said. "I happened to search the body an' the room. I found three loose checks on the Northern & Southern Bank—that's where you keep your private account, ain't it? An' this——"

Very leisurely he took out a fat and worn leather case from his pocket, laid it flat on the desk and rummaged in the inside. After a while he found what he was looking for—two folded sheets of paper, evidently torn from a school exercise book. He smoothed these flat and Luke saw a succession of signatures, one under the other: "Luke Maddison—Luke Maddison."

"Looks almost as though you'd been scribblin' absentmindedly." The detective's shrewd eyes were on the young banker. "But at the same time I couldn't imagine a business man like you doin' anything so silly! If you'll excuse the liberty. I called at the Northern & Southern Bank yesterday afternoon, but they were reticent—'reticent' is a good word—an' referred me to you. But by an underhanded an' despicable trick I found that young Mr. Leferre cashed a check the other day for eighteen thousand."

Luke broke in here.

"Yes—I gave him a check for that amount."

The Sparrow was frankly skeptical.

"Did you now? Maybe you'd like to show me the counterfoil of that check?"

For a second Luke was taken aback.

"If there were any reason for doing so, I could," he said coldly, "but I see no reason."

Mr. Bird was not abashed; he leaned his huge arms on the table, and when he spoke his voice was very serious.

"I've no right to ask—I'm not the sort of man who would attempt to pull a bluff on a gentleman like you. I'll put my cards on the table. That check was met in notes and I want to know where those notes went. There's a bird in London I want to catch. I've got one of the best little cages for him that was ever built, an' whilst it's empty so is my heart. If that check was a forgery it might get the deceased a bad name, but it would make it very easy for me to pull in a certain man for 'uttering'—I'll tell you the truth, Mr. Maddison: I want that man's finger prints so much that I wonder I don't knock him down in the street an' take 'em!"

Luke's eyes were averted: he gave no sign until the detective had finished.

"I'm sorry I can't help you," he said. "The check was drawn by me and signed by me."

Mr. Bird rose with a sigh.

"You're too kind to the criminal classes, Mr. Maddison," he said. "No wonder Gunner Haynes thinks you're a good feller—six months he got yesterday for bein' a suspected person. What a man! When I tried to pump him about your friend he wouldn't let on that he knew him even."

"Morell?" Luke was thrown off his guard, as he saw by the Sparrow's grin.

"That's the name. What's the use of talkin' at cross-purposes? He's the——"

"I know nothing about Morell." Luke was emphatic. "He was a friend of Rex's—of Mr. Leferre's. I'd rather not discuss him."

The Sparrow sighed again, gathered up the papers on which the unfortunate Rex had practised the signature, and stuffed them back in his pocketbook.

"Nobody helps the police," he said dolefully. "All hands are against the natural guardians of the children of the poor. I'll be getting along."

He offered a limp hand and went heavily out of the room. The door had hardly closed upon him before the telephone bell rang, and for the first time since the tragedy Luke heard the voice of the woman he loved.

"Will you see me to-morrow, Luke?" Her voice was very low.

"Now, if I may—darling, let me come to you now!"
But her level voice denied him.

"To-morrow—after this ghastly business. Luke, did
Rex owe you any money?"

The unexpectedness of the question threw him off
his balance, and when Luke Maddison was flurried he
was invariably incoherent, for the same reason as others
are incoherent in the circumstances—he thought too
quickly for speech.

"Yes—but it isn't worth discussing. He was heavily
insured, you know, and I don't think the policy is in-
validated. . . ."

He heard the quick breath and grew panic-stricken.

"I was thinking of you—that there was no need to
worry about his affairs. He owes me practically nothing.

"Will you see me to-morrow?"

Before he could reply he heard the click of the hook
being depressed.

CHAPTER V

"I SEE no reason in the world why the wedding should be postponed, Luke."

The hideous business of coroner's inquisition was only a day old, and an accountant's statement that the dead boy's affairs were involved was accepted and no details were asked.

Margaret Leferre could not understand herself; her own calm astonished her. Had she ever loved this suave man who stood before her, apparently agreeing, as though Rex were his dearest friend? Sometimes she was afraid that he would read her loathing of him in her eyes—she was amazed to find herself telling him now, with the greatest calmness and in a tone that was sadly sweet, that she saw no reason why the ceremony should be postponed.

"My poor darling!"

He took her in his arms, and she did not resist. Rather, she raised her cold lips to his, and hated herself. But the Judas kiss was his, not hers—that was a tattered comfort.

"There is nothing in the world I would not do to make life a little more smooth for you," he was saying. "If money could buy you happiness I would beggar myself!"

She smiled faintly at this. Here was a man ready to betray his gods.

He had ruined Rex; he had always hated him. She remembered half-forgotten phrases of his, little irritated comments upon Rex's carelessness in financial matters.

He put her at arm's length and scrutinized her a little sadly. The pallor and the soft shadows beneath her eyes gave her an unearthly loveliness.

"Naturally I've been worried sick. What a fool I was on the 'phone to talk of insurances—it was indecent. I just didn't know what to say——"

"Luke, are you awfully rich?"

She was always staggering him with questions like that.

"Why—yes, I suppose I am. The bank isn't doing terribly well—on the trading side. We are merchants as well, you know—but I have over half a million private fortune. I thought you knew."

She smiled faintly.

"I have never asked you. I'm worried about—poverty. We have been poor—desperately. My father left us nothing, poor dear. It must be wonderful to be so rich—to have command of money—never to be bothered about bills, never to feel the frantic urge to go out and earn something."

He was regarding her in open-eyed astonishment.

"But I never knew, my dear, how awful! I thought you had an income?"

She shook her head. This time she was not acting.

"If money will give you a sense of security, and of course it will, I'll—why, I'd give you control of every cent I have in the world——"

He saw her incredulous smile and was angry with himself, as though in that gesture of unbelief he detected some reservation, some gesture of insincerity in his offer.

"Why not? Thousands of men put all their property in their wives' names. It is a sane thing to do—it keeps a man steady and it will make us really partners. Wait."

He was at the 'phone—as eager, as enthusiastic as a boy pursuing some new and delightful idea.

"Luke, is that your lawyer you're calling?"

Conscience overwhelmed her with a sudden fear; she realized for the first time the enormity of her treachery and was terrified.

"Yes, Hilton—it is Luke Maddison speaking . . . you had the draft of the antenuptial contract? Well, include everything! You have the list of my securities? . . . Yes, all. And the cash in bank—everything. My interest in Maddison's . . . no, I'm not mad!"

"You are!"

She was standing by him now, her face white as death. The words came tremulously.

"You're mad, Luke—I didn't mean it."

He smiled and kissed her, and there was something in his eyes that made her shrink back—something that recalled the words of Danton Morell.

"You are his first obsession at the moment!"

She stood there, her hands gripped, her breath coming quickly and more quickly, and heard him override the protests which came from the other end of the wire. Presently he hung up the 'phone and turned to her, a smile of triumph on his flushed face.

"You are Maddison's!" he said grandly. "Lock, stock, and barrel, darling—I am what old Bird calls a child of the poor."

Even she could not realize that he was speaking prophetically.

CHAPTER VI

To WHAT end was life moving for Luke Maddison?
In his rosy dreams he saw nothing but the smooth path
of it. For him there must come, in a cycle of pleasant
inevitability, years that were to be made up of amusing
house parties, Ascots, Deauvilles, Lidos. He would wander at will from St. Moritz to Cannes, from Cannes to
town; there would be a make-believe of business, with
the indispensable Mr. Stiles mumbling his forebodings,
but the bank would go on whether Luke was there or
not.

He had trodden these ways before—but alone. Now
he was to have his heart's desire. It was almost unthink-
able that she would be with him—all the time, in all the
places, in all the seasons. Margaret Leferre stood for
womanhood *in excelsis*. Not the weakling woman that
had been so favoured of the poets; she was to be something more than a wife. Here was a comrade to be
trusted. Toward her he felt a tenderness more poignant
because of the shadow of sorrow in which she lay. She
was definitely a charge now, someone to be protected, to
be shielded.

On the morning of his marriage he went to his office
at the earnest solicitation of his manager. There were
certain documents which demanded his personal atten-

tion. He went with the greater alacrity since his lawyer had called at his flat that morning to protest hopelessly (since the deed was signed the day before) against the antenuptial agreement.

"Luke, I'm beginning to think that you're the biggest kind of fool that I've met in my professional career. Yes, yes, I know that Margaret is the sweetest girl in the world and the most trustworthy—all the decency of the Leferres seems to have run to her side—but don't you realize what an awful mess you may be making of things? Suppose she died without making a will—I *know* it's a ghastly suggestion—I tell you I know it is—but suppose——"

"I'll suppose nothing so horrible, Jack!" said Luke hotly.

They were boyhood friends, he and the keen-faced young lawyer who overlooked his affairs.

"I believe that a wife should have a share in her husband's fortune——"

"A share!" snarled Jack Hulbert. "You dam' fool, she's got it all!"

They came as near to quarrelling as they had ever done.

It did not soothe Luke's irritation that Mr. Stiles was in his most pessimistic mood.

"We can cut our losses, but it is going to cost you a lot of money," he said gloomily; "and after this, Mr. Maddison, I hope you're going to leave well enough alone. Speculation is all very well for——"

"I know, I know!" Luke's nerves were a little on

edge. "I quite agree to cut out speculation—the truth is, I was led rather against my will to take up these options."

He could not confess that his amazing lapse had been due directly to poor Rex. Mr. Stiles would hardly have believed that his shrewd young employer could have been led into dealings so remote from the normal business of the firm by a youth with no particular experience in the markets. Yet this had been the truth.

"What are our losses?" asked Luke.

Mr. Stiles had the exact amount.

"Ninety-seven thousand six hundred and forty pounds," he said impressively, and Luke smiled.

"I happen to know that I am worth considerably more than that," he laughed. "In fact, Stiles, I am a much richer man than I thought."

He "happened to know" because, for the purpose of the ante-marriage bond, it had been necessary to make an equally exact schedule of his holdings.

"All right, send a check, I will sign it."

Mr. Stiles went out, and Luke made a rapid examination of the papers that remained to be signed.

He was meeting Margaret at the registrar's office at two o'clock. Danty was to be there—he frowned at the thought, but had not objected. Danty, in some mysterious way, had ingratiated himself into Margaret's confidence; perhaps, thought Luke, it was his close friendship with Rex which had made this not only possible but almost inevitable. There was to be no bridesmaid; the second witness was to be Mr. Stiles.

His hand was on the bell push to summon the manager to remind him of his duty when the bearded man came in.

"Do you want to see a man named Lewing?" he asked.

"Lewing? Who is he?"

From Mr. Stiles's expression of disparagement he gathered that Lewing was not of any great account.

"He's a queer customer," said Stiles. "I'd have sent him off, only he said that he came from Gunner somebody who evidently knows you."

For a moment Luke was puzzled. Gunner? He knew a man who was in the artillery . . .

Then in a flash he remembered Gunner Haynes. He had forgotten all about the unfortunate hotel thief whom he had tried to save—had not even read in the newspapers what had been his fate.

"Show him in."

The man who followed Stiles into the room was tall and spare of build. His deep-set eyes had in them a furtiveness that was almost animal. He glanced quickly round the room, and it almost seemed to Luke that he was pricing every article within view against the night when he might enter and take away such movables as would show him a profit.

"Mornin', sir."

He held his head downwards and sideways, looking up from under his heavy and untidy eyebrows.

"Like to speak to you private, sir," he said in his husky voice.

Luke glanced at the manager and signalled him to leave the room. Mr. Stiles left with the greatest reluctance.

"Sit down, will you?"

Not taking his eyes from Luke's face, the visitor stretched out a hand and drew a chair to him.

"Well?"

The visitor sat down.

"Gunner's got three moon for bein' a suspected," he said in a low, hoarse voice. "The Sparrer spoke up for him, but the beak handed out the three moon. The Gunner's appealin' to the sessions."

Luke nodded.

"He has got three months' hard labour and is appealing? I hope he gets off. Did he send you to me?"

Lewing nodded slowly. He had the appearance of a man who was lying and expected to be found out at any moment.

"Yes. A few quid would do him a bit of good. He wants a mouthpiece. The Sparrer says he'll get off—an' the Sparrer knows."

"Who is the Sparrow?"

A slow smile dawned on Mr. Lewing's face.

"He's a busy—a detective. Bird by name——"

Luke nodded. He remembered Mr. Sparrow, whose activities were apparently not wholly confined to inquests.

"I was inside meself—for breakin' an' enterin'," confided Lewing, "but they couldn't prove nothin' so I got out. But me an' the Gunner's like brothers. He was in the next cell to me at Brixton an' he told me to pop up an' have a talk with you—a few quid would help him."

Luke was puzzled. His acquaintance with the redoubtable gunman who called himself Haynes was a slight one, but it had struck him, during their brief interview in the Carlton, that the Gunner had the manners and certainly the vocabulary of a gentleman, and that this mean sneak-thief who was looking at him stealthily from the other side of the table was hardly the type of man in whom the Gunner would confide his commissions.

Luke felt in his pocket and took out a few pound notes.

"I suppose you know Mr. Bird very well?" he asked as he counted the money.

The man grinned.

"The Sparrer? I should say so! He's always goin' on about the children of the poor—but he's always laggin' 'em! He pretends there's a lot of poor people who are sufferin' because of the likes of—" he was about to say "me" but changed his mind—"of fellers who go on the crook. That's silly. If you can't do work you've got to do something: you can't starve. The last time the Sparrer started talkin' to me about it I says: 'Look here, Mr. Bird, why don't you go after the children of the rich an' make 'em pay their whack to these children of the poor?' He couldn't answer me. He was dumbfounded. I'm always beatin' people in arguments."

He seemed rather proud of this accomplishment; was not without his vanities, even if he had to lie about his triumphs.

"Here is ten pounds. Give that to your friend. I can't help him much more. I'd like to know what happens to him, and he can write to me here."

A dirty hand like the talon of a bird shot out and clutched the money into a ball.

"If you see the Dicky, don't tell him I called—the Sparrer, I mean. Some calls him one thing an' some another. An', governor, if you ever want to see life or bring any other swells to see it, you might pop down to Rotherhithe one night. Ask for Harry Sidler—I got it writ down somewhere."

He fumbled in his waistcoat pocket and produced a dirty-looking card. Amused, Luke took it and read:

> Harry Sidler,
> next door The Cap and Bells.

Beneath was the inscription:

> Best prices given for old iron.

Lewing was staring at him, his teeth showing in a mirthless grin.

"Old iron!" he chuckled hoarsely. "That's not bad! If you want to see the children of the pore—that's the place to see 'em!"

He rose from his chair and with a nod stole across the room and vanished through the half-opened doorway. Vanished from life, thought Luke, but in this he was mistaken.

CHAPTER VII

THAT morning had been one of great mental distress to Margaret Leferre. Three times she had taken up the telephone to call Luke; three times she had put down the instrument. And then Mr. Danty Morell had called. Almost she did not receive him. She was in that state of mind when his appearance gave an ugliness to reality of which she would rather have remained unconscious.

Daybreak had come to her after a night of dreams; horrid dreams of the dead Rex, of Luke, of lawyers gabbling through the esoteric terms of a marriage deed. And out of all these disturbing dreams one fact had emerged: she hated Luke—hated him with an intensity that overbalanced all reason. She tried to recall the time when he had meant everything in the world to her, when her pulse quickened at the sound of his voice and the day seemed a little brighter for his presence. Desperately, and for the sake of her own dwindling self-respect, she endeavoured to recapture those hours when he was as a very god to her. She tried to find excuses for him, and in doing so she was unconsciously fanning the flame of her resentment. She had grown to hate herself for the tremendous treachery she contemplated. It made matters no easier that she found herself committed to a conspiracy with a man who a few months before had been a stranger.

In this mood Danton found her. He was soberly attired; even in his black silk hat there was rather a suggestion of memorial service than wedding.

She began without preliminary; she was so far involved that there was no need for pretense.

"I can't go through with this, Danton," she said—she had never taken kindly to "Danty," and after a few embarrassed attempts to carry off the familiarity she compromised with the more stately Christian name. "I have made up my mind to call up Luke and tell him. It is horrible—I can't do it."

He was too clever to attempt a contest. Moreover, he had expected an eleventh-hour penitence.

"Exactly what is horrible?" he asked. "There are certain horrible aspects of the affair which have rather depressed me. Naturally I cannot discuss those with you, but—well, it is rather horrible that you hate him and must sacrifice yourself. When Luke told me that the honeymoon was to be spent in Paris I didn't like it. Though why you should go on a honeymoon at all I don't know. You remember the Fletcher girl who broke her leg as she was stepping into the carriage? Naturally one hates suggesting things, but—I know a doctor who would certify a sprained ankle. . . ."

She shook her head, but obviously she was thinking over this suggestion. She must have the climax of the drama at once. Must at the very door of the registrar's office tell Luke the truth about the marriage—or there

must be no marriage. With the ink still fresh on the
antenuptial contract she must tell him that she had deliberately set herself to ruin him. There must be no lingering—a quick finale whilst the hatred was not within
her, before some sentimental spirit of mercy undid the
work and left her tied to a man she secretly loathed.

Danty saw her weakening. There was need to flog her
animosities to fullest activity. He had a weapon to his
hand: he had most carefully reserved this to the last.

"I suppose you wonder why I am so bitter about Maddison," he said.

There was no reason in the world why he should suppose anything of the sort. He had left her with no doubt
in her mind that he hated Luke for more reasons than
she could remember. He was too skilful a strategist to
have suggested that he regarded Luke Maddison as a
rival. That would have removed him from the sphere
of disinterested friendship and discounted every move
he made, every argument he employed. And yet, with
every day that passed, he found it more and more difficult to conceal his growing passion for her. She was so
different from the women he had known, so far removed from the Millie Haynes type; a lady, one of the
class against which he had warred incessantly. He had
to school himself to maintain the rôle of platonic friend.
A single false move would have brought him to disaster.

"I hate him because I loved Rex," Danty continued,
"and he will never leave Rex alone. The poor boy is not
beneath the earth before he makes the most shocking
accusation against him——"

"What?" She was on fire again.

"Forgery! You wouldn't believe it possible, but Luke told me confidentially that a few days before Rex's death he had forged a check for eighteen thousand. A stupid accusation, as I told him—for I was with Rex when the check was given to him by Luke Maddison."

She sat motionless, her chin held up, a new light in her eyes.

"He said that?" She spoke in so low a voice that she was almost inaudible. "That Rex forged——but he couldn't have! How beastly!"

He saw her lip quiver and knew that it was his moment. Bending toward her, he began to speak, quickly, eagerly. He spoke of things which in other moments she would have instantly resented, and she listened unmoved: in her cold fury she became elemental—somewhere within her a weak, protesting voice told her that she should not listen, but it grew weaker and subsided into a murmur of unease.

At two o'clock she stepped from her car at the door of the Marylebone registrar's office, and Luke, waiting in the room of that official, turned to greet the palest bride that had ever entered those commonplace portals.

She spoke not at all, only answered the questions that were put to her. With a shudder she felt the ring slip upon her finger.

It was all over so quickly that she could not believe that the first act of her vengeance was played. Somebody put a pen into her hand, and a squat forefinger showed her the place where she must sign her name.

For a long time she held the pen, and when she wrote it wavered in her fingers and the scrawled signature looked like nothing she had ever seen.

Leaving for Paris that night—the Meurice, or was it the Bristol? There was some confusion in her mind about these details; anyway, they did not matter if she kept her courage. The two o'clock wedding had been an inspiration. She went back to her house—Luke was coming to dinner; they were to leave immediately after to catch the night boat from Southampton.

"Wife! It's wonderful—unbelievable!"

Luke's voice was tremulous. They were alone in her pretty little drawing room, and he was sitting by her side, his arm around her. She was very still and unyielding, but he thought that he understood this.

Luke was bubbling over with excitement—he was like a boy who had received a new and wonderful present.

"I say, did you see that queer-looking man standing on the pavement as we came out? A fellow named Lewing—a thief of some kind. I wonder if he came to pick pockets? I'll bet he did; touched his hat to me as I came out."

She was not listening, and, after he had gone, could remember nothing that he had said except something about Rex. It was indecent of him to mention the boy. Danty rang her up, but she would not see or receive him. She must go through now without help. Luke was coming at seven. At six she called him on the telephone, and had one panicky moment when she feared that he had already left his flat and could not be found. Then she heard his voice.

"Darling, isn't it odd? I can't believe it—I still think of myself as a crusty old bachelor——"

"Luke, I want you to do something for me." She found her voice at last. "No—no, don't interrupt. It's a big thing. I don't want to go away to-night, not for a day or two. I want to be alone, not to see you. My nerves are in a terrible state; I think I am on the verge of a breakdown."

As she went on, he listened with a growing sense of alarm and dismay. And yet he was not thinking of himself.

"I've been a selfish brute. Of course, darling, I quite understand."

The conversation did not occupy five minutes of time; he could hardly realize what was happening, to what he was agreeing, before he was sitting at his writing table staring blankly at the telegraph forms by which he was to cancel so many pleasant arrangements.

Danty, waiting at Waterloo Station with a full view of the barrier, watched the mail-boat passengers filter through to the platform. He saw the barrier close and the red tail lights of the train disappear into the darkness, and went home humming a little song, for Mr. and Mrs. Luke Maddison were not among the passengers.

CHAPTER VIII

THE general manager of Maddison's Bank was not a man who could easily be taken by surprise. He had the fatalistic qualities which are peculiar to all men engaged in the business of finance. The vagaries of markets, the incidence of bank rates, and the fluctuations of trade left him unmoved. He had once been held up by an armed robber and did not so much as change colour.

Yet he stared with amazement and was physically incapable of coherent speech when he saw Luke Maddison walk through the outer office toward his private room.

"It's all right, Stiles," smiled Luke: "You're not seeing a ghost."

Mr. Stiles recovered his speech.

"I thought—um——"

"You thought I was on my honeymoon, but I'm not," said Luke as he preceded the manager to his room.

He stopped on the threshold at the sight of a burly figure disposed in the easiest armchair.

"Mr. Bird called, and I was—er—I thought you wouldn't mind if I saw him in your office."

Luke Maddison was already shaking hands with his visitor.

"Thought you might turn up," said the Sparrow

cheerfully. "I noticed you weren't on the honeymoon express."

Luke laughed.

"You were at Waterloo, I suppose?"

"Me and about fourteen crooks various," said the detective, "but only two of us interested in the boat train. All the rest were low, common luggage pinchers, but they didn't stay long. Me and him held on to the Paris Limited till it went out."

"Who was the 'him'?" asked Luke, but Mr. Sparrow was not informative.

"Nothing wrong, Mr. Maddison? Yes, I know that your good lady is far from well, but nothing serious?"

It was queer to hear Margaret referred to as "a good lady," and Luke found himself laughing quietly.

"I come up to see you about a cheap little lob-crawlin' roustabout," explained the Sparrow. "If it's not asking you to betray a criminal's confidence, I'd like to know what brought Lewing to you yesterday?"

Luke hesitated. He was loath to say anything which might get the man or his principal into trouble.

"He didn't come for money perhaps—on behalf of the Gunner?" Mr. Bird was watching him keenly. "I thought so. The Gunner's appealin', that's true, an' I think he'll get away with it. I was discussin' it in the exercise yard at Brixton Prison, and this Lewing must have been walking round and overheard. What did you give him?"

As nearly as he could recall Luke gave him the gist of the interview. The Sparrow was amused.

"The Gunner wouldn't talk to a man like Lewing. Haynes belongs to what the newspaper writers call the aristocracy of crime. If you'll prosecute I'll pull him in."

But Luke was in no sense agreeable to such a course.

"All right—leave him. He'll go around workin' against the children of the poor till one day he'll fall an' I shall be on top of him."

The phrase again attracted Luke's attention, and he asked a question. The Sparrow pursed his thick lips.

"People like you, Mr. Maddison, don't understand. Look out of your window now"—he pointed, and Luke walked to the window. "See that girl—typist or somep'n. Two pound a week. She's one of a family of six (I'm makin' all this up) an' lives in Bermonsey. Every hand's against her. You don't think so? I'm tellin' you. They rob her, they lay in wait for her. They crowd round busses an' pinch her purse. Maybe some smart-lookin' lad asks her to go to the pictures—then one evenin' she'll go to supper in a flash night club. See that man? Old feller? Brought up a family on nothin'—he's a workin' carpenter by his bag. Do you know what they'll do to him? They'll get him tight, pinch his tools, and turn out his pockets. That's why I'm drawin' so much a week—for protectin' the children of the poor. Do you get that?"

"But I thought that thieves only went after the rich?" said Luke.

Mr. Bird guffawed.

"What have the rich got? Their money's in safes.

They've servants and telephones, and the law's on their side. A thief would rather rob the poor than rob anybody. They're helpless. I'll tell you, Mr. Maddison, you've no idea what the poor are like, and you've no idea of what the rats are like. I could take you to a place in South London where they live in herds—little wicked thieves—just like in books. Livin' together in cellars and old warehouses. They'd hold your face down in the river mud till you were dead—that's if they had twenty pounds to split between four of 'em."

Luke shivered.

"It doesn't seem possible."

Mr. Bird smiled broadly.

"I hope you'll never know how possible it is—what about that Lewing?"

Luke shook his head, and the Sparrow, heaving himself from the chair, grunted his disapproval of such mercy.

"He's one of the worst. Breakin' an' enterin', did he tell you? He's got the heart of a worm—he wouldn't break or enter anything more dangerous than a veal an' ham pie! He's a shore thief—I'll tell you all about it one day."

During the talk Stiles had appeared in the doorway twice. He was obviously worried, frowned at Bird, and by such signs as Luke understood signified his desire for an early interview. The detective was hardly out of the office before Stiles came in.

"That check you signed yesterday for ninety-seven

thousand—the bank manager says he wants to see you urgently. He wouldn't tell me what it was about, after I had told him you were still in town."

Luke frowned.

"But it was on my private account," he said.

"That is exactly what I told him. I explained that you were transferring that amount to the bank account, but he says he must see you."

The bank was not very far distant, and ten minutes later Luke was in the manager's office. He had first to receive the congratulations of that official and to explain his presence in town. Margaret was feeling better—he had telephoned to her early that morning, and her message was reassuring.

"Now about this check, Mr. Maddison." The manager became suddenly businesslike. "You realize, of course, that it cannot be honoured?"

"What?" Luke looked at him incredulously and the manager laughed.

"Sounds queer, doesn't it? Especially queer to me when I realize that I am talking to the head of Maddison's Bank; but it is a fact. It is the merest formality, of course, but you as a banker will realize that banking is based upon formalities——"

"Will you please tell me what you mean?" said Luke impatiently. "I have six hundred thousand——"

"You had," smiled the manager; "but you seem to forget, Mr. Maddison, that you settled all your money and your securities on your wife!"

And then it dawned upon Luke Maddison that he was

a penniless man. His smile grew broader, his chuckle became a roar of laughter in which the manager joined.

"That is the best joke I've heard." Luke wiped his eyes. "Of course, I had forgotten. I will see Mrs. Maddison"—he lingered on the words—"and ask her to oblige me with a check for the amount."

"Early," warned the manager. "You know, of course, that I must return this check unless I have her authority to pay?"

If Luke Maddison's smile was a little contemptuous, he was justified by his own standards.

He did not even trouble to see Margaret at once. Before lunch he remembered and telephoned.

"I want to see you, darling," he began.

"Why?" It was difficult to disguise the suspicion she felt.

"I want you to sign a little document," he said gaily.

So that was it! Danty had warned her. Only she had never dreamed that she would be asked to renounce her marriage portion so soon.

"A document?"

"I want you to transfer some money to me," he said. "It is the merest formality—I've discovered that I have rather less than I need."

She thought quickly.

"Very well, come to the house at three o'clock."

He forgot that the bank closed at three-thirty and agreed. After all, it did not greatly matter if the check was returned. It was merely a transference from his personal account to the bank's.

He was, true to his methods, five minutes late, when he was shown into her little sitting room. The first thing that struck him was that she was dressed. He had pictured her resting in her negligee—in bed even. She was not as pale as she had been. It was when he went to take her in his arms that he had his first shock.

"Don't kiss me—please!"

It was not a request; it was a peremptory command.

"Why—what is wrong, darling?"

She shook her head impatiently.

"Please tell me what you want."

Her tone turned him cold. It was hard, almost antagonistic. He could hardly believe the evidence of his senses.

Stammering like a schoolboy, he told her in disjointed sentences of the situation which had arisen, and she listened and did not speak until he stopped.

"Ninety-seven thousand pounds," she said. "A tenth of that would have saved Rex."

He could only stare at her uncomprehendingly.

"It was rather dreadful to see a man make a god of money, Luke, and to know that for its sake he is willing to sacrifice even a young life."

To him her voice sounded like the clang of a bell; to herself it hardly seemed that it was she who was speaking.

"And to accuse this poor dead boy of forgery—to add that infamy to the other!"

"I—you are speaking of me?" he said in a whisper. She nodded.

"Of you. I knew that you were coming to get your money back—that is why I did not go with you to France. I wanted it to happen here. Here, where I have friends and can meet you on even terms."

A pause, and then:

"Luke, I am giving you no money. You gave it to me—it is mine. Not a penny can you have—not a penny!"

She wished he would speak during the silence that followed. She wished he would rave, curse her, do all the things that were consistent with her picture of him. But he said nothing. He was not even looking at her, but was studying the pattern of the carpet. Presently he jerked up his head.

"Good-bye," he said, and turned on his heel.

She heard the door close on him, and then there came to her a realization that made her brain reel. She loved him.

CHAPTER IX

LUKE MADDISON walked into his office so calmly that Stiles, who from his glass-partitioned office saw him pass, did not dream of the devastating catastrophe which had shattered the life of his young employer. Stiles glanced up at the clock and grunted his satisfaction. Evidently the matter of the check had been satisfactorily adjusted.

The house 'phone rang and he took up the instrument. "Will you come in?"

Luke's voice was even; not by so much as a tremor did he betray his emotion.

There was nothing remarkable to betray. He was astounded at his own amazing calm, and it was some time before he had discovered a reason for his abnormal serenity. He was living entirely in the present, not daring to look backward, indifferent to what waited on the morrow.

Stiles, who had known him from a child, saw something in his face that he had never seen before, and was alarmed.

"Anything wrong, sir?" he asked anxiously.

Luke Maddison pursed his lips as though he were going to whistle.

"I don't know. I haven't quite got things into perspective. Sit down, Stiles."

64

Again he pursed his lips, staring past his manager; and then, in measured, deliberate tones, he told the man just what had happened. It was not a moment for reticence, nor did he feel the necessity for covering up or excusing Margaret's action. He was dealing with definite and final facts, and he set them forth with a sort of cold-blooded precision, as he would have set forth the values in a prospectus.

Stiles heard but at first could not comprehend the magnitude of the disaster. At last he made a little moaning sound, and this seemed to appeal to some latent sense of humour in Luke Maddison, for he smiled.

"You'll have to do the best you can, Stiles. I suppose one has friends in the City who would help, but I haven't the faith to go to them—faith in anything. No, I'm not stunned, I'm destroyed. But I'm not feeling sorry for myself—I wish I could. That at least would bring me back to realities."

"What are you going to do?" Stiles' voice was little above a whisper.

Luke Maddison shook his head.

"I don't know exactly," he frowned. "What does one do in these circumstances? Go away and shoot lions! Isn't that the usual course for broken-hearted men to take? I don't know."

Stiles glanced at his watch and got up from the table.

"I'm going to see the bank," he said, with remarkable energy. "I think we can lodge those Artificial Silk shares against an overdraft."

Luke made no comment. He heard the staccato ex-

plosion of Stiles' voice—the old man invariably got that
way when he was excited. He was conscious that Stiles
had gone and shut the door behind him.

For ten minutes he sat at the desk, looking straight
ahead, trying hard to reëstablish touch with life. Then
he rose, took his hat from the stand, mechanically drew
on his gloves and went down the private staircase into
the street.

As he opened the door of his flat he heard the telephone bell ringing, and had time to stop the butler as
he was going to it to answer.

"Leave it, will you, please," he said.

The 'phone was in his own little study leading from
his bedroom. He lifted the receiver and put it on the
table. Then, locking the door, he changed his clothes.
He took the first garments that came to him; was unaware, till he was dressed, that trousers and coat were a
bad match. Counting the money in his pockets, he found
he had a little over fifty pounds. He grew thoughtful at
this. Was that his or hers? It was a ridiculous problem,
yet he battled it out for a long while; but all the time
realities avoided him. He could only think of Margaret
as A, himself as B. There was C, which stood for money
—did this belong to A or B?

He threw the notes on the table, retaining the silver,
and went out into the hall. He was taking down a light
overcoat when the butler appeared at his elbow to ask
the inevitable question.

"No, no, I'm dining out to-night." And then, with the
open door in his hand, he remembered. "I left some

money on the table in my study. Take half for yourself and half for the cook—I shall not want you after this week."

He left the man petrified with amazement and dismay.

Why he gravitated to the Embankment he could never tell; it seemed a natural objective. He had no thought of suicide, no intention of finding that gross way to forgetfulness. Walking slowly by the parapet, he came to a halt before Scotland Yard and eyed that Gothic building incuriously. That big detective was there, the Sparrow—the Sparrow, who righted so many wrongs, could hardly disentangle the problem which deadened the mind of Luke Maddison. The "children of the poor"! He smiled mirthlessly. He was one of the children of the poor, the natural charge of that big man. To protect the children of the poor and punish the wrongdoer. Who had done wrong? Margaret? He tried hard to apportion all blame to her, to hate her. He shook his head and walked slowly back toward Blackfriars.

Opposite the Temple station he rested again. There was a narrow street running up to the Strand—Norfolk Street, wasn't it? And his lawyer had his office there. Why not see him and tell him all that had happened? It was the sane thing to do. But then Luke Maddison realized that he was not sane. He was the maddest being in the maddest world.

He went on toward Blackfriars and came to a halt before the tram station. There was a long queue of people waiting to board the cars which arrived empty and went rolling along the Embankment crowded with humanity. Husbands and wives, possibly; young men going back to sweethearts who loved them; girls who had faith in some men or other and were ready to make every sacrifice for them. To Luke Maddison every car that drew away was laden with happy people, their day's work ended, the recreations and pleasures of the night before them. Old men, young men; girls looking trim and smart; young men smoking big pipes, with a newspaper under their arms; bespectacled students—they hypnotized him, these great, blazing tramcars. He watched men and women mounting to the top, tried to identify them through the glazed windows.

He was standing with his back to the parapet, his elbows resting on the stone.

"Are you waiting for anybody?"

The voice had authority, though it was quite kind. He looked up to meet the suspicious scrutiny of a City policeman. The City police do not like to see men lingering indecisively, one hand on the parapet, the swirling black river below—especially a white-faced man, with a tense face and an almost horrified stare.

"N-no," stammered Luke, "I'm—just watching."

The policeman was looking at him curiously, as though he was trying to remember his face.

"I've seen you before somewhere, haven't I?"

"I dare say," said Luke, and turned away abruptly.

He followed the homeward-wending crowd across Blackfriars Bridge. It was dark and cold, and he struggled into the overcoat which he had been carrying on his arm. He remembered somewhere in the borough that he entered a little coffee-house, redolent of burning lard.

At eleven o'clock it began to rain, a fine drizzle that very soon soaked through the light coat. He was walking aimlessly along York Road in the direction of Westminster. A man ahead of him was walking more slowly, a slouching man with his hands in his pockets and his coat collar turned up. Luke was wearing rubber-soled shoes, and came up to the walker before he was aware of his presence. He saw the night wanderer lurch sideways with a snarl, stoop forward as though he were going to run, and then something in Luke's face or appearance checked his flight.

"Hullo!" he said huskily. "Thought you was a busy."

Luke recognized him.

"You're Lewing, aren't you?"

The man peered into his face.

"Blimey, if it ain't Mr. What's-your-name?—Maddison! What you doing down here? You should have come and seen me down Tooley Street: this ain't my pitch."

Twice he looked back furtively over his shoulder.

"You thought I was a detective?"

The thin lips of the man twisted in a leer.

"That's what I said. No, I thought you was one of Connor's lot. They chased me out of Rotherhithe tonight, said I'd been 'nosing' on 'em. That's why I'm round here. Connor's crowd always thinks that someone's been nosing if one of his gang's dragged."

"Nosing? You mean spying?"

"Giving 'em away to the police," explained Mr. Lewing. "Connor's brother got caught the other night and they got a yarn down Tooley Street that I'd done it."

Luke began dimly to understand.

"Come down here."

The clawlike hands of Lewing caught him and dragged him down a narrow, ill-lit street.

"I'm nervous to-night," he said, and here he was speaking the truth, for his voice became a little whimpering gasp. "You're a gentleman, Mr. Maddison. You'd help a pore feller to get away. You know what Connor is—he'd knife you for twopence. Bumping off, he calls it—he's an American; at least, he's been in Sing Song. . . . Sing Sing, is it? Anyway, it's a stir. A couple of quid'd get me out of London."

"I haven't got a couple of pounds with me," said Luke.

He was already weary of the companionship, and, but for being in his present condition, would never have submitted to being dragged into this foul little street.

"Perhaps I can call at your office in the morning?" Lewing's voice betrayed his anxiety. And then, as he remembered: "I give that ten pounds to the Gunner——"

"You gave nothing to the Gunner," said Luke coldly. "Mr. Bird told me all about you."

There was an embarrassed silence.

"Anyway, I'd like you to stay with me, sir," said the man. "I called you a busy just now, and you look like a busy. If any of them Connors see me with a busy they'll——"

They had just turned the corner into an even narrower street, and Lewing stopped suddenly. Four dark shapes, two on the pavement, two in the roadway, confronted them. Luke surveyed them curiously. They all seemed to have caps drawn over their eyes; each man had both hands in his pockets.

"Here, what's the idea, Joe?" Lewing's voice was a whine. "This gentleman is taking me round——"

The leader of the four laughed harshly.

"You've got to have a busy with you, have you?" he said with an oath. "You ain't satisfied with nosing on us Connors, but you got to carry Scotland Yard strapped under your arm. That's yours, Lewing!"

To Luke it only seemed that the man had edged a little closer to Lewing as he spoke. Lewing coughed and fell groggily against Luke.

"Get the busy," said a snarling voice.

Luke swung back but not quite in time. He saw the glitter of steel and felt as though a hot iron had been drawn across his breast; and then a curious weakness came on him, and he leaned back against the wall and gradually slipped into a sitting position. His last conscious impression was the clattering feet of running men; four dark shapes vanished into a greater darkness, and he was left alone, with something that sprawled across the pavement, staring with unseeing eyes at the flickering light of the street lamps.

CHAPTER X

AT NOON the next day Mr. Danton Morell called with all the news procurable—and that was not much.

"He seems to have disappeared from London, but I shouldn't be very much alarmed about that," he said.

Margaret Maddison sat white faced by her writing table, playing with a pen. She had not slept at all since Luke's butler had wakened her at midnight to ask for information about his master. Early that morning she had weakened sufficiently to ring up Luke's office, only to find that she had communicated her own alarm to Mr. Stiles.

"Naturally he wants to worry you," said Danty with a little smile. "That's part of his scheme. I dare say if you had told old Stiles that you were ready to give a check for——"

"I told Mr. Stiles that I'd give him a check for any money he wanted," she said.

Her voice was a little cold and hard. Danty grew alarmed. He was evidently on the wrong track; it was not easy to find the right one.

"Then, if I may say so, you were extremely foolish. After all, you know the man; you know exactly what poor Rex thought of him; you went into this with your eyes open——"

"I know." She was impatient. "I would do it again, I think—perhaps in another way. I was rather—brutal."

She rose from the table and walked slowly across to the fireplace, took a cigarette from an enamelled box on the mantelpiece, lit it, only to throw it into the fire.

"I am worried, Danton," she admitted. "I haven't the stamina for hate. I haven't even the illusion that I've done right."

"Stiles took your check, of course?"

She shook her head.

"No; he said it wouldn't be necessary. I think Luke must have told him about—everything. He was very sharp with me, almost rude."

"Fire him," said Danty promptly. "Don't forget that you own the bank——"

"I do not own the bank," she interrupted. "My lawyer rang me up this morning to say that by an omission the bank property was not included in the contract—and I am glad. Of course I shall transfer back to Luke every penny I have taken from him."

"Are you mad?"

He almost shouted the words.

She had not seen this Danton before, and she stared at him in amazement. He realized his mistake instantly.

"I'm terribly sorry," he said, almost humbly. "I'm thinking of you; I'm thinking of how easily his disappearance may be a trick, as I'm perfectly sure it is. It is like you to want to give him back his money, but suppose you do, what then? You're married to him; he's hardly likely to give you grounds for divorce, and the net result of your generosity would be that you would be penniless, dependent on his charity for every farthing."

She thought for a long time on this, looking down into the fire. It was difficult to know what Margaret was thinking about: her face was set; the side view he had of her eyes told him nothing.

"I wanted to hurt him, and yet I was very frightened. If he had only said something, if he had only abused me . . . it was awful!"

She closed her eyes as though to shut out the memory of Luke's face.

"He'll be back to-night," said Danty cheerfully, "and then you'd better settle it among yourselves. I'm almost beginning to regret that I gave you any advice, and yet God knows I did not act from self-interest."

"Why, of course not." She held out her hand impulsively and he took it. He was now mastering the situation.

Yet he was puzzled, and all the way home he was trying to find a likely explanation for Luke's disappearance. He had formed an estimate of Luke Maddison's character, and his own prognosis of what would follow Margaret's revelation was, frankly, that the man he hated would take one of two courses: he would either display an immense sanity and consult his solicitors, or he would go the way of Rex Leferre.

A newspaper placard attracted his attention; he tapped on the glass and stopped the cab to buy a copy of the journal. "Race Gang Murder," said the contents bill, and Danty was interested in gang fights. The scene of the tragedy was unknown to him. In his more humble days he had worked North London. The Borough and Lambeth were *terra incognita*.

As a result of a stabbing affray, arising, it is believed, from a quarrel between members of rival race gangs, a man named Lewing was killed, and his companion, whose identity the police are anxious to establish, is now lying in a dangerous condition at St. Thomas's Hospital, suffering from a knife wound in the breast. The Flying Squad is combing South London to find the assailants, who are believed to be members of a dangerous criminal gang operating in the Borough.

Danty tossed the paper on to the floor of the cab. It was one of those commonplace crimes which have no especial interest for the well-to-do classes, and just now he was on the verge of becoming one of that exclusive set.

It may be said that he had no exact plan as to what part he would play in the present situation. He could make money more easily with Luke out of the way, and with this fool girl Margaret controlling a fortune, than he could if he were working under the cold blue eyes of Luke who hated him. He had not disguised the fact, when he discussed Rex and the forgery, that he believed Rex was more victim than instigator of the crime.

His disappearance was really a sensible relief. It was hardly likely that his relationship with Margaret could have continued if she were in love with her husband and were guided by him. All that Danty planned was that Luke should cease to be a factor; and he had planned well. Whether he took his profits in one shape or another was a matter of indifference, except—the growing fascination that Margaret was exercising over him. He never saw her but there grew a stronger desire for another relationship than confidential friend. Once he had touched her hand by a well-timed accident. She had let her hand rest against his long enough to encourage the hope that he might go farther; but when he had followed up this opening she had left him in no doubt about her feelings. Margaret had the disconcerting habit of candour.

"I hope you aren't going to be very silly, Danton, and imagine that you're in love with me," she said.

This was in the days when Rex was alive, and when her pulse beat a little quicker at the sound of Luke Maddison's footstep.

Danty shrugged his shoulders. Women change; their charm is their inconsistency.

He stepped out of the taxi and turned to pay the driver.

" Morning, Mr. Morell."

Danty brought his head round slowly. Where had the Sparrow come from? He had a most alarming trick of appearing from nowhere. As a matter of fact, Mr. Bird had been standing in the roadway but had been momentarily screened by the taxi.

"I thought I'd like to have a little chat with you," he beamed. "Seen anything of Mr. Maddison?"

It was on the tip of Danty's tongue to disclaim any acquaintance with Luke Maddison's movements.

"Not since the marriage," he said.

"Maybe he's gone away alone on his honeymoon,"

said the Sparrow, smiling broadly. "I can't keep track of these modern ways of going on. I suppose you haven't been on a honeymoon for a long time, Mr. Morell?"

His keen, bright eyes, half hidden behind the puffy eyelids, fixed Danton Morell like a gimlet. Danty did not flinch.

"I've never been married," he said.

He could easily have ended the interview by brushing past the detective and walking into the vestibule of the building—it was his error that he submitted to the cross-examination.

"A pleasure to come," said the Sparrow brightly. "I was having a little talk with Gunner Haynes about you."

In spite of his self-control, Danton Morell felt the colour leave his face.

"Oh, were you?" he said defiantly. "And who is Gunner Haynes?"

"A low criminal," said the Sparrow in melancholy tones. "I meet 'em—it's my job. There's a lot of things I like about the Gunner. First of all I like him because he never carries a gun, and secondly I do admire his memory! Got the memory of a horse, that old Gunner! He's the sort of fellow that remembers the colour of the socks he was wearing the day the Armistice was signed. I shouldn't be surprised if they were khaki. What colour socks did you wear that day, Mr. Morell?"

There was something so deadly in that question that Danton held his breath. On Armistice Day he had been serving a sentence of eighteen months in Peterhead Jail. Had the Gunner recognized and betrayed him? He had only to consider this possibility to find a reason for its rejection. If Gunner Haynes knew he was alive and get-at-able, he would tell no police officer. Very surely and expeditiously he would settle his own account.

"I can't tell you what kind of socks I was wearing," he drawled. "Are you interested in the hosiery business?"

Mr. Bird nodded solemnly.

"Especially gray socks," he said; "gray woolen socks with a little broad arrow on the ankle."

It was in perfect good-humour, and could not, by any effort of the imagination, be described as offensive. Before Danton could speak he went on:

"I suppose you can't oblige me with information? I'd like to know why Mr. Maddison went away yesterday, and where he's gone. I'm thinking of sending him a birthday present. How long are you staying in London, Mr. Morell?"

The question was asked abruptly; the eyes behind the heavy lids seemed to brighten when Danty answered.

"About a month."

"I was thinking perhaps you'd be going next week."

With a little nod he turned and went off in his heavy, ponderous fashion. Danty looked after him, biting his lip. He had received a warning. Though he would rather have the warning from the police than the more ungentle warning which Gunner Haynes would have delivered.

He was still pondering the detective's words when he was dressing for dinner that night. It couldn't have been the Gunner—Bird was guessing, hoping to surprise a confirmation of his suspicions.

Margaret and he were dining together that night, and when she 'phoned to him that afternoon he thought that she was cancelling the engagement, and had two convincing arguments to make her reconsider her decision. But she had merely 'phoned to ask him if he had any further news.

She was infinitely more cheerful when he saw her that night; was reaffirmed in her old determination.

"You'll hear from him to-morrow," smiled Danty over the coffee. "He's not the sort of man who gets very far from the City of London, where the money is made!"

She sighed.

"I'm afraid you're right," she said.

At that moment two eminent surgeons stood, one on each side of a bed in St. Thomas's Hospital. One of them folded his stethoscope and looked down at the unconscious patient with a little grimace.

"You haven't found this man's name, constable?"

The detective officer who sat by the bed shook his head.

"No, sir."

The surgeon turned to his colleague.

"Pneumonia undoubtedly, Sir John," he said briskly. "The lung is badly pierced—the pneumonia symptoms were to be expected, don't you think?"

He beckoned the third of the party, the house surgeon, who was attending another patient on the other side of the ward.

"This fellow will probably die to-night," he said, almost brightly. "I don't see what you can do except to make him as comfortable as you can. Rather a superior-looking fellow to be a member of a gang."

The unconscious man smiled and muttered a word.

"Sounded like 'Margaret' to me," said the interested surgeon. "Pity you don't know who he is, you might have notified his wife—I hardly think there's time now."

CHAPTER XI

IT WAS the thirteenth day after the disappearance of Luke Maddison, and a day of fate for his wife, since it put a period to the long and agonizing hours of doubt and uncertainty, of self-reproach that at times approached self-loathing. Twice she had been on the point of acquainting the police, and twice had Danty stopped her.

It was a time of worry for Danty also, but from quite another cause.

What had puzzled, and to some degree comforted her, was the fact that Mr. Stiles, the manager of Maddison's Bank, had shown no particular anxiety. She guessed, or knew, that Luke had told him of her act, for when she had offered her check it had been almost peremptorily refused. What she did not realize was that in the days before she became a factor in Luke Maddison's life, and largely determined his actions, Luke was in the habit of disappearing into the blue. Invariably it was from Spain that Stiles had received a postcard notifying him of the imminent return of his employer. The country had a fascination for Luke Maddison. He spoke the language like a native. He was one of the few Englishmen who understood and enjoyed the punctilio of bull fighting, and he loved nothing better than to retire to some lodging in Cordoba or Ronda and, making that his headquarters, rove the countryside for weeks on end.

Stiles was uneasy, but he had that hope left, that in this great crisis of his affairs Luke Maddison had gone back to the scenes of his happy holidays.

During all this period of waiting Margaret Maddison had kept to her house. She was not seen in the fashionable restaurants she usually patronized, and her few friends never doubted that she was on her honeymoon. Danty had advised that she should take the car and go by night to a remote Cornish village and stay there till what he described as the "scandal" had blown over; but she was too worried about Luke to follow this counsel.

A telegram had come to her on this twelfth morning, and she had just 'phoned to Danton Morell asking him to call, when her butler came in with a card upon a salver. Margaret read the name and frowned.

"Miss Mary Bolford?" Who was she? "Tell her I'm not at home."

"I told her that, madam," said the man, "but she was rather cool about it. She said she knew you were in, and that she insisted upon seeing you."

Margaret looked at the card again. In the left-hand corner where the address is usually inscribed were the words: *Daily Post-Herald*. She realized the futility of denying the interview; was in some terror, being wholly unacquainted with the ethics of journalism, that if she refused to see Miss Mary Bolford that interesting reporter (as she guessed her to be) might invent an interview, with painful consequences.

"Show her up, please," she said.

She expected something rather mannish, or at best a girl who had developed her intellectual side at the expense of her appearance, and she was not prepared for the pretty girl in the neatly tailored costume who walked into the drawing room, displaying none of the nervousness nor showing the apologetic manner which Margaret expected.

"Are you Miss Bolford?" asked Margaret, in surprise.

The girl nodded her head and smiled.

"I'm a reporter: I suppose you gathered that from my card, Mrs. Maddison?"

Mrs. Maddison! It was the first time she had been called by that name, and somehow it seemed to bring home to her the tragedy of those past twelve days.

"I told the butler to say I was out to everybody. I am not feeling very well, and I'm staying in town———"

"That's what I've come about—may I sit down?"

Margaret pointed to a chair, and the girl reporter settled herself comfortably.

"I realize that you think we're being terrible, prying into your private affairs, but that is our business," she said, with almost offensive brusqueness. "Newspaper readers love a romance, whether it is happy or unhappy, and we have news that your honeymoon was interrupted and that your husband had to go abroad—or has he gone abroad? Mr. Stiles—that's the manager of the bank—suggested that he had, without saying as much."

Margaret did not speak for a second, and then:

"My husband is abroad, yes."

"Do you know where he is?"

Margaret was not prepared for so open an attack and for a second was nonplussed.

"Yes, I think I do," she said at last; "but I am not aware that that is a matter of public interest."

Mary Bolford looked at Margaret straightly and searchingly. She had rather nice gray eyes, and they were not at all hostile. The girl shook her head.

"I'm sorry, Mrs. Maddison, but I think I can best help you, as well as help myself, if I am perfectly frank with you. We have a story that you quarrelled with your husband on your wedding day and that he——"

"Ran away?" suggested Margaret coldly.

"Well, not exactly that. The truth is, I've a very good friend at Scotland Yard, and he came to me to-day to ask if we on the newspaper had any information as to Mr. Maddison's whereabouts. And of course we haven't. Mr. Bird was not terribly communicative—Mr. Bird is Inspector Bird of the C. I. D.——"

"What is the C. I. D.?" asked Margaret mechanically. She was fighting for time. The mere mention of the detective frightened her—if she stood in terror of anything it was that kind of loose talk which is as loosely described as scandal.

The girl reporter explained. Again Margaret thought quickly.

"Suppose I were to tell you that we quarrelled? Is that a matter of public interest, too?"

To her surprise, she discovered that accidentally she

had produced an explanation for Luke's disappearance which might be accepted without question.

"Of course not! You must think I've an awful cheek to come at all. The last thing we want to do is to pry into a purely personal matter. If that is the explanation I can only apologize and make a graceful exit!"

She rose briskly; but in those laughing eyes Margaret read sympathy.

"You see," she went on, "if Mr. Maddison had been called away on his wedding day to conduct some big financial deal, or from almost any cause other than— well, the cause you've given, it would have been a really interesting story. I'm terribly sorry, Mrs. Maddison." She held out her hand impulsively and Margaret took it.

"I think I'm rather sorry, too," she said, and sighed.

And then Mary Bolford saw her face grow hard.

"I was sorry yesterday—perhaps I'm not as sorry to-day. That's rather cryptic, and I hope you won't attempt to interpret it."

She walked with the girl to the landing, and waited till she heard the door close upon her.

Danty had arrived during the interview; she had heard the butler show him into the small anteroom that adjoined the drawing room. She opened the door.

"Come in," she said.

"Who was that?" asked Danton Morell, a little anxiously. "Fenning said that it was a reporter. What has she come about?"

Margaret smiled wryly.

"She was trying to find something romantic in my marriage," she said. "I'm afraid even she'll never find it—read this."

She opened a drawer of the desk, took out a folded sheet of paper and handed it to him. It was a telegram addressed to Margaret Maddison:

You can hardly expect me to come back to you. In a few months I will furnish you with sufficient evidence to enable you to secure a divorce. I am not entirely without money, therefore I am not entirely without pleasant consolations.

It was signed "Luke," and had been handed in at Paris at eight-thirty that morning.

"That's that," she said. Her tone was light, but there was an agitation in her heart which she had not imagined possible.

Consolations! And this was Luke Maddison, the idealist—a vulgar philanderer, who had fled to—consolations!

"I'm rather surprised that you got this," said Danton gravely. "I shouldn't have thought he would have troubled to wire."

She shrugged her shoulders.

"Stiles probably knows his address, and may have telegraphed to him that the police were making inquiries——"

"The police?" Danty's voice was sharp. "Who told you the police were inquiring?"

She related all that Mary Bolford had told her, and saw his face grow troubled.

"The Sparrow—that's the name they've given Bird. He hasn't been here?"

She shook her head. He was very thoughtful; stood for the space of a moment rather tense, his eyes narrowed, his mind very far away.

"What are you going to do?" he asked at last.

"Immediately? I'm leaving for Madeira on Saturday. The sea voyage will be good for me, and I shall be spared the experience of passing through—Paris." Her lips curled at the word.

She saw he was perturbed, and instantly he blurted the reason.

"I don't think I could get away on Saturday," he began, and she smiled.

"There's no need for you to get away, Danton. I am going alone. I want to think things out."

He was dismayed, though he did not show his feelings.

"How long will you be away?"

"A month perhaps," she said. "I'm going to ask you to be an angel and to look after things for me—I will probably give you a power of attorney; you'll make much better use of it than I made of Luke's!"

Had she been looking for it, she would have seen relief in his face. Danton was rather obvious beyond a certain point.

"I'll do anything, of course," he said.

The rest of their conversation was general, and he left very soon after. When he had gone, she opened the morning newspaper, more interested in the weather prospects than anything else. On the centre page of the *Post-Herald* she saw the photograph of a haggard and unshaven man. It had evidently been taken in a hospital bed. His eyes were closed; the photograph just showed the edge of the sheet a few inches under his chin.

"Do You Know This Man?" demanded the head-line.

She glanced at the letter-press, and saw that it had reference to a murder that had been committed in South London, and that he whose picture was shown had been present and had only escaped death by the narrowest of margins. Not even his dearest friend would have recognized Luke Maddison, for the photograph had not been taken until the eleventh day of his detention in hospital, and it had been taken in a very poor light.

CHAPTER XII

MR. BIRD was discussing in a casual way the gang murder which had scarcely agitated Scotland Yard.

"I saw the photograph of that other bird in this morning's paper," he said. "Looks like the leadin' man in *Saved from the Sea*—that's a great film, superintendent: you ought to see it. Brought tears to my eyes, and I'm no light crier." He knitted his brows. "Maybe it wasn't that picture at all. Have you got the feller?"

Superintendent Kalley shook his head.

"No, nor are we likely to. If we roused Lewing from the dead he'd swear he didn't recognize the man who knifed him. This other fellow will be the same."

The Sparrow pursed his lips.

"I'd like to go over and take a look at this invalid—is he going to die?"

Kalley spread out his hands, thereby expressing his complete indifference.

"God knows! But I wouldn't advise you to break in on Gennett's 'manor'—he's rather touchy, and he's got charge of the case."

Professional etiquette therefore kept Mr. Bird from the casualty ward of St. Thomas's Hospital. He found, however, a copy of the statement that the dying man had made. It was brief and unilluminative.

I do not know who killed Lewing. I was with him when he was stabbed, but I only know him slightly. I should not recognize any of the men; they were strangers to me and I did not see their faces.

Beneath this was a note in brackets:

"This man refuses to give his name."

The Sparrow read and was slightly amused. He did not like the inspector in charge of the case.

"Gennett's going to tie himself into knots over this —good luck to him!"

Later that afternoon he met Miss Mary Bolford by arrangement, and they had tea together. For the Sparrow was of an age when he could with impunity meet the prettiest and the youngest of girls without exciting any other comment than the one he employed himself.

"We're a regular Beauty and the Beast show, me and you, Miss Bolford. How did you get on?"

"With Mrs. Maddison?" Mary sighed and shook her head. "I don't know. It made me feel quite unpleasant. They quarrelled on the day of their marriage. Of course I don't know why."

"Maybe the brother," said the inspector. "You know what relations are——"

"But he's dead."

The Sparrow nodded solemnly.

They were in one of the busiest teashops in the Charing Cross area, and all the time customers were coming and going. Mr. Bird had secured for himself a small table in an alcove, and from here he commanded a view of the shop door. There was no especial reason why he should take this trouble, for he neither expected friends nor enemies. He was, however, intensely interested in his fellow humans, and, moreover, he cherished a dream that some day a man badly wanted by the police—any man would do—and for whom they had searched in vain, would walk into his view. He was something of an optimist.

"Quarrelled, eh? That's a warning to you, young Mary Bolford—never get married. I was only saying to-day——"

She saw his mouth and eyes open in astonishment. He was staring at the door, and, turning her head, she looked.

A man had strolled into the café, his felt hat at the back of his head, his hands in his pockets. He was rather dour-looking, and yet his face was strikingly attractive.

"Well, well, well!" muttered Mr. Bird. "This is where Justice falls off the top of the Old Bailey and hits the man they couldn't hang."

"Who is he?" she whispered.

"A bad lad," replied the Sparrow under his breath. "Want to meet him?"

She nodded, and at that moment the eyes of the stranger and the detective met. A slow smile dawned in the saturnine face, and at the request of Mr. Bird's beckoning finger he came slowly across, took off his hat when he saw the girl, and, after a moment's hesitation, sat down.

"Hullo, Gunner!" said the Sparrow, mildly reproachful. "Have you broke jail?"

"I certainly have," smiled Gunner Haynes, and calling a waitress to him ordered coffee.

"A friend of mine—a newspaper lady," introduced the Sparrow. "Being a member of that unlawful profession, she can meet the best jewel thief in England without blushing!"

She met the Gunner's amused eyes and smiled.

"In case you don't know who I am," said Haynes ironically.

"They quashed that conviction?" And, when the Gunner nodded, Mr. Bird emitted a long and extravagant groan. "I've lost my faith in the court of appeal," he said despairingly. "I know exactly why you were in the hotel, whose sparklers you were after—there's no justice in the world, Gunner."

The Gunner stirred the coffee that the waitress had brought, and laughed. It was a soft, musical laugh, altogether out of character with the man she saw.

"You had a poor case, Mr. Bird, and you'll be the first to admit it. I'd like to meet that man that tried to—do me a turn."

"You were going to say 'warn you.' " The Sparrow looked at him keenly. "Well, you can't, because he's on his honeymoon."

"Maddison, wasn't it? I remember the name. Is he the banker? You can answer freely, Mr. Bird: I'm not going to touch him. He's got a good mark in my book."

"That'll get him to heaven," said Bird sardonically,

and then became his businesslike self. "What's the game now, Gunner? Are you a reforming character? If you are, I'll give you a ticket for the Prisoners' Home of Rest."

But Gunner Haynes was not listening.

"Who did he marry—that pretty girl that was at the dinner that night, sitting at the head of the table? Gosh! she was lovely! Reminded me of——"

He stopped dead and Mary Bolford saw his face twitch.

"—somebody I knew. Good luck to them!"

"Wish them good luck separately," said Mary Bolford; "they parted on their wedding day."

He looked at her quickly.

"What did she do to him?" he asked, and in spite of herself Mary Bolford laughed.

"You're assuming a lot, aren't you? Doesn't it strike you that he may have done something pretty awful?"

He shook his head.

"That kind of man couldn't do anything pretty awful—I'm telling you, young lady! I know men; I understand the good in them and the bad in them—I've lived on men all my life; my knowledge of their weaknesses and their strengths has been my only asset. I don't understand women. And that's where you're wrong, Bird— I'm telling you this over the table—I wasn't after that woman's stuff, though I admit I was curious to see it. I was after a diamond bracelet as big as a leg-iron. There was an old fool staying there who was mad about an actress—or at least she called herself an actress, but I've seen her! He must have been a hundred—maybe a hundred and twenty. No, I've got money enough to live on." He glanced slyly at the Sparrow. "Money enough to buy a machine gun and justify my title. Where's this man Maddison?"

He addressed Mary Bolford.

"Ask me," snapped the Sparrow, his cold eyes upon the crook. "I'm the information bureau round here! If you want to tell the story of your life, I dare say Miss Bolford will fix it for you, but I didn't bring you in here to make light conversation, Gunner."

Haynes saw the little look of pain that came to the girl's eyes and laughed.

"He's right—of course he's right," he said. "Let me give you a word of advice, Miss Bolford." His voice was strangely gentle; even the Sparrow looked at him a little astonished. "Never be afraid of hurting a crook's feelings, because you can't. A man who's had ten minutes' conversation with the police after his arrest, when they're not certain where the stuff is hidden, has been insulted by experts!"

The Sparrow nodded gravely.

"Before you get sympathetic with an ex-convict," the Gunner went on, "find out what he's been in for—and, what's more important, how many times he's been in. It doesn't matter what his crime is: if he's been in twice you can cut him out as an object of pity—I've been in three times."

The eyes were smiling, but the mouth was strangely hard. He was looking at the girl all the time, drinking in her fresh, unspoiled beauty. He turned with a sudden jerk, raised his finger to the waitress and took the check. Then he rose, offering his hand to the Sparrow.

"Bird and I are in the same war." He was talking to the girl. "Only we're on different sides. My side always loses, but has most of the fun."

With a jerk of his head he turned, walked slowly across the shop and disappeared into the street.

CHAPTER XIII

THEY put Luke Maddison in a private ward, and one morning they left a little temperature chart within his view, and he saw that his name was Smith.

"How long have I been Smith?" His voice was extraordinarily strong, remembering that only a few days before he had not been able to speak above a whisper.

The good-natured nurse grinned cheerfully.

"If we don't know people's names we call them Smith—preferably Bill," she said. "But you're going to be good, aren't you, and tell us yours?"

He shook his head.

"No, I don't think so. Smith is a very good name, borne by some very nice people. If my name had been Smith I might have been a better man," he added whimsically.

Since they had moved him into the private ward the burly-looking policeman who had loomed out of his dreams, and seemed part of them, had been taken away. That day they thought he was dying a police magistrate had been summoned to take his deposition; but he had told nothing which was of the slightest consequence or value. Moreover, he had heard one detective say to another that he would not be of the slightest value as a witness at the inquest. So he could afford to lie and watch the hours pass, and the pale light of the sun move across the green wall, and night come and the lights.

From where he lay he could hear the distant jangle of the trams; came to know the bell of one, and marked its comings and goings. He did not think of Margaret for longer than a few seconds. Resolutely he put her out of his mind. Once he had an idea of sending for Stiles, but the appearance of the manager would have betrayed his identity, and he was anxious to save the name of the bank—or was it Margaret? Again and again he told himself that he would not raise his hand to save Margaret—but he knew that he was lying. It was for Margaret's sake that he was content to remain Bill Smith.

They brought him newspapers, but he refused to read them. That was another reason why Bill Smith was so acceptable. If Maddison's Bank had suspended payment, there was an extra good reason why he should never be Luke Maddison again.

He was curiously apathetic as to the state of the bank, curiously apathetic about almost everything and everybody. There was a time when he believed and hoped he was dying, and that in the final oblivion of things he would find the complete and absolute forgetfulness which his aching heart craved. But his heart was no longer aching. Presently the time would come when he would leave hospital, and then——? He was apathetic as to the prospect, too. What did anything matter? Perhaps he would sell flowers, like that jolly girl he had seen in St. James's Street one snowy day. Or he might become a soldier; he was not too old, and he had been a member of the O. T. C. when he was at Eton. Or go abroad. He smiled faintly. "And shoot lions?" asked his own sarcastic voice.

He did not care really what happened after. It was his sixteenth or seventeenth day in bed—he was not sure which—when the sister came in.

"A friend of yours wishes to see you," she said. "He says he knows you."

Luke frowned.

"A friend?" he repeated. "I'm sure he's mistaken me for somebody else."

"No, he particularly asked for you. He said the man who was stabbed; of course, I didn't tell him your name was Smith, because it isn't."

"Oh, yes, it is, sister—I'm profoundly curious; let him come in."

Who was it? For one moment of lunacy he had pictured a penitent Margaret. He would have instantly laughed at the thought, except that laughing hurt his chest.

The man who came in he had never seen before. His shabbiness was relieved by a collar of such surprising whiteness that Luke guessed it had been bought for the occasion, as also had the violent necktie. He was a man with a very small face, sharp featured; his heavily lidded eyes glanced furtively left and right before he came stealthily to the bed.

"All right, sister." His voice was high and husky

(Luke remembered that Lewing's voice was that way, and wondered if this was a relative).

"Is this your friend?" asked the nurse.

The man nodded.

"That's him all right, miss."

The nurse disappeared, and the man bent over the bed. He smelt musty and unsavoury, as though his clothes had been stored in a damp place.

"Joe says that as you didn't squeak he's going to make things right for you."

"Didn't what?" asked Luke.

"Squeak. Don't be funny! When you come out, see him." He slipped a dirty piece of paper under the pillow, and Luke heard a well-remembered rustle. "There's a fiver there for you. Joe says he'll look after you."

"God bless him!" said Luke soberly, "for if ever there was a man who wanted looking after, it's me!"

The day before his discharge from hospital the sister asked Luke Maddison if he would like to see a barber. He fingered his bristly face, and his smile was almost one of boyish amusement.

"No, I rather like myself," he said. "Can I indulge in the vanity of a mirror?"

She brought a small hand glass, and he saw reflected in the polished oval a strange, untidy-looking man with long hair and a shapeless beard. The face was still pale, the nose pinched, but the eyes shone as brightly as ever.

"Good lord!" he murmured, and whistled.

"You're not very pretty, are you?" said the good-humoured sister.

"I never was," answered Luke cheerfully. Then suddenly he frowned. "Is that infernal policeman coming back again?"

She shook her head.

"No, he has given you up as a bad job. The inquest on that poor man was finished last week. Didn't you read the newspaper?"

Mark hadn't read the newspaper.

"I can't read," he said, but she laughed at this.

So the inquest on "that poor man" was concluded, and presumably the coroner had accepted his statement that he met Lewing by accident and was walking with him when the assault occurred. A long time later he read the newspaper account, and saw himself described as "William Smith, of no fixed abode." The paragraph ran.

The man is still in a critical condition, and witness said that it was unlikely that he could give evidence for a month, or that he could throw any light upon the murder.

That afternoon Luke spent sitting in a chintz-covered armchair looking out across the river. Opposite were the Houses of Parliament. It was curious that he knew personally at least fifty men whose presence in that building was indicated by the Union flag on the clock tower—fifty men, any one of whom would come flying across Westminster Bridge to help him. But he did not require help.

He reviewed his position with the calm detachment of a third party. All the objectives in life had been wiped out by a terrific gunfire. He was homeless in the truest sense, for there was no place or being that stood for comfort or happiness. He was in the centre of horizons that showed no beacon light to indicate a destination. In the acid bath of his experience ambition had been burned out; the very desire for life had gone. He would have cheerfully and gratefully died.

It was curious that he seldom thought of Lewing's death or of the knife thrust that had brought him, on the point of dissolution, to an operating room stinking of disinfectants. He had no grievance against the man who knifed him; was rather amused than otherwise to find himself unconsciously the victim of a vendetta in which he had no part.

He read again the slip of paper that the mysterious man had left with him.

Go to Mrs. Fraser, 339 Ginnett Street, Lambeth. She will look after you.

He chuckled faintly at this. So there was somebody in the world who wanted to look after him. It was rather funny.

The first time he had read this short message he had all but torn up the paper and thrown it away; until his last day in hospital he had not the slightest intention of interviewing the lady—she only came into consideration after he had exhausted all the possibilities of conduct. To go back to the office was impossible. He had a country house somewhere, but he dimly remembered having made this over to Margaret in the deed.

He could go abroad, of course, but that would cost money. He had not the slightest intention of touching again any of the strings which would lead him back to the old life. That episode had finished. There was interest and adventure somewhere in the world—who knew if it might not begin in the shabby purlieus of Ginnett Street?

He left the hospital on a sunny afternoon, and could walk out without assistance, for he had carried no baggage. He was strong enough to walk, for he had taken an appreciable amount of exercise on the terrace of the hospital; but he had lost weight and his clothes hung loosely upon him.

Ginnett Street was not discovered without difficulty, but he found it at length; an unsavoury thoroughfare in the Borough. Number 339 was a greengrocer's shop that stood at the corner of a narrower street, in which was a gateway leading evidently to a small yard at the back of the premises. The shop was not particularly inviting; faded bills pasted on the window announced that the best household coal and firewood were procurable. The interior was dirty and dingy. Behind the counter was a shelf where, in sloping compartments, were a number of dyspeptic-looking potatoes, whilst a few weary and rusty cauliflowers were displayed for sale in the window. In one corner of the shop was a heap of coal and a weighing machine—evidently the people of Ginnett Street purchased their coal by the pound.

He pushed open the door; a cracked bell clanged, and after a while there emerged through a door leading to the shop parlour a sharp-featured woman with brassy hair, who greeted him with all the superficial unfriendliness which he discovered was the normal attitude of the small tradesman in this neighbourhood.

"I am Mrs. Fraser," she said.

"I was told to call and see you," he began, when she interrupted him quickly.

"Are you the man from the hospital—Smith?"

Luke smiled and nodded. She lifted the flap of the counter.

"Come in, will you?" Her tone was respectful, almost fawning. "I thought you wasn't coming out till to-morrow."

She led the way into a frowsy little parlour and closed the door communicating with the shop carefully.

"It's lucky I had the room done up for you to-day," she said. "I'm a rare one for getting things done in time. Will you come this way, Mr. What's-your-name?"

Curiosity impelled him to follow her. At the first sight of that dingy shop he had been tempted to turn back, to find a new foothold to life; but now he went after the woman almost gaily. For that was the ineradicable weakness of Luke Maddison: a consuming curiosity as to what would happen next.

At some time or other there had been built a small annex to the house; the floors were firmer, the doors seemed heavier. She opened one of these and showed him into a room, the comfort of which was rather stag-

gering. He expected to see something particularly un-
inviting, and it is possible that, had this been the case, he
would have declined the lodging and gone elsewhere.
But the bed was neat, the sheets spotless; the furniture,
though plain, was ample, and a small fire burned in the
grate. "To air the room," she explained, almost apolo-
getically, and led him to understand that this luxury was
impermanent.

On the table were a few sheets of writing paper and
a pen and ink. Their presence puzzled him, till the
woman explained.

"A Certain Person thought you'd like to write to
your friends, especially as you didn't write any letters
from the hospital."

"How the devil do they know that?" he asked in
astonishment.

Mrs. Fraser smiled cryptically.

"He knows everything," she said.

Evidently He was a person to be reverenced.

"You don't want to have anything to do with that
Lewing lot any more," she said, and all the time she was
speaking her pale eyes were fixed on his searchingly.
"The police broke up that crowd last week, and good
luck to 'em! That Lewing would have twisted his own
mother out of her insurance money!"

"A bad lad, eh?"

"If you'd done any jobs with him, as sure as death he
would have shopped you—especially you being a gentleman born."

"Let me put you right, Mrs. Fraser," said Luke. "I was not a member of Mr. Lewing's gang or any other gang——"

"I know. He knew that. But Lewing was always boasting about the people he could get hold of, and he was shouting the odds about you and how you could drive. Are you a driver?"

"A motor-car driver? Yes, I am a pretty good driver," smiled Luke.

"Won races, haven't you?" she asked in her monotonous tone.

As it happened, Luke had won a private owners' race at Brooklands though he could not by any stretch of imagination be described as a racing motorist.

"I thought so," she nodded. "Boasting, that was Lewing's downfall."

Luke remembered a little conversation he had had with the dead man.

"He's a friend of Gunner Haynes, isn't he?"

An extraordinary change came over the woman. She made a little grimace and blinked quickly, as though she had been confronted by a bright light.

"I don't know anything about Mr. Haynes," she said, obviously on the defensive. "The least said, soonest mended. We've never had any trouble with Mr. Haynes and we don't want none."

There was something in her tone that told him beyond doubt that fear was the basis of her respect for Gunner. He was "Mr." Haynes to her; she was obviously anxious to say nothing that might be construed as disrespectful. Luke wondered why.

She bustled off soon after to get him a cup of tea, and he pulled up a chair to the table. The writing paper was a great temptation; yet to whom could he write? He did not think of Margaret.

When a mouse gets into a beehive and is killed by the outraged occupants, they find him too heavy to move, and so they cover him with wax, and he becomes part of their dwelling: a great lump that once lived but now has no significance. He had embalmed and covered Margaret in the same way. She was just an obstruction, to the circumvention of which he had grown accustomed.

But Stiles——? What would Stiles be thinking? And then for the first time there occurred a dreadful thought. Suppose Stiles thought he had committed suicide? Suppose the newspapers were full of stories of a "millionaire"—all people in his position were millionaires for newspaper purposes—and rivers were being dragged and descriptions being circulated? He turned cold at the thought.

Mrs. Fraser came back with a cup of tea which proved to be drinkable. He made a desperate effort to obtain the information he could have had by searching a newspaper file. She listened to his questions and shook her head.

"No, there's no news. There was a murder up in Finsbury, and that fellow was hung who killed the old woman."

"I seem to remember," said Luke carelessly, "when

I was in hospital, hearing the nurses talk about a rich man who disappeared—his bank went broke or something; there was a talk of suicide."

She pursed her lips and shook her head.

"I never heard of it; and I should have noticed that, because my poor mother lost all her money when the Webbick Bank went broke. . . ."

He breathed more freely when she had gone. Possibly Stiles had refrained from communicating with the police except as a last expedient.

He drew a sheet of paper to him and dipped the pen into the ink.

CHAPTER XIV

THE last person in the world that Danty Morell wished to see was Inspector Bird. If there was any compensation for that meeting in Green Park, it was that Mr. Bird was accompanied by a very pretty girl, whose face was curiously familiar to the connoisseur of beauty.

Danton was strolling aimlessly along the margin of the pond watching the ducks, his mind intent upon a scheme which he had formulated that morning. When he saw that the Sparrow had a companion, he hoped that the detective would have sufficient sense of decency to pass him; but apparently Mr. Bird was deficient in this quality. He stood, a stout, stolid figure, his eyes twinkling through his puffed eyelids, a smirk of satisfaction on his face, as though he were meeting a long-lost friend.

" 'Morning, Morell—I'd like you to meet this gentleman, Miss Bolford."

His tone was so friendly that Danty was momentarily taken off his guard. He smiled ingratiatingly.

"I think I've met you before," he began.

"And you'll meet her again," boomed the Sparrow. "This young lady's a reporter—ever been to the Old Bailey, Miss Bolford?"

She laughed.

"Twice. I don't want to go again."

"You *can* go there too often," admitted the Sparrow. "Once is too often with some people, eh, Morell?"

Before the wrathful man could reply:

"Any news of Mr. Maddison?"

"He's in Paris," said Danty shortly.

"Thought he was." The Sparrow nodded. "When I see that servant of yours getting off the boat train I said to myself, 'I'll bet Maddison's in Paris. I'll bet he's sendin' lovin' wires to his wife all the time that servant of yours is there.' Do you know Mr. Stiles?" His head drooped on one side so ludicrously like a sparrow's that Mary Bolford had to make an effort to keep her face straight. "Manager of Maddison's Bank?"

"I've heard of him; I've met him, I think," said the other curtly.

"Good fellow, but not talkative," said Bird. "The more you talk to him the less he says. He's just like ten oysters singing the Hallelujah Chorus—maybe eleven. What he doesn't know about the whereabouts of Mr. Maddison he doesn't say."

"So far as I know," said Danty in a loud voice, "Maddison is in Paris, having a very good time."

"Not before the child," murmured the Sparrow, closing his eyes in anguish. "I suppose he said so in his wire? I'm betting ten million pounds it wasn't a letter."

"You'd better ask Mrs. Maddison," said Danty, and would have walked on had not the detective's hand detained him.

"There's one thing I'd like to know—have you met the Gunner?"

He saw the man start.

"The Gunner?" he stammered. "Do you mean Haynes—the fellow who was charged the other day? He's in prison, I understand."

"You don't read your newspapers." The Sparrow shook his head sorrowfully. "Here's Fleet Street spendin' millions of pounds a year, thousands of honest, industrious reporters workin' like hell to get as much of the truth as makes good readin', and you don't read 'em! Gunner's conviction was quashed—he's floating around London somewhere."

Danty had regained control over his features now and his face was like a mask.

"I'm really not interested in the criminal classes," he said.

"I'll bet you're not!" said Mr. Bird admiringly. "I'll give you a tip, Morell—avoid the wide, open spaces where men are men in the daytime and frequently dead at night. I never found the Gunner's well-known gun, but maybe he knows just where to lay his hand on it. So-long!"

He watched Danton walking furiously along the path, and turned with a broad grin to his companion.

"That man's nearer to being a crook than I am to being a detective," he said.

"He's the man who asked me to call at his house after dinner and have coffee with him," smiled Mary.

"I'll bet he is! Why, of course!" said Bird. "I'd forgotten that little episode outside the bank." He scratched his chin. "Who was with him then?" he asked with sudden interest.

"A young man; I'd never seen him before, but you said he was a speculator or a gambler or something."

The Sparrow's lips pursed in a whistle.

"They were in that bank together," he said softly, "at about three in the afternoon, when a check was cashed for umpteen thousand pounds! Everything is very curious and mysterious."

But when she endeavoured to satisfy her own curiosity and solve the mystery, he was as uncommunicative as Mr. Stiles.

Danty strode on furiously, his smooth complacency disturbed. He had counted on the fact that the Gunner would be in prison for at least three months. And in three months much could be done. His big coup could be projected and brought to fruition, and he could be well out of the country, with enough money to last him for years, before Gunner Haynes started forth on his quest.

As he reached the Mall he stopped suddenly with a blank sense of dismay. Why had the Sparrow warned him? There was nothing to connect him with the arrest of the Gunner, unless—the police had betrayed him! So the Gunner knew. It was strange that Haynes had made no attempt to see him during all the weeks he had been at liberty. Danton Morell took comfort from that thought, and went on to keep his appointment.

Margaret was out when he arrived; he had to wait

for an hour in her drawing room before she returned. That in itself was a bad sign. He had made the appointment and did not dream that she would fail to keep it. He hinted as much when she came in, and recognized his mistake.

In these days Margaret was never in the same mood for ten minutes together. She who had been so tractable and so easily influenced, who was ready to accept the most deadly charges against the man she had loved, without any attempt at independent investigation, was now peculiarly difficult to convince at all. He was constantly meeting new barriers, new reservations; he had to combat, as it were, another nature which he had not even suspected. She was in her most austere mood this morning.

"You must have mistaken the time," he suggested. "I said eleven o'clock——"

"I know you said eleven o'clock, but I was detained."

He swallowed something.

"Been shopping?"

She shook her head. She seemed to be more intent upon the book whose leaves she was turning than upon Danton and his appointment. He saw it was a Continental Bradshaw.

"I thought you were bored with Madeira? You're not going away again?"

She did not answer. She had found the place she wanted and her finger went down a column of figures.

"I'm not going away," she said; "I am sending a man into Spain—Mr. Stiles thinks that if Luke went anywhere it would be to Ronda, though of course he wouldn't have had time to reach there yet."

He stared at her in amazement.

"Stiles? Have you seen him?"

She nodded.

"Yes."

"But I thought he was rather rude to you the last time you spoke to him?"

A faint smile curled the finely moulded lips.

"He was inclined to be rude to me to-day—but I persevered," she said quietly.

"But, my dear Margaret! You surely aren't going to do anything as undignified as to run after Luke? After his wire and his barefaced admission of consolations——"

"Luke has not been in Paris," she said evenly. "Mr. Stiles had a note from him this morning, saying that he had been in London but would probably go off to Spain for a little time. He asked Mr. Stiles to send his Spanish check book to the Carlton in Madrid. Luke has an account at the Spanish National Bank which apparently he has only just remembered."

There was a long silence. Danty was too wise to insist upon the authenticity of the Paris telegram.

"You're sending a man to Ronda?"

She nodded.

"But what can he do?"

"He can tell me when Luke arrives—then I shall go out to him."

The man stared at her open mouthed.

"You'll go out to him?" he repeated incredulously. "Do you really mean that you've forgotten . . . Rex, and Rex's letter?"

She was standing by her little writing table, looking down at the pad, very lovely, very thoughtfully—a slim, gracious figure of a girl.

"When Rex—" she hesitated—"shot himself he could not have been in his right mind. He must have been mistaken. It wasn't possible that Luke could have done this thing. I've been thinking it over day and night."

Danty could adapt himself to circumstances, but when those circumstances were centred in a woman's caprice he found his task an almost superhuman one.

"You disbelieve your brother, then?"

She raised her eyes slowly to his.

"I even disbelieve myself," she said.

"And me?" he challenged.

She hesitated.

"I think you were very zealous for me," she said, "and I probably let you into my way of thinking; and Rex was very fond of you."

He smiled bitterly.

"Is that all?"

"What did you expect?"

There was genuine surprise in her voice. Danton Morell knew that it was not the moment to put his fortune to the test. He threw out his hands and smiled.

"I'm sorry—one is human with human ambitions, human thoughts, human hopes."

Before she could check this, he went on:

"I suppose I was prejudiced against Maddison. I always thought he was a weakling. I have still suspicions that he is. If one of us has prejudiced the other, it is I who have prejudiced you."

Instinct told him that he was saying the right thing, and that now for the first time he was attuned to her mood. But he had his own business to settle.

"I was talking to you the other day about this Argentine Power Scheme I was organizing—you remember I showed you the report and the figures. You said you would like to take a few thousand shares."

She nodded.

"I wanted to talk to you about that," she began, but he interrupted her.

"Well, I've had a cable this morning. I have been trying to persuade one of the biggest supporters of the scheme to stand out—I was virtually pledged to give him a big holding—and he has agreed. I can now let you invest a hundred thousand pounds——"

"I'm sorry"—her tone was so definite that he turned cold—"but I can't even take the few thousand. I have handed to the custody of Mr. Stiles and Luke's lawyer every penny I had from him—that is why I went to see Mr. Stiles."

CHAPTER XV

DANTY looked at the girl in horrified amazement. His consternation was almost comic.

"You've given back all the money he gave you?" he stammered.

She nodded, her steady eyes on his.

"Why shouldn't I? I have enough to live on," she said. "Mr. Stiles, as trustee of the fund, is making me a sufficient allowance."

He could only gaze at her, dumbfounded. All his fine schemes had been blown away as a feather of steam is blown by a gale. She saved him the trouble of speaking and gave him time to recover himself, for she went on:

"Luke has never been in Paris since he went away— some interested person must have sent that wire. I almost feel as though I willed it to be sent, to give me some excuse for the terrible way I treated Luke." She smiled. "I should be awfully uncomfortable if I thought my money made any difference to you in your scheme, Danton. Happily, you're a rich man."

Danty nodded slowly. He had that morning received a warning letter from his banker, for he had been spending money and losing large sums at his favourite gaming house in the faith that his financial position would soon be unassailable.

With an effort he recovered his balance and forced his voice into a tone of indifference.

"I'm not sure that you're wise. Did you consult your lawyer?"

She shook her head.

"In matters of conscience one does not consult lawyers," she said quietly.

It was difficult enough even to make intelligent conversation. Her attitude was a dead wall built across his easy path, and at the moment it seemed unscalable. He had to play for time now; his native cunning told him that so long as he had her on his side there was no reason why he should lose hope. He had dreamed of hundreds of thousands; he had been certain of tens of thousands; there was still an odd thousand or two for the picking and possibly a greater haul if he played the game shrewdly.

"When do you expect to leave for Ronda?"

"In two days' time," she said, quickly—so quickly that he realized she had worked it out to the hour. "As soon as I am certain that Luke is in Ronda I shall go to him."

"Exactly what will you say to him?"

He could not resist asking this question, though he realized even as he spoke the words that he was guilty of a tactical error.

He saw her stiffen; that cold look came back to the beautiful eyes.

"That is entirely a matter between Luke and me,"

she said. "I have made this mess, I am afraid, and I must get out of it."

In his desperation he blundered again.

"You owe something to Rex's memory," he said. "I don't know what you're feeling about Luke, but there's a fact that can't be blinked. Luke could have saved your brother's life; instead, when he found he was ruined, he hounded him still further into the mire. His god is money——"

"Yet he gave me everything," she said quietly; "and when I refused him money, he went away without a word. Don't you realize, Danton, that had he gone to his lawyer, had he gone to the courts—had he done any-thing—I must have given him the money back, not be-cause he had any legal right to it but because I would not have dared to face a public inquiry. He may have been mean, he may have been terribly cruel, but I cannot right one wrong with another. That is the consideration which made me give back the money to Mr. Stiles," she went on in a voice less tense, more agreeable, almost friendly. "We shall have to thresh out this business of Rex—it's very ugly and hurtful, and I can't think of it calmly even now. Luke may have some explanation; there may be a very excellent reason why he refused any further help to poor Rex. At any rate, it's my job to find the truth."

He was almost livid with a fury he could hardly dis-guise. His lips curled in a sneer.

"It seems to me that the result of your reconciliation —I suppose that's what it is coming to—will be to leave me in the lurch and put me wrong with anybody. Financially it may ruin me. Luke had a big influence in the City, and even now the mere suggestion that I was antagonistic to him is making a big difference."

To his surprise she laughed.

"Danton," she said, almost gaily, "you're making me feel a pig! You don't imagine I would allow a friend of Rex's to suffer because of the help he tried to give me?"

Danton Morell was puzzled. Why was she so cheerful? And then he remembered—she would be in Ronda in a few days, would be united with her husband. The thought made him wince; he was beginning to understand how big a place this girl had made for herself in his life. It was not like Danton Morell to allow any woman a foothold in the cold thing he called a heart; but insensibly, and for some reason which he could not understand, she whom he had intended as a dupe had become a factor. It was almost unbelievable.

And with this came another realization that momentarily left him aghast. She was in love with her husband!

He had opened his lips to speak when there came a discreet knock at the door and the maid entered.

"There's a gentleman wishes to see you, madam—a Mr. Haynes."

Had Margaret been looking at him, she would have seen Danty's face go pale.

"He says he knows Mr. Maddison slightly," the girl went on, "and he wants particularly to see you."

Danty gaped at her.

"You didn't tell him I was here, did you?" he began, and saw the look of astonishment in Margaret's face.

"Do you know him?"

He nodded, and glanced significantly at the girl.

"Just wait a moment outside, will you?" said Margaret, and, when the maid had gone and the door was closed: "Who is he?"

"He's a man I don't wish to see, and a man I don't think you ought to see. He's a criminal, the fellow who was arrested that night at the Carlton. If you take my advice you'll send him away."

She hesitated.

"If he knows Luke——" she began.

"He doesn't—that's just a trick to see you. He'll probably want money, and he's a pretty dangerous man."

"Then you'd better be here when he comes," she said, and saw by his consternation that this was not an acceptable suggestion. "I'd better see him," she said. "Will you wait in the little drawing room?"

Margaret in that mood he could not combat; he agreed sulkily to her suggestion, and was in the little drawing room when he heard the quick step of the Gunner pass the closed door.

Margaret was unprepared for the type that came into the drawing room. The tanned, hawk face had a strength and a certain refinement which she had not expected.

"Are you Mrs. Maddison?" drawled the visitor, and she inclined her head slightly. "My name's Haynes— the police know me as Gunner Haynes. I am a jewel thief among other things," he said.

His tone was as calm as though he were announcing himself the member of an honourable guild.

"I met your husband once; he tried to do me a service—I should like to do him one, Mrs. Maddison."

Again she nodded.

"Mr. Danton Morell is a friend of yours, isn't he?" he asked.

"Yes," she said coldly. "Why?"

She saw his lips twitch.

"I was wondering . . . Mrs. Maddison, would you think I was impertinent if I asked you why your husband left you?"

Her steady eyes met his.

"Do you think you would be?" she asked quietly, and saw that faint smile of his.

"I should be a little worse than impertinent. And yet, Mrs. Maddison, I have a very deep interest in your husband's affairs. I have many bad qualities, but disloyalty is not one of them. Your husband went out of his way to warn me, at a moment when he knew the police were coming to arrest me. If ever there was a white and wholesome man, that man is Luke Maddison. I ought not to have asked you the question and I could not very well expect a satisfactory answer. The only thing I am anxious to know is this: have you any idea where your husband is?"

"Do you wish to find him?" she challenged.

He shook his head.

"No, but I'd like to know exactly where he is. I have a very special reason for asking this. Is he in London?"

She shook her head.

"He's in Spain at the moment, but I'm afraid I cannot give you the address."

"Mr. Morell—is he in Spain? Pardon me, Mrs. Maddison, but if I have a reason for asking you the one question, I have a doubly important reason for asking the other. Morell is the kind of man that no decent woman should know——"

She walked to the table and pressed the little onyx bell push. This time he smiled.

"That means you're going to turn me out, and I don't blame you. I'm afraid I've blundered this interview, which I intended should be very discreet and diplomatic. I particularly wished to know where Mr. Maddison was——"

"I have told you," she said, as the maid appeared in the doorway.

"As far as Danty Morell is concerned——" he began.

Her hand pointed to the door.

"I am not prepared to discuss my friends—even with the criminal acquaintances of my husband," she said, and she heard him chuckling as he went down the stairs as though at a very good joke.

She waited till she heard the street door close, and went in search of Danty, but he was not in the small drawing room. The maid told her he had left within a few seconds of Gunner Haynes's arrival. Danty was not a man who took unnecessary risks.

She had some business to do in the West End of London, and as the afternoon progressed she ordered the car to drive her into the park. Near the Marble Arch she signalled to the driver to stop and got out. She wanted the walk and the solitude that the park gave her. Here she could think more clearly.

She walked slowly along the asphalt path that runs parallel with the roadway. As she did so she saw a car coming slowly along the tan on the other side of the road. It was an electric brougham containing two people: a beautiful-looking girl, fashionably dressed; by her side, his face half hidden under a broad-brimmed Stetson hat, a bearded man of striking appearance. Ahead of her was walking a stout-looking man, and by his side a rather pretty girl. As she overtook them she heard the stout man say:

"Take a look at that swell woman! That's Jean Gurlay—the biggest crook in London, my dear."

Those ahead of her she recognized as the Sparrow and his companion, and, not wishing to be seen by them, sat down on a garden seat, her eyes following curiously the electric brougham. She saw the machine turn at the Marble Arch and come slowly along by the side of the curb, and she watched with a detached interest the beautiful girl and the bearded man, whose head was turned toward his companion. As they passed she heard the man say:

"This is all very mysterious. What does it mean?"

In an instant she was on her feet, pale and shaking; she had recognized the voice of the bearded man. It was her husband.

CHAPTER XVI

LIFE in Ginnett Street might be rather amusing, thought Luke Maddison.

It was his third day in his lodging, and he was not averse to his new life. He had discovered unsuspected physical weaknesses as he had made his way from the hospital, and was glad of a rest, the freedom from worry, the utter irresponsibility of this queer life into which he had obtruded.

Mrs. Fraser did not bother him with her presence. She brought in a surprisingly interesting collection of books to read, supplied him with plain but very wholesome meals, and gave him the freedom of the house, though she suggested that he had better only go out at nights. He was mystified by the attention she was paying him, though he realized that she was acting on behalf of the unknown Connor.

Some of the mystery was cleared up on the third day when she asked him a number of questions about Australia, a country to which he had never been. When he said as much she smiled cryptically.

"If that Lewing had had as much sense as you and had kept his mouth shut, he might have been alive and well to-day. If he'd had the sense to keep his mouth shut, nobody would have known anything about you. But he was a rare one to boast, was Lewing, God rest him, always boasting what his crowd could do against our crowd, though he must have known that we had all the money."

Gradually it came out. Lewing had boasted of a man who was coming from Australia to work with his "crowd." Luke gathered that the new man had a fairly hectic reputation in the Dominion, but that he had never been convicted.

"The moment Connor heard you were coming, he said: 'That's the man for us—get him.' He reckons that Sydney bank affair was the cleverest job that's ever been done."

Now Luke discovered his identity, and began to piece together the little scraps of information he had had from time to time. If Lewing was not the brains, or the leader, of the Borough gang, he was at least a person of considerable importance. It was he who had arranged for the Australian's services, and apparently had recruited him by correspondence.

Luke learned that the gang warfare in South London had a special significance. The Borough gang were mainly river thieves, and several of the members had grown rich out of the cargoes they had broached.

"Now let us get this straight, Mrs. Fraser. You're under the impression that I'm an Australian criminal. When I say 'you' I mean your principals."

"My how much?" asked Mrs. Fraser, puzzled.

Luke explained.

"Well, I'm not the man you were expecting," he insisted. "The fact that I happened to be with Lewing the night he was killed means nothing—it was the purest fluke. I can certainly drive a car, but I'm afraid I can be of very little use to your friends, who, I gather, are on the wrong side of the law."

She smiled cryptically at this.

"What I like about you, Mr. Smith," she said, "is that you know how to keep yourself to yourself."

It was late that night that he saw the redoubtable Connor. As he shook hands with the stranger he shuddered, for he had heard that deep voice before on the night when Lewing met his end.

"I shan't want you for a day or two, Smith," said Connor brusquely. "Everything being done for you? That's right."

His tone was commanding; it was the same voice that had challenged Lewing, but more cultured. Before Luke could explain who he was, or at any rate explain who he was not, the man had taken his departure. A day or two later came another surprise. There walked into his room as he was sitting at the table, a book before him, his head upon his hands, a pretty, fair-haired girl, who eyed him with a certain amount of amused interest.

"Connor sent me down to see you. Did your new clothes arrive?"

Luke shook his head and smiled.

"No," he said. "Am I getting an outfit?"

She looked at him critically.

"And you want a barber. I'll have one sent up to you

to-night. That beard of yours wants trimming. Could you bear taking a little drive with me to-morrow?"

He laughed again.

"I could bear worse things than that," he said, wondering who she was or whence she had come.

She was well but not too smartly dressed, and he guessed that her attire was designed so that she should not attract too much attention.

"This is a hole you're in!" she said contemptuously, looking out onto the street. "It must be hell here. How these people manage to exist I don't know."

He said nothing to this; he had gained a working knowledge of these children of the poor; had watched in the earlier hours of the dawn the street doors open and discharge the workers; had seen the brave, drab wives battling to make a sixpence do the work of a shilling. At eight-thirty their daughters, neatly attired, in flesh-coloured stockings and cheaply smart coats, went forth to the City to add theirs to the meagre family resources. The children of the poor! The victims of a thousand preying vultures! For the poor are robbed as the rich are never robbed. There existed a dozen gangs of little sneak thieves, who would pick their pockets in omnibuses, snatch their bags, sneak into their houses when they were out, to collect a few pence worth of their poor belongings. He had seen one night a gang of three young ruffians attack a middle-aged workman, knock him down and empty his pockets. He had heard of glib men who had come down this street, pretending they had been sent by some absent husband to fetch tools he had left behind; and once, to his great joy, he had seen a swift car rush through the street and discharge half-a-dozen detectives to the arrest of a bully who had lived on the wages of infamy.

The police gave them what protection they could. He had seen a wife-beater lying stark and unconscious on the pavement after a detective had used his rubber truncheon on him. But as a rule these human parasites that preyed upon the poor escaped unharmed.

The girl turned from the contemplation of misery.

"Meet me near the Guards Memorial in Green Park. I shall be in a car and will pick you up," she said.

She looked him up and down, admiration in her eyes.

"You've got a good voice," she said. "You'd pass for a swell."

The clothes came that night; they fitted him remarkably well, and when the promised barber had finished his work and Luke was arrayed in his new clothes, he was almost reconciled to the beard.

In the interest of his new, strange life he found it fairly easy to forget. The spirit of adventure was on him. Margaret belonged to a dim, almost unbelievable, past. She was of the substance of dreams.

He went gaily to the rendezvous on the following afternoon, and was delighted to find how springy was his step. He had hardly taken his place in front of the Guards Memorial when he saw an electric brougham approach and, catching the girl's signal, stepped to the side of the road as the car stopped.

She was in excellent spirits.

"It's a great idea to let yourself be seen in a certain kind of car," she said. "You don't know what I mean? I'll bet you don't!"

They crossed into Hyde Park, made a slow progress near the edge of the sidewalk, and he found himself enjoying the novel experience. She was very pretty, though older than he had thought.

"Do you see that fat man over there? That's the Sparrow. You want to keep away from him."

He started at the name.

"You mean Bird?" he stammered, and looked guiltily in the direction she indicated.

He saw Mr. Bird. He was walking with a very pretty girl, but the woman who was at that moment seating herself on one of the park benches he did not recognize.

As the brougham turned and came back on the other side of the road, she said suddenly:

"There will be a car waiting near the Cavalry Barracks. I hope you can drive?"

"Another car?" he asked in astonishment.

She nodded.

"I want to try you out."

He laughed.

"All this is very mysterious," he said.

The car was waiting for them, a closed light car of English make. There was nobody in attendance, but without hesitation she stopped the brougham and gave the driver instructions.

"Here it is," she said. "Get in."

Luke sank into the driver's seat and put his foot on

the self-starter, and she came in after him, slamming the little door behind her.

"Grafton Street," she said, in a businesslike tone. "Pull up opposite the Rean Club."

He thought she was testing his driving ability, for he had to pass through three traffic blocks before he brought the machine to a standstill at a place she indicated.

"Now you understand," she said, dropping her voice and speaking rapidly, "I'm going in to see my husband."

She looked him straight in the eyes.

"If he makes a fuss I shall expect you to help me. If he doesn't make a fuss, we'll drive quietly away down Albemarle Street, make for Vauxhall Bridge and Tooting Common."

"Your husband?" he stammered.

She gave him one quick look of suspicion.

"That is what you tell the flattie if there is any fuss."

What a flattie was she did not explain, and was gone before he could ask her. He kept the engine running according to her instructions. She was gone some twenty minutes. Presently, looking out, he saw her turn the corner from Bond Street and walk with apparent unconcern toward him. As she stepped into the car, a man in his shirt-sleeves darted round the corner, flew at her, and gripped her by the arm. She tried to wrench herself free, and before Luke realized what he was doing he had struck her assailant and sent him tumbling to the pavement.

"Drive!" she snapped, and mechanically Luke Maddison sent the machine leaping forward.

They crossed Oxford Street, down St. James's Street, through the park, and were over Vauxhall Bridge before he partly realized what had happened.

"Why did that fellow grab you?" he asked.

"My husband—I had a row with him," she said calmly. And then: "I knew Connor was wrong," she said, and whistled. "If I hadn't had my wits about me and started that husband story, I'd have been half-way to Holloway!"

He saw her look at every policeman they passed, out of the corner of her eye, and his heart was beating faster as they came to the edge of Tooting Common, and at her command he stopped the car.

"We'll get out here," she said. "You can go back by bus, I'll take a taxi. If Connor comes to-night, tell him I've got the stuff."

She turned to go, but he caught her by the arm.

"What stuff?" he asked sternly.

And then he saw the flat case she carried under her leather coat.

"My God!" gasped Luke Maddison. "You stole that!"

There was amusement in her fine eyes as she nodded. "Of course I did, you poor simp!"

A taxicab was passing and she hailed it. Slowly his grip on her arm relaxed. He watched the taxi recede like a man in a dream, too stunned even to think. He could never remember that journey back to Lambeth. He had crossed Westminster Bridge when he saw a newsboy with a placard: "Daring West End Robbery." He stood dead still, gazing open-mouthed at the contents bill, and then he felt in his pocket and dropped a penny from his trembling hand into the newsboy's palm.

He dared not look inside the newspaper until he was in a quiet street. Then he read:

DARING WEST END ROBBERY

Bearded Man and Pretty Girl Rob Taffanny's of £20,000 Diamond Necklace.

A daring robbery was committed this afternoon at Messrs. Taffanny's jewel shop in Bond Street. At about 3:50 a well-dressed woman walked into the shop and asked to be shown some plain gold rings. Whilst the assistant's back was turned, she must have broken a glass case with a rubber-headed hammer. When he came back, he found not only the woman but a valuable diamond necklace had disappeared. He flew out into the street and overtook the woman as she was entering a motor car. He was immediately struck down by her companion, who is described as a man of great height, with a fair, well-trimmed beard, dressed in a gray tweed suit. . . .

"That's me!" groaned Luke Maddison, and almost swooned.

CHAPTER XVII

LUKE MADDISON sat in his little room in Ginnett Street, his head upon his hands, his mind a great confusion. Mrs. Fraser had not been in the shop parlour when he passed through, and was apparently unconscious of his return. But this was not the fact, he discovered, when, a quarter of an hour afterwards, she came in with a cup of tea.

He had a feeling that she was well aware of what had happened that afternoon, although she made no reference to his terrifying adventure until she seemed at the point of departure.

"Connor says that the only danger is that some of the Lewing mob may put up a squeal."

"What is a squeal?" asked Luke, and she smiled amiably and admiringly.

"What a one you are! But perhaps in Australia they don't have these expressions."

He leaned back in his chair.

"Do you know what strikes me, Mrs. Fraser?" he said calmly. "That every person in this street who reads the description will recognize me? About a hundred people must have seen me walking down Ginnett Street——"

She shook her head.

"I know everybody in the neighbourhood and what they're doing," she said calmly. "The only man who saw you is old Joe who runs errands for me. Connor says you ought to cut that beard of yours and get another suit. I'll take away the one you're wearing, if you'll change."

"Into what?" he demanded with some asperity.

"There's a blue suit in the drawer; it came when you were out this afternoon," she said, and went away.

For a quarter of an hour he sat and watched his tea growing cold, his mind vacillating between horror and amusement. He, Luke Maddison, was a thief, a gangster, an active member of an organization which had robbed Taffanny's! He knew Taffanny's rather well; he had bought Margaret's engagement ring over the very glass counter that had been smashed. He was helpless—the idea of going to the police and betraying his associates never occurred to him. There was only one thing to be done and that was to steal away at the first opportunity. He had written for his check book to be sent to Ronda, and it was a simple matter to reach Spain. Was it, though?

With a gasp he realized that he had no passport! And without a passport it was impossible to reach Spain, of all countries, where every man and woman who passed across the frontier were closely scrutinized. If he had not dismissed his servant it would be easy to creep back to his flat one night, pack a bag, and fade away into a Continental limbo. But probably his solicitor had the key of the flat. A new hope awakened. Hulbert had an apartment in St. James's Street. He was a bachelor and accessible.

Luke dismissed from his mind his experience of the afternoon. That was something not to be thought of without a shudder—he was whistling cheerfully when Mrs. Fraser came with a pair of bright, new scissors to collect the gray tweed suit he had discarded, and to bring him a pair of brown shoes, so hideously bright that they dazzled him.

"Connor says you'd better leave your moustache," she suggested.

"Where is Connor? Is he on the premises?"

She shook her head.

"No, he 'phoned me."

"I didn't know you had a 'phone," he said, in surprise.

Mrs. Fraser smiled cryptically.

"We've got lots of things here that people don't know anything about," she said.

She came back a little later with a tube of shaving paste, a brand new lather brush, and a razor which had evidently been purchased recently, for when he opened the case he found it still inclosed in oil paper. Shaving was a painful process in spite of this, but apparently the results were satisfactory, for when the woman brought him some food later she stood in the doorway and gaped her approval.

"Well, I should never have known you, Mr. Smith," she said, "and I'll bet your best friend wouldn't know you!"

As to this Luke was perfectly convinced. What an extraordinary change a moustache made in a man's appearance! To him it lent a touch of the sinister—he stood gazing, fascinated, at his reflection in the mirror.

Mrs. Fraser seemed more inclined to be conversational than she had been before; asked him if he was married, and before he could answer announced herself as a widow.

"At least, practically," she amended the statement. "My husband got a lifer two years ago."

She was quite cheerful about this calamity, and Luke gathered that life had not run any too smoothly for the woman.

"He asked for it," she said. "Shot a copper and nearly killed him; and naturally, Connor wouldn't stand for that. Connor says a gun's all right for the heads but not for the unders. Fraser was that kind—flash! He tried everything——"

"Had he been in prison before?"

She smiled amusedly.

"Why, of course! He did two stretches."

Luke did not ask what a stretch might be: he had a vague idea that it meant penal servitude.

"He did one stretch," said the communicative Mrs. Fraser, "for a swindle up in Manchester—he and Danty were in it——"

Luke's jaw dropped.

"Danty?" he said incredulously. "Who is he?"

"He's a con man—you must have heard of him. I think he's straight now, but you can never tell. He lives up west, knows all the swells, and has got a flat in Half Moon Street. He and Gunner Haynes used to work together——"

"Gunner Haynes—you know him?" asked Luke quickly.

From her expression and tone he gathered that Haynes was a person of some importance in the hierarchy of the underworld.

"No, I don't know him, I've only heard of him. But what do they call Danty now?" She frowned in an effort of memory. "I had it on the tip of my tongue—a swell name. Danton Morell—that's it! Connor told me only the other day about him."

The room seemed to swim before Luke Maddison's eyes. Danton Morell—a confidence man, an ex-convict? It was incredible! And then suddenly he had the stunning realization that Danty Morell was his wife's best friend!

"What is he like in appearance?"

"Danty? I've seen him two or three times. . . ."

She described Morell in her homely language. There was no doubt at all that this was the man! It was more vitally necessary than ever that he should escape from this environment and reappear as Luke Maddison.

His vague plans became definite. He could leave the house that night, seek out Hulbert, and tell him the truth.

At nine o'clock that night he was preparing to leave when an unexpected difficulty arose. He was just about to turn out the light when Mrs. Fraser appeared. She closed the door behind her, and from her manner he gathered that something serious had happened.

"Two of the Lewing crowd are down below," she said in a low voice. "I haven't had a chance to call up Connor; the 'phone is in the parlour, and they came in before I knew what was happening."

She had something hidden under her apron, and when she withdrew her hand he saw that it was a small Browning pistol.

"Put that in your sky," she said urgently. "You don't know what these fellows are after."

"In my——?" he began, bewildered.

"In your pocket," she said impatiently. "Do as you're told."

Mechanically he took the pistol from her hand and slipped it into his hip pocket. The one thing he did not wish to challenge was a scene with two members of the rival gang. It was vital that he should get away from Ginnett Street with the least possible delay, and if this pistol helped him it was welcome.

"They want to see you——" she began.

And then a voice came from the foot of the narrow stairs.

"Come on, Smith!"

There was menace in the tone. Mrs. Fraser flung open the door.

"Wait!" she said sharply. "Who do you think you are?"

Luke heard a grumbling voice and the slam of the

door which separated the foot of the stairs from the parlour. And then, at the beckoning jerk of the woman's head, he followed her down the stairs.

There were two men in the parlour. One stood with his back to the fire, the other significantly near the door that gave egress to the shop. They were respectably dressed. Luke realized that if he had seen them in the street he would have thought they were decent artisans. There was certainly nothing sinister in either face. One was tall and rather stout, the other a slightly built man, who wore as his necktie the colours of a cavalry regiment.

The big man who stood with his back to the fire lowered his chin to his breast and looked at Luke from under his eyebrows.

"Is this Smith?" he asked.

"That is Mr. Smith," said Mrs. Fraser primly.

"What's the idea of your coming here and pretending you're somebody you're not?" asked the little man by the door with extraordinary rapidity.

His big companion silenced him.

"You shut up. I'll do all the talking, Curly," he said. "You did that job to-day, didn't you, Smith?"

"I've done many jobs," said Luke coolly.

"You're pretending you're a fellow named Smith whom our governor brought over from Australia—no, I'm not talking about Lewing: he was nobody. Swank killed him, and he's well dead. But you're not Smith." He pointed a finger to the man at the door. "That's Curly Smith."

"I'll say I am!"

The little man was quivering with anger; he spoke with a shrill cockney whine.

"You've been using my name"—he qualified the name with a violent adjective.

The stout man by the fire rebuked him.

"There are ladies present," he said, with such solemnity that Luke almost laughed at the incongruity of the reproach.

"The point is," said the big man, who, Luke discovered, was named Verdi, "you was picked up when Lewing was chived, and you got yours too, and naturally Connor thought you were the man that Lewing was supposed to meet off the boat in the London Docks. And instead of going to meet him, Lewing got cold feet, because he thought the Connor lot were after him for a squeal. But you're not Smith, and I'll take my oath you've never been to Australia."

"Him!" Curly Smith was quivering with contempt. "That feller couldn't get a living in Australia!"

He suddenly tugged a newspaper from his side pocket.

"Do you see what you've done for me?" he hissed, and thrust the paper under Luke's nose.

Luke Maddison read the paragraph which the grimy thumb of the man stabbed.

In connection with this robbery the police are seeking information concerning a man named Smith who landed a few weeks ago from the Orient liner *Pontiac*.

"Do you see what you've done?" repeated Smith savagely. "You've got the dicks after me!"

His hand strayed to his trousers pocket.

"Steady your mitt!" growled Verdi. "This bird's got a gat—what do you think the old woman went up to see him about?"

Mrs. Fraser flamed at the insult.

"Old, am I, you fat snail! We'll see what Connor says to that! He'll be here in five minutes."

Verdi glanced uneasily at the door.

"Bluff," he said. "Anyway, Connor can't complain if we come round to make a few inquiries. We're entitled to a bit of information."

"Do you want to see me any more?" said Luke, and moved toward the door.

Curly Smith stood squarely in his way.

"We want to know——" began Verdi.

"You know all you're likely to know," said Luke curtly.

He took another step forward, but Smith did not move. Suddenly Luke's hand shot up, gripped the little man and swung him across the room. It was not a moment to compromise or to argue; instinctively he knew he was taking the right line as he pulled the door wide open.

"Get outside, both of you!" he said.

Verdi shrugged his broad shoulders.

"That's all right," he said. "We don't want any unpleasantness."

He was smiling when he came abreast of Luke; but Mrs. Fraser had slipped to the other side of the table, and saw the life preserver he carried in his right hand.

"Look out!" she cried shrilly.

As the deadly little stick rose, Luke struck for the man's jaw, and he went over with a crash against the wooden partition which separated the shop from the parlour.

For a moment he was stunned, and in that time Luke had jerked the life preserver from the man's hand (a leather cord attached to it was twisted round his wrist) and had dropped it into his pocket.

"Come on, you." He beckoned Curly Smith, and the little man sidled nimbly past him.

Verdi was on his feet by now, a little dazed, blinking with his pale blue eyes at the man who had knocked him down.

"All right," he said, and went heavily after his companion.

Luke closed the door with some difficulty, for the fall of the man against the partition had thrown the door out of true. Mrs. Fraser was very pale and her breath was coming quickly.

"I've never known them Lewings to do that before," she said. "I wouldn't be surprised if they didn't start a fire."

They had taken this course once before, Luke learned to his horror and amazement—that explained the new annex to the house.

339 Ginnett Street was obviously Connor's head-

quarters. The place had never been raided—for the matter of that, it had never held a pennyworth of stolen property.

He learned now, in the burst of confidence which apprehension inspired, that although the rival gang was called Lewing's, the dead man had had very little to do with its organization. There had been a coterie of irresponsible larrikins and shop thieves, and this had been the nucleus of a more important gang, of which Lewing, at the moment of his death, was the merest servant.

"He was just a little thief and a nose" (this was an informer, Luke learned), said Mrs. Fraser. "Why, he was in stir a few days before he was killed."

Luke nodded. He remembered the occasion of Lewing's first visit to him. He had been in Brixton with Gunner Haynes, and had come in a fraudulent spirit to collect money on behalf of the Gunner.

"There's going to be some trouble—the Lewings have never done this before," repeated Mrs. Fraser. "I must let Connor know about it—you going out?"

Luke was going out, and never intended returning. This latter piece of information he did not pass to his hostess.

"Have you got any money? Oh, that reminds me." The woman searched in a leather bag which she carried beneath her apron and produced a small package of notes. "Connor sent this—it's fifty," she said. "It's only on account. That stuff has got to be cut four ways, and you'll get your share. Connor's always straight about money. You could trust him with a million pounds."

"I don't want this."

"Put it in your pocket," she commanded, and as he did not wish to prolong the conversation he obeyed. "Have you got any small money?"

"I have plenty," he said, almost impatiently.

"Small money," she insisted, and he had reason to be thankful for her insistence.

He had not, and again she dived her hand under the apron and produced some silver and coppers.

"If you try to pass fivers in this country you'll get yourself into trouble," she said. And then: "Are you Australian?"

"No," said Luke.

She was troubled at this, but her face cleared up.

"I expect Connor knows all about it."

Evidently the word of Connor was something more than law.

She accompanied him to the door of the shop. When she found it was raining she went back herself to get his mackintosh.

"Watch out for the Lewings," she warned him, "and keep that gat in your pocket where you can reach it."

She fussed over him as a family nurse might and was not satisfied till he had taken the automatic from his hip and dropped it into the slip pocket of his waterproof.

Why was a pistol called a gat, he wondered. Probably it was an abbreviation of gatling, and was obviously an Americanism.

There was nobody in the street, but he took the precaution, on Mrs. Fraser's advice, of making a wide detour, and ten minutes later he was walking across Westminster Bridge.

Parliament was sitting; the clock in the big tower pointed to twenty minutes to ten.

First he must see Jack Hulbert, that sane young solicitor of his. It struck him that there was a possibility that Jack might not be alone. The telephone, of course! He stopped at the first public booth and put through a call. And here it was he was thankful to Mrs. Fraser for her coppers.

The voice of Mr. Hulbert's servant answered him.

"I want to speak to Mr. Hulbert," he said, and to his horror the reply came:

"Mr. Hulbert is not in England, sir; he has gone to Berlin for a holiday and will not be back till next week. Who is it speaking?"

Luke for the moment was speechless; when the question was repeated he had an inspiration.

"Can you tell me if Mr. Luke Maddison's flat is occupied—is his servant there?"

The tone of the man changed.

"Who are you, and why do you want to know that?" he demanded.

Luke rang off without explanation. He might have told the man who he was, but he was chary of confiding in servants, and it was particularly undesirable that he should betray his presence in London to anybody except to Jack.

And then a thought struck him and he called the number of his own flat. He waited for fully five minutes listening to the faint buzz of the call, and then the operator said:

"I'm sorry, sir, there's no reply from that number."

Luke made a slow way to the Mall, and walked slowly toward Buckingham Palace, oblivious of the rain which was now falling in earnest. There was only one thing to be done, and by the time he reached the end of the Mall he had made his plans. He had often remarked jokingly how easy it was to burgle his flat. Recently there had been erected a new fire escape at the back of the block in which he had his residence, and access to the yard where the escape touched earth was by no means difficult. He could climb the wall from the mews which ran at the back of the flat; he knew exactly how the window could be forced.

CHAPTER XVIII

MARGARET MADDISON was preparing for bed when the street bell rang. She opened the door of her room and listened: somebody was talking in the hall below; she heard her footman's voice and a deeper one, and then somebody said:

"You'd better go up and tell the lady. I must see her . . . Scotland Yard."

She sent her maid down to find out what was the matter, and in a few minutes the girl came back.

"It's an inspector from Scotland Yard, madam. He wants to see you on a matter of importance."

"Is it Mr. Bird?" she asked anxiously.

Why she should be anxious at all she could not for the moment understand. Later she realized that it was the knowledge that Scotland Yard was a carrier of unpleasant news, and that possibly something might have happened to Luke, which sent her down to the drawing room so quickly.

It was not Bird but a stranger, who introduced himself as Divisional Inspector Gorton.

"I'm sorry to bother you at this time of night, Mrs. Maddison," he said, "but we've got a report sent to us by the servant of Mr. Hulbert, the solicitor—I believe he is your husband's solicitor?"

She nodded, and drew a quick breath.

"Is anything wrong—I mean, with Mr. Maddison?"

"No, ma'am, it's not serious—in fact it may be nothing at all. But this valet of Mr. Hulbert's says that he had an inquiry from a strange man to-night as to whether your husband's flat was occupied—he also said that you had the key of the flat."

Margaret nodded. The key had been in her possession since a few days after Luke's departure. His man had brought it; it was at that moment in her desk.

"I understand Mr. Maddison's abroad?"

"Yes, he is in Ronda," she said quickly. "You can have the key."

Inspector Gorton hesitated.

"I'd rather like you to come along with us, madam," he said. "I promise you there's not the slightest danger, but we do not like searching houses until there is a representative of the owner present."

"What do you expect to find? I'll come with pleasure," she said.

"You can wait outside in your car, madam. What do we expect to find? Well, there is a possibility that the man who called up intended burgling the flat, and we want to be on the safe side."

She went upstairs and finished dressing, putting on a raincoat, and accompanied the policeman into the street. A car was drawn up, with two or three men sitting in the back, and she was invited to take her place by the side of the driver.

They came very quickly to the entrance of Luke's flat.

"No, no, I'll come up with you," she said. "I've only been in it twice, but I'll probably be able to help you find your way about."

It was not a pleasant experience, walking into that familiar hall, looking at the dusty furnishings. The place was peculiarly Luke's, had something of his aura, and it gave her a little pang to realize that Luke might never come here again.

"There's a fire escape here, isn't there? Where does it touch?"

"The kitchen," she said.

The inspector sent one of his men to search that apartment; and then suddenly he sniffed.

"Somebody's been smoking a cigar here, and smoking it recently," he said.

Margaret too had smelt the faint fragrance. At that moment the detective sent to look at the kitchen came running back.

"The window's been forced!" he said.

Again Gorton nodded. Evidently he expected to hear this.

"Which is Mr. Maddison's room?"

She pointed. A key was already inserted in the lock. The detective turned the handle. The door did not move: it was bolted on the inside.

"Out you come, son!" he said in a loud voice as he rapped on the panel. "It's a cop!"

He turned to the girl.

"You'd better go downstairs, Mrs. Maddison—we're going to break in this door!"

Luke Maddison, standing on the other side of the door, listening, heard the words and gasped. His wife was there—the one person in the world who must not see him!

CHAPTER XIX

WITH her heart beating a little faster, Margaret passed down the stairs. When she reached the street she found that the driver of the police car had summoned a taxi, which was drawn up behind the tender.

"Is anybody there, miss?" asked a police officer.

"Yes, I think there is," she said breathlessly. "At least, the inspector thinks so."

"You'd better get into the cab, miss," said the police officer. "I suppose Mr. Gorton expects a bit of a fight."

"Do you often have cases like this?"

"About every other day," he said cheerfully. "We're one of the Flying Squads."

Apparently it was quite usual for the Squad to be called to buildings where suspected burglars were. They moved with the celerity of a fire engine and were as alert.

Inspector Gorton waited until Margaret had left the building, and then he rapped again on the panel.

"Open this door, my son."

The bolt was slipped back, the door flung open. The inspector saw a man with grimy face and disordered clothing standing in the doorway, and instantly he was seized.

Luke was taken aback. He had expected an opportunity of parleying, even of taking the detective into his confidence. Resenting the sudden seizure, he tried to shake off the detaining hands, and in the next instant was flung violently to the floor. Somebody passed their hands scientifically behind his coat.

"He's got a gat," said a voice.

The pistol was passed to Inspector Gorton.

"I can explain the gun," said Luke.

"I dare say you can." Gorton snapped back the jacket of the automatic and detached the magazine. "Loaded —you'll get a ten stretch for this, my lad. Fan him, one of you: he may have another."

In two minutes Luke was searched and everything was taken from him.

"Where did you get this money?" asked the inspector.

"It was given to me——" began Luke, and there was a roar of laughter.

"What is this?" said Gorton, examining something in his hand.

That morning, before he had left on his fatal expedition, Mrs. Fraser had handed him a little blue-covered book.

"A driving license, eh? You weren't by any chance driving a car to-day round about Bond Street, were you?"

Luke's heart sank within him. And then he heard one of the detectives say:

"That's the fellow! He had a beard this afternoon. I saw him driving with a woman in the park."

He whispered something to Gorton and the inspector nodded. All the time Luke was thinking rapidly. That simple explanation of his was no longer possible. If he declared himself to be Luke Maddison, he must also explain what he had been doing since he disappeared. The realization of that came with shocking emphasis. And he knew that below, Margaret was waiting and would recognize him instantly in spite of his moustache.

Ahead of him was the open door leading to the hall. To the right the little room he had used as a dressing room. The window was right above the first landing of the fire escape. Luke had a horror of fires, and it was his favourite amusement to plan out how he would escape from a burning building. If he could get to that room. . . . It did not seem possible.

Somebody spoke from the landing outside. It was the hall porter, who had called to discover what the commotion was about. The two detectives who were guarding the door turned their backs for a moment, and in that instant Luke Maddison leaped. He was something of an athlete; had played for his fifteen at college, and had nothing to learn about the art of avoiding a tackle. He dashed through the door of the dressing room, banged it tight, and shot in the bolt as the weight of two men was flung against it.

This was no moment for caution. He flung up the

window and his legs went out almost in the same motion. In another second he dropped into the darkness. He had calculated well. The steel platform of the fire escape clanged under his feet. In another instant he was flying down the steps and was over the wall before the first of the detectives reached the head of the escape.

A man was lounging in the mews: he turned with a shout as Luke dropped. But Luke was off like the wind. His long stay in the hospital had thrown him out of condition, but he had all the technique of a runner. As he emerged from the narrow entrance of the mews he saw a cab passing, and leaped on the running board.

"Paddington," he said, and swung himself deftly inside.

Evidently the driver was in some doubt as to whether he should continue. He went about two blocks and then pulled the car up by the side of the curb.

"Where have you come from?" he asked. "I can't take you, guv'nor. You look as if you were running away from somebody."

"I was," said Luke.

It was not a moment to argue. He threw a two-shilling piece into the man's hand, turned down a narrow street conveniently near, and doubling back, reached the main road. Here he found a taxi moving at leisure, and a driver who did not question his *bona fides*.

"Scotland Yard," he said.

He had made a sudden resolution. He would go to the Sparrow, tell him the truth, and trust to that shrewd man to see him through his troubles.

The cab drew up at the entrance of Scotland Yard and Luke went swiftly down the declivity and into the gloomy entrance hall. A police officer on duty challenged him and he stated his requirements.

"Mr. Bird's been gone for two hours, sir. I think he's gone into the country. Would you like to see anybody else?"

Groaning inwardly, Luke shook his head.

"No, I don't think anybody else would be of much use to me," he said.

"You wouldn't like to see Mr. Gorton? He'll be back soon," said the police officer, quite ignorant of the fact that the one person in the world whom Luke did not wish to see was that same Gorton.

He came out on to the Thames Embankment at one end of the Yard as Gorton and his Flying Squad came in at the other. Turning left, he walked toward Waterloo Bridge. At Charing Cross Underground he made another attempt to get into touch with the Sparrow. There was a chance that the policeman was wrong and that Bird was still in town. He went to the telephone directory, but there were so many Birds that it was impossible to tell which was which. And then he remembered one of his initials—an unusual "Z" (Mr. Bird's middle name was Zachariah). He scanned the list again and going into the telephone booth, gave a number.

At first he thought his luck was in.

"Yes, this is Mr. Bird's house," said a voice, "but he's out of town. Who is it speaking?"

"It is vitally necessary that I should get in touch with

him as soon as possible," said Luke urgently. "Can you tell me where I can find him?"

"Who are you?"

"Will you tell him it's Mr. Maddison speaking? I have been to Scotland Yard . . ."

He felt a sudden draught. The door of the telephone booth was ajar; an unconcerned man was standing near by, and apparently had no interest either in him or his conversation. Luke shut the door again, and then, to his annoyance, found that whoever had spoken for Mr. Bird had hung up her receiver. Still, that was a start. He almost felt a sense of relief as he came out on to the cold Embankment and pursued his way toward Waterloo.

He had not gone twenty yards before two men, walking quickly, overtook him and fell in one at each side.

"Hullo, Smith! Connor wants to see you."

He had never seen the man before. His tone was offensive and peremptory.

"And who may Mr. Connor be?" asked Luke coolly. "My name is not Smith, it is Maddison."

"That's all right, sir," said the other more respectfully, "but Mr. Connor does want to see you pretty badly."

"Where is he?" asked Luke after a moment's thought.

"At the top of Savoy Hill—there goes the Squad."

A car flashed past at that moment; the red light disappeared along the Embankment.

"They call 'em busies and they *are* busy," said the second man bitterly.

They did not go up Savoy Hill but turned aside, passed one entrance of the Savoy Hotel and up a steep and narrow street. They turned again to the right.

"Where is Connor?"

"I'll tell you in a minute, when I've got a light for my fag," said the smaller of the two.

He struck a match, and Luke's eyes instinctively went to it. That is all he remembered. He did not feel the pain of any blow, but dropped limply to the pavement under the impact of a rubber cosh.

His head was splitting when he came to his senses. He was lying on the hard floor of a jolting motor car; he discovered afterwards it was a tilting Ford wagon that bore innocuously enough the name of a respectable firm of greengrocers. The two men were squatting by his side; one was smoking, and they were carrying on a conversation in a low voice.

". . . That's what Connor told me," said one. "But then, Connor always thought this nut would put up a squeal."

Luke lay motionless; his head was throbbing, but he felt no other discomfort. Apparently, although he could guess there was a bump as big as an egg on his skull, the blow had not drawn blood.

The car stopped. There was the creak of a gate being opened, and then they went forward again, jolting over uneven ground; presently the car stopped and the engine was shut off.

"Are you awake?" asked a voice.

"I'm awake all right," said Luke.

"Then get out of this. Why was you so foolish, Smith?"

A mild question from a man who, only ten minutes before, had stunned him.

He slithered out of the back of the car and came to his feet on soft, muddy ground. The cold night air made him reel; one of the men caught him by the arm and guided him into what looked to be a small cottage. To the right he saw the gleam of the river. A tug was moving, her green starboard light reflected in the water. So quickly she was moving that he guessed she was going downstream. He must therefore be on the Surrey side of the Thames.

He could see nothing but a high wall to his right, and far away a blood-red advertisement sign. The door banged on him. There was a smell of dampness, but apparently the cottage had some sort of furnishing, for he walked upon something that might have been a carpet, and when a door was opened on his right and he was pushed in, he found himself in a room not only furnished but overfurnished.

Connor was sitting at a table shuffling a pack of cards. He looked up as Luke entered the room.

"Did you have to cosh him?" he asked pleasantly.

The man who held Luke's arm grinned.

"He wouldn't be sensible," he said.

"Sit down." Connor pointed to a horsehair sofa against the wall, and Luke was glad to accept the invitation. "Tried to put up a squeal, did you, Smith?"

There was nothing unfriendly in Connor's tone, but he did not cease shuffling the cards as he spoke.

"I thought you were a man when you did that bust —yes, one of my lads saw you get into that flat, and saw you when you bolted. But you're nothing better than a dirty squealer. Went into the Yard and asked for the Sparrow, did you? Is he a pal of yours?"

"I know him," said Luke.

Mr. Connor nodded pleasantly.

"And then you tried to get him on the 'phone—what was the squeal about? Don't trouble to tell me: I know. I never trusted you from the first, Smith—I don't trust Australians."

Despite his aching head, Luke could not but smile at this libel.

"I shouldn't think they trust you a great deal, do they?" he asked.

"Not much," said Connor.

He cut the pack into two, shuffling them scientifically, and all the time his eyes were on Luke.

"So you know the Sparrow? That's good. I'll bet you know Danty, too."

Luke started.

"Danty Morell?" he asked.

Why had Danty gone out of his mind? Why had he forgotten that Danty was the confidant of his wife— that his one desire, in seeking freedom from the sinister environment in which he found himself, had been to expose that confidence man?

"Know Danty, too!" Connor's voice was almost admiring. "And Pi Coles?"

Luke nodded.

"Yes, Coles—that's his servant."

Connors smiled broadly, and there were grins on the faces of the other two men.

"Pi is his servant all right. You seem to know the whole darn shoot! I'm telling you, Smith, that a man that knows Danty and the Lewing gang, and calls at Scotland Yard to see his friend the Sparrow, isn't a healthy fellow to have around the house."

There was a long pause, and then he added:

"That's why you're not going to be around the house."

He looked up at one of the men thoughtfully.

"When is high tide?"

"Four o'clock."

Connor nodded. Again his dark eyes fell on Luke.

"You a good swimmer?"

"Fair," said Luke coolly.

"We'll give you a little dip to-night," said Connor. "Put him in the cooler, Harry."

The man who had struck him gripped Luke by the arm and pulled him to his feet. The throbbing was easier now; he did not reel, had recovered something of his strength; but this was not a moment for its exhibition.

Evidently the building was not an extensive one. It had been the weighing room of a company that had once owned the wharf and small warehouse which Connor used as a headquarters.

Connor carried on a legitimate if unprofitable business. He was a dealer in certain building material, and barges came regularly but at rare intervals to this wharf and were unloaded. He bought and sold scrap iron, cement, any commodity which offered an immediate profit. The wharf could be, and was, hired for a fee.

A few paces from the door of the sitting room they came to another. Luke could not help wondering whether the little chamber into which he was thrust had been used before for the same purpose. It had no windows, but in other respects was curiously like a prison cell. It might have been employed for the storage of coal, but there was nothing in it now, not even a bed or a stool. In the light of the man's electric torch he saw that the walls were of brick and whitewashed. Then the door slammed on him; he heard a bolt shot, and he was left alone with the unpleasant knowledge that it would be high tide in five hours, and that Mr. Connor, in his amiable way, had planned "a dip" for him.

CHAPTER XX

Margaret had waited a long time for Mr. Gorton to come out, and when he appeared he was in so great a hurry that he could only tell her the bare fact that he had found a man in the room and that he had escaped. It was the hall porter who supplied her with greater, and in some respects less accurate, information.

"Yes, madam, the police found a man in Mr. Maddison's room. I caught a glimpse of him just before he got away. Good-looking fellow with a moustache, and, according to the police, a pretty desperate burglar— they found a revolver on him. Perhaps you'd like to go up and see the flat, madam?"

Margaret hesitated.

"Yes, I will," she said, and the man took her up in the lift.

A detective had been left in charge of the disordered room; apparently she was expected, for he displayed some relief on her arrival.

"You don't want me to stay, madam? Inspector Gorton told me that he'd like a list of anything missing, and he'll come and see you in the morning."

He showed her the room where the "burglar" had been. Drawers had been pulled out, a desk had been broken open (Luke had lost the key) ; papers littered the floor.

"Mr. Gorton doesn't know even now what he was looking for," said the detective. "There was a gold watch in one of the drawers, but he didn't touch that. We know he was after the clothes."

He showed her a big suitcase into which clothing had been thrown pell-mell. There was a dress suit, half-a-dozen shirts and collars, a wad of pocket handkerchiefs, and a suit of pajamas.

"But he must have spent a lot of time over the desk," said the officer. "One of my mates said that he had something like a book between his shirt and his skin. He'd just felt it when he broke away and made his escape."

"A book?" said Margaret quickly. "How very odd!"

And then her eyes fell upon an envelope on the floor and she recognized it immediately. It bore the official stamp of the Passport Office, and Luke had had it in his pocket the day before the wedding, and had shown it to her in that half-shy and half-amused way of his that sometimes irritated her. It was his new passport, decorated, rather prematurely, with a portrait of his wife. He had opened it in her presence, and she had been rather annoyed because he had light-heartedly forged her name in order to present her with the document on her wedding day.

She picked up the envelope; there was nothing inside it—this, then, was the book which the burglar had stolen—why?

There were several sheets of notepaper on the floor.

She picked up one, read it and gasped. The date had been scrawled in on the top line, and it began:

My dear Hulbert, I am in a most terrible——

It was Luke's writing! It was Luke who had been there that night. She found another sheet covered with smudged writing; this also was addressed to the solicitor, but the three scrawled lines were undecipherable. He had deliberately crossed them out. Evidently he had sat down to write a letter to Hulbert, had made two attempts and then had changed his mind.

It was so like Luke: he could never resist the temptation offered by a sheet of note paper—he must write to somebody, he had often told her.

Luke had been here; Luke was the burglar. But why?

She turned to the detective, and it was on the tip of her tongue to make the revelation when he said something that struck speech from her lips.

"He must have been a pretty bad man, that fellow— one of our men recognized him as the chap who was driving a car this afternoon when Taffanny's was robbed. He gave one of the shop assistants a punch in the jaw——"

"But that's impossible!" she said indignantly. "This man——"

"Ah, you've read about it in the papers—a bearded man. That's right, madam, he's taken his beard off this afternoon. Johnson—that's the officer—saw him driving with a girl round the park."

Again speech died on her lips.

"They got her to-night," said the communicative detective. "Mr. Gorton's pretty certain she'll put up a squeal—I mean to say, she'll tell who her companion was. From all accounts he's a man who's been seen about with her a great deal in the past year or two."

She was stunned, bewildered; she could only shake her head in feeble protest.

"It couldn't have been the same man," she said at last.

"Do you know him—the fellow who was here?" The detective looked at her keenly.

"No, no," she said hastily. "I only thought . . . it would be such an extraordinary coincidence."

"I've got an idea Mr. Gorton knows him." The detective shut the door behind her as she walked out of the room. "I heard him telling the sergeant that he might be the fellow who was knifed the night a man named Lewing was killed. If that's the case, he's only been out of hospital a few days."

She offered the officer some money; he refused it with great firmness and escorted her to her taxi. She was reminded by the fare, when she reached her house, that she had been two hours absent.

Her maid was waiting up for her and she sent her down to make some coffee. Turning on all the lights in the drawing room, she opened her desk and presently found a bundle of Luke's letters. She compared their beginnings with the two scraps of paper she had brought from the flat. There was no question at all: it was Luke's writing. The "My dear" began characteristically in the middle of the page in every case.

It was Luke! And it had been Luke that afternoon in a car with that impossible woman! Luke who had assisted at the robbery of Taffanny's!

She was not shocked; it was too tremendous a discovery to produce emotional phenomena of the commonplace kind. She accepted Luke Maddison, banker, burglar, hold-up man, companion of questionable ladies, with the calmness of a scientist who had happened upon a new and interesting discovery.

Here was an immense happening. To display anger or humiliation would be absurd. One has no regard for a sense of decency when fleeing from an earthquake and its tumbling walls.

She went to bed; and such is the serenity of a resolute mind that she slept dreamlessly. In the morning while she was sitting at breakfast came Inspector Gorton; she listened calmly to his confession of failure.

"The fellow ran like a hare. He must have been a trained athlete," he said. "I'm pretty sure now that he is the fellow who was knifed in a gang fight in South London. Lewing was killed."

"Who was Lewing?" she asked.

Gorton shrugged his broad shoulders.

"Nobody in particular, although he gave his name to a gang. The real leader of that crowd is a gentleman named Danty Morell—though he hasn't taken any very active . . ."

She had put down her cup. He saw how white her face was.

"Danty Morell? You don't mean Mr. Danton Morell who lives in Half Moon Street?"

Gorton smiled.

"Perhaps I oughtn't to have said that, but I thought Mr. Bird had told you. You know Mr. Bird? I hope you don't know Mr. Morell!"

"I know him very well," she said; her voice was steady and she was smiling. "But you may rely on my discretion, Inspector—I feel almost like a Scotland Yard officer myself."

She had her hands folded in her lap so that he could not see how they were trembling.

"He may, of course, have turned over a new leaf," said Gorton, uneasily conscious that he had said the wrong thing. "Some of these fellows do. I know there's been no complaint against him at the Yard for a very long time. Morell isn't his name, of course—I forget what it was, but the Sparrow—I mean Mr. Bird knows. Wonderful fellow, Danty! He can talk the hind leg off a donkey. They say he's the cleverest confidence man that ever operated in Europe. Perhaps he's made enough money to retire."

Danton Morell! How had she come to know him? She tried to trace back the friendship. Of course, it was her brother—her poor brother—who had introduced him. Rex knew so many queer people. She trusted him— she had trusted Danty. She had believed him implicitly,

believed him when he told her that Luke had hounded
her brother to his death, believed him when he had produced that pitiable note written on two small sheets of
notepaper—that at least was genuine, for she knew
her brother's writing.

She was viewing a new world, or viewing it from
a new angle; and somehow she was able to cope with
problems which the day before would have terrified her.
Of that new gift she was unconscious—she could only
feel the effect.

Gorton, who had had very little sleep on the previous
night, accepted her invitation to join her at breakfast,
though he confined himself to a cup of coffee and a roll.

"You found nothing missing, I suppose? The officer
I left in charge told me you'd been there looking round.
Where is your good husband now, Mrs. Maddison?"

She swallowed something.

"In Spain, I think. I am going to join him in a day
or two."

"None of the wedding presents were at the flat?"

She shook her head.

"We had no wedding presents," she smiled.

He finished his coffee, folded his serviette, and got
up from the table.

"Now I've got a very unpleasant job which I wish
somebody else was going to do," he said.

"You're going to arrest somebody?"

He shook his head.

"No, that wouldn't be unpleasant—I enjoy putting
these fellows behind bars; and the day I catch that enter-

prising gentleman who came to your flat last night will be one of the happiest I have known for years! No, this is something gruesome which would shock you, so I shan't tell you."

"I'm beyond being shocked," she smiled.

"It's nothing really," said Gorton. "Only there was a very high tide last night, and the river police found the body of a man who had evidently been drowned in the night. I'm going down to see if I know him. From the description I had I shouldn't be surprised if it was our burglar."

She had said she could not be shocked. She was shocked now, and clasping her hands together so tightly that they hurt—it was only the pain that prevented her from fainting.

CHAPTER XXI

DURING the hours which Luke Maddison had spent in his prison house, it was curious that he should think so little on serious topics. He was face to face with death in its most hideous aspect—it was impossible to mistake Connor's intention—and yet for the main part his mind was occupied by the veriest trivialities. If he thought of Margaret at all it was only in a detached and impersonal way and to find an explanation for her presence with the police at his flat that night. She must have had the key; the police went to her—but why?

Then he remembered his conversation with Hulbert's servant, who had obviously been suspicious and must have communicated at once with the nearest police station.

He thought of the drive across London in that uncomfortable van, and spent quite an hour trying to locate exactly the building in which he was confined. Driving along the Embankment on his way to the City, he must have often seen the very wharf, the very building. He went to the City twice a week, to directors' meetings, and he loved the Embankment in the early days of spring, when the green was bursting from the trees, and sunlight dappled the pavements with moving arabesques of shadow.

In such circumstances as his all a man's past life should come before him. Luke made an effort to satisfy the convention, but grew bored after five minutes.

He wandered round and round his cell, feeling the walls in a grim spirit of humour, seeking for those loose bricks which inevitably occur in the prison houses of heroes. Not that he was any hero, he decided. He was a smash-and-grab man—liable, probably, to three years penal servitude, certainly to disgrace. He decided that it was not in any spirit of altruism that he wished to save Margaret's name from being dragged into this sordid affair. It was because it would intensify his own sense of foolishness.

Exactly what would Connor do? He was almost curious to know.

There was a church clock close by; he heard it striking the quarters and the hours, and the last notes of three were still quivering on the air when he heard the sound of a key in the lock, the door was opened, and the two men who had been his captors invited him forth. Their tone was friendly, almost courteous.

He followed the first, and was followed by the second, into the room. Connor had evidently been sleeping on a folding bed. He sat on the edge of his untidy couch, rubbing his fingers through his hair and yawning prodigiously. On the table were four cups of steaming coffee and some sandwiches.

"Sit down, Smith. We've got to think out what we're going to do with you," said Connor, coming to his feet with a yawn.

He drew up a chair to the table and fell into it; pulled a cup of coffee toward him and took a sandwich.

"Help yourself to milk and sugar."

He pushed a cup toward the prisoner. Luke was looking round the room interestedly. Stacked on a chair were four great bars of something white and crystalline, which he guessed was salt, and on the floor was a long length of heavy chain.

Connor followed the direction of his eyes.

"Want to buy a bit of salt?" he asked good-humouredly.

His question seemed to tickle his two companions, for they chuckled deeply.

"I am not in the salt business," said Luke with a smile.

He sipped at the coffee; it was raw stuff, but the warmth of it was grateful, for the night was cold and he had grown chilly in the brick-lined room.

"What are we going to do with you, Smith, eh?"

Luke took a big gulp of coffee and leaned back in his chair with a laugh.

"You can listen to a very interesting story," he said, "and you can also earn yourself a thousand pounds."

He saw a faint ghost of a smile come to Connor's face.

"Go on," said that tousled man.

Then Luke told everything, but without referring to Margaret. He gave his name, his address, told how he came to meet Lewing, related the story of Lewing's little fraud and of his meeting him on that night——

"But what were you running away from?" asked Connor.

This was difficult to explain, for Luke had perforce to leave out the motive for his strange action. He could neither tell of his marriage nor of Margaret's staggering conduct; and without these facts he felt he was being unconvincing. Nevertheless, with this handicap, he struggled on to a finish. Connor shook his head.

"I've heard all about you, Smith—there never was a con man who couldn't tell a tale. But if you're a specimen of the Australian man I wonder you're not starving! Drink up your coffee and have some more. I want to find a way of settling this business without unpleasantness."

Luke finished the coffee and put down the cup.

"Now, I'll tell one," said Connor, and his voice was no longer pleasant or amiable. "You've been to the police and you've tried to double-cross me. And now you think you'll get out of it with a silly story! . . . Squealer . . . police find you . . ."

Luke heard only scraps of the talk: he was desperately sleepy. His head sank forward on his breast, and though he strove with all his will-power to rouse himself, he could not so much as open his eyes. He did not even realize that he had been drinking laudanum——

"Hold him up," said Connor.

One of the men caught Luke as he swayed sideways and lowered him to the floor. Connor pushed back the table and jerked his thumb in the direction of the salt. Two blocks were put on the floor under Luke's legs, and with a knife one of the men scooped a deep depression in two of the corners. The other blocks were laid on top. Connor lifted the heavy chain, wound it carefully round and round the salt, fastening the last two links with a piece of wire.

They discussed their grisly work without emotion.

". . . You want to be careful it doesn't slip over his feet, Harry," said Connor. "Tighten that chain a bit —not too tight or you'll break the salt."

At last it was finished and Connor straightened his back.

"Get that old plank to lay him on," he commanded, and the bigger of the two walked to the door and pulled it open.

Connor saw him start back and his face wrinkle.

"Who's that?" he asked sharply.

The man who was in the passage walked into the room at his leisure. Connor saw him and showed his teeth like an angry dog.

"Hullo, Gunner! What the hell are you doing round here?"

Gunner Haynes looked from Connor to the unconscious man on the floor.

"Ingenious but not original," he drawled, his thin lips curling in contempt. "You're dropping him in the river, of course, and the water will dissolve the salt, the chains will fall off, and the verdict will be 'Death from misadventure.' What a pity!"

"What's the pity, Gunner?" asked Connor.

"That I happened to butt in," said Haynes. "Who's the victim?"

"There's no victim," said Connor loudly. "This poor fellow is ill and we're taking him off to the hospital."

The Gunner nodded.

"I thought you might be pickling him," he said, shook his head and repeated: "Ingenious but not original. No marks of violence on the body, nothing to show that he didn't drown, as people do drown, by accident. I'm sorry to have spoiled your amusement, but you'll have to let him go."

"Why?" asked Connor.

"Because," said the Gunner deliberately, "I'm in it! You don't catch me as accessory before, after, or in the fact of murder. It's not my graft, Connor. Remove that interesting apparatus."

Connor smiled. His hand dropped quite naturally out of sight below the level of the table.

"If you pull a gun on me," said the Gunner, not a muscle of his lean body moving, "I shall shoot you through the stomach. It'll take you five days to die, and it's a very painful death by all accounts. I shall then go out and explain to the police why I shot you, and there will be no flowers from Scotland Yard."

One of Connor's assistants moved a step toward him.

"Look here, Gunner——" he began, mildly enough.

Haynes's fist shot out so swiftly that the man could not counter the blow. He went down with a crash. The Gunner stood motionless, watching.

"Both hands in sight," said Haynes. "Lay 'em on the table, Connor."

He had no weapon in his hand, but none knew better than the livid man on the other side of the table how quickly the Gunner could draw, with what devilish accuracy he could shoot.

"What's the fuss?" he growled. "This bird doesn't mean a thing to you."

"Unlace him," smiled the Gunner. "I'm sorry to butt in, as I said before."

"What did you come here for, anyway?" asked the other savagely.

The Gunner looked up at the ceiling.

"I forget exactly," he said untruthfully. And then: "Who is this man?"

"Man named Smith. He squealed on me to-night, and then tried to carry it off with a tale about being a banker—he's got a nerve! Luke something or other."

Gunner Haynes bent down and peered into Luke's face.

He recognized the sleeping man instantly.

"Luke something or other, eh? Where did you pick him up?" As he spoke he beckoned one of the men. "Take that chain off," he said.

The man glanced uneasily at his chief, but Connor nodded.

"The trouble with you, Gunner, is that you will interfere with other people's graft. If you want to know who he is, he did that job to-day in Bond Street."

He related "Smith's" biography; Gunner Haynes

knew that he was speaking the truth. He was puzzled, but not greatly. He had lived too long on the seamy and shadowy side of life to be surprised at anything. Men had lived double lives before; but this was the kind of double life which Haynes thought belonged to the realm of imaginative novelists. A banker who amused himself in smash-and-grab raids was wildly fictional—but possible.

There might be, he thought, a woman somewhere in the background. Where women touched life, the inexplicable became almost daylight-clear.

"What are you going to do with him?" asked Connor, as the man stooped and with scarcely an effort lifted the unconsious Luke onto the chair.

The Gunner did not answer the question. Instead, he propounded one of his own.

"Have you any slush in this place?" he asked and saw a look of alarm come into the imperturable face of the other.

"Slush?" said Connor quickly. "No—why should we? I don't deal in that kind of stuff."

"No forged French banknotes?" The Gunner shook his head in anticipation of the answer.

"What do you mean, Gunner?"

A smile lit up the saturnine face.

"You asked me why I came here, and I'm telling you. They're raiding your place to-night. I only got to know it an hour ago. I thought I'd come along and tell you. I don't know why, but that's my nature—helping poor crooks!"

He saw the three men glance at one another, and the alarm in Connor's face was patent.

"We had a parcel over from Paris the other day," he said uneasily. "Harry, get it up."

He looked at the huddled figure of Luke.

"You're making a big mistake about this bird," he said. "You let him get into the hands of the police, and he'll put up a squeal that'll make you deaf!"

Stooping, the Gunner put his arm about Luke Maddison and lifted him bodily. He turned and strode through the door, down the narrow passage, and into the untidy yard. He had already located Connor's van, and he was on the point of hoisting his burden into its interior when he heard a stealthy scraping against wood. It was the sound that a man makes when he is climbing—somebody was getting over the gate.

He sat Luke on the ground, propped him against a wall, and went noiselessly toward the entrance of the yard. Stooping to get a skyline, he saw the head and shoulders of two men above the gate. It was enough; he need see no more.

Returning as quickly as he came to the place where he had left Luke, he lifted him and went cautiously and gingerly down the slope toward the water. There would be a boat here. Presently his keen eyes discerned the dim shape of it as it moved uneasily on the rising tide.

He had considered the possibility of leaving Luke to be discovered by the police, and had rejected that plan. He owed a debt to this man—he could not leave him to discovery and disgrace. If what Connor had said was true, Maddison, in his capacity of brigand, was as much wanted by the police as Connor himself.

He drew the boat to the broken stone causeway with the heel of his boot, and put Luke aboard by the simple process of laying him level with the edge of the wharf and rolling him onto the boat. It took a few minutes to balance him. As he himself stepped astride of the man, he heard the sound of voices in the yard, saw the flicker of electric lamps. Untying the painter, he pushed off with his hand, dragged an oar from under the reclining figure and paddled his way to midstream, keeping a sharp lookout for the river police.

He saw the launch coming downstream at full speed, and drove his boat into the shelter of two moored barges as the tiny steamer swung in a semicircle.

"A bit late," muttered the Gunner.

He was free from detection now, unless he met another patrol, and finding the second oar, he pushed Luke down between the two seats and sitting, rowed steadily downstream.

In an hour there would be daylight; already the eastern sky was whitening. The Gunner knew a safe landing near Rotherhithe; the tide was turning and would, he judged, carry him to safety.

He judged wrong, and saw, before he had reached London Bridge, that he could not make his destination in the darkness. He took his decision quickly. Stooping over the side of the boat, he filled his hat with water and dashed it in the face of the slumbering man. Luke shivered and groaned, and the Gunner repeated his experiment. He heard the moaning voice of the man at the bottom of the boat.

"My head . . ."

"Keep quiet!" hissed Haynes. "I'm taking you to London Bridge Stairs."

There was no answer, and the Gunner prodded with his heel at his uneasily moving cargo.

"Do you hear me?"

"Yes, I hear you. What has happened?"

Haynes did not reply, but pulled at his oars, and in a minute Luke heard the jolt of the boat striking against the stone.

"Can you get up?" The Gunner's hand gripped Luke's wrist and drew him to a sitting position.

With the boathook he drew the little skiff against the steps and came to land. It took five minutes before Luke could follow him. His knees gave under him, and he wanted all the support that his companion could give him.

"Sit on the steps," commanded the Gunner, and Luke obeyed. "Now try to stand."

For five minutes Luke sat crouched up, his face in his hands, and then the Gunner's voice aroused him.

"There are too many people passing over the bridge to please me," he said. "We had better get up before it's light."

He assisted the half-unconscious man to rise to his feet. The Gunner's grip was firm as they climbed the steep flight until they emerged flush with the footpath. The people who were hurrying across the bridge took little notice of them, and gripping his companion by the arm, the Gunner led him down toward Tooley Street. When he saw a slowly moving cab he hailed the driver and bundled Luke inside.

"My friend's a bit under the weather," he explained to the cabman with a smile. "Drive me to Lennox Street, Clerkenwell."

There was a large block of model buildings in Lennox Street, and for years the Gunner had had his secret headquarters in a fairly large flat on the ground floor. It was a place to which he very seldom came, and of whose existence the police were ignorant. It was his *pied-à-terre,* jealously preserved for emergencies. He had slept there two nights before, and the woman who came in daily had made the bed. Upon this he laid Luke Maddison.

"They must have given you a pretty large dose," he said. "I'll make you some coffee."

Luke shuddered.

"Coffee—ugh!"

"Gave it you in that, did they? That's probably why you're not dead."

He pulled down the blinds before he lit the gas; then, going out into the little kitchen, he made coffee as only a man who had fended for himself on the Continent, and who had kept house in places as wide apart as Biarritz is from Munich, could brew that delicious beverage. When he came back Luke was sitting on the side of the bed, his head in his hands.

"A couple of aspirins ought to put you right," said

the Gunner, and went in search of the little white pellets.

Luke gulped down the medicine, and then for the first time became conscious of his benefactor.

"Aren't you Gunner Haynes?" he asked.

Haynes smiled.

"That is my name."

"Where is Connor?"

Again that cryptic smile.

"In jail, I hope," said the Gunner. "Now, Mr. Maddison, are you well enough to talk?"

Luke looked up eagerly.

"You know me, then?"

The man nodded.

"I knew you the first time I saw you. There's one thing I want to ask you—is it true, the story that Connor told? That you were in that smash-and-grab raid at Taffanny's?"

Luke nodded.

"I drove the car. I hadn't the slightest idea what they wanted me to do or what it was all about until it was too late."

"So you're the bearded man?" mused the Gunner. "That certainly is amazing. I'm not asking you to explain——"

"I'll explain as soon as my head stops splitting," groaned Luke.

It was after two that afternoon when he woke from an uneasy sleep. His head was still thick, his mouth tasted like a limekiln, but after a cold wash at the kitchen sink he was near to his normal self; and over a cigarette and a cup of tea he told the story from start to finish, and this time reserved nothing.

The Gunner listened in silence, making no comment until he had finished.

"Did you tell Connor this story?"

Luke nodded.

"Yes, except that naturally enough I didn't speak about my wife and the—money. Why do you ask?"

Gunner Haynes pursed his lips.

"I don't know. Connor is a pretty bad man. Your only hope is that he's sent down for a stretch—by which inelegant word I mean a term of penal servitude. If he gets away with this police raid, supposing they find nothing on the premises—and like a fool I gave him plenty of warning—Connor is the sort of man who would investigate the most unlikely story if he thought there was a chance of money in it. And that is going to make your reappearance a rather difficult matter."

He lit another cigarette and stared past his guest.

"Tell me why your wife hated you—you rather glossed over that part of your yarn."

Luke was silent for a long time.

"I don't think it's very difficult to understand," he said. "She thought I was responsible for the death of her brother. He shot himself."

"But why did she understand that?" persisted the Gunner. "Allowing that Danty Morell is a very plausible gentleman, she would hardly take his bare word." He thought for a moment, then asked suddenly: "When that boy shot himself did he leave any message behind?"

Luke shook his head.

"I heard of none—nor was anything mentioned at the inquest."

"Who found his body?"

Luke considered.

"Morell was in the room and made the discovery."

The Gunner nodded.

"And immediately after that Mrs. Maddison's manner changed. Of course, you weren't married then, but that is a fact, isn't it? If that is a fact, it means that Danty carried some evidence to the young lady that was quite sufficient to make her play this trick——"

"I'm not blaming her," began Luke.

He saw a flicker of amusement in the man's eyes.

"You are?"

"Well, not exactly," drawled the Gunner. "I've given up blaming people. There's no profit in it."

He flicked off the ash of his cigarette carefully into his saucer.

"You can't make a sudden reappearance; you can't even get to Ronda and be sure you'll get away with it," he said. "You've got yourself mixed up with two bad gangsters—Connor and Morell."

He rose and paced up and down the small room, his eyes narrowed, his brow corrugated in thought.

"It's Connor that's worrying me. If he's held for trial, that problem is settled. If he isn't, and suppose you come back from Ronda, he'll be able to trace all your movements. Have you got your passport?"

He saw Luke thrust his hand inside his shirt, and a look of blank dismay come to his face.

"I've lost it somewhere."

Gunner Haynes's lips clicked impatiently.

"If you lost it at Keel's Wharf then you're in the soup," he said. "There's only one thing to do and that is to get your passport back. There's another thing: I want to see the letter that that boy wrote before he shot himself."

Luke shook his head.

"I don't believe he wrote a letter, and if he did it was certainly destroyed."

Ten minutes later the Gunner left the house on his quest. His first call was at a police station near to Keel's Wharf. He knew the inspector in charge, and between them was that curious camaraderie which it is so difficult for the "layman" to appreciate—the understanding between the criminal and his ruthless enemy.

In point of fact the Gunner met the divisional inspector as he was coming out of the station.

"I hear you've had trouble at Keel's Wharf," he said.

The inspector looked at him with a smile in his keen eyes.

"Is this hearsay or information, Gunner, or direct observation?"

"Come again," said the Gunner, with elaborate innocence.

"Connor says you were on the wharf a few minutes before, and that if anybody was toting slush it was you.

He said you came with a parcel, that he refused to entertain the deal, and that you got away by boat."

Now the police do not always speak the truth. It is a lamentable statement to make. They have to deal with liars and cunning men. But the Gunner trusted the man to whom he was speaking.

"I was on the wharf, yes," he said. "As a matter of fact I came to see him about another matter altogether —you know that forgeries are not in my line. I heard the raid and I got away by boat. I gather that you did not pull him?"

The inspector shook his head.

"No; there was nothing there. Connor and his friends seem to be doing an extensive trade in salt. Do you know anything about that, Gunner?"

"If I did I shouldn't tell you," said Haynes coolly. "So you didn't drag Connor, eh? That's a pity."

The detective looked left and right and lowered his voice.

"If you particularly want him dragged, you'll tell me what I can drag him on——"

Again the Gunner shook his head.

"You want me to give you a little information? I'm not that kind of bureau! Is Connor still at the wharf?"

The inspector nodded.

"I think I'll call on him. I haven't seen you, Pullman."

He came to the wharf and found Connor in a very cheerful frame of mind. If he was at all disconcerted to see Gunner Haynes, he did not reveal the fact.

"You owe me four pounds," said Connor. "That's

the price I paid for that boat which you pinched. You're not staying long, are you? Because I'm expecting a lady visitor."

"Who amongst your friends has this courtesy title?" asked the Gunner offensively.

"Nobody you know," said Connor carelessly. "A lady named Mrs. Maddison—who has recently lost her husband."

CHAPTER XXII

Gunner Haynes looked at his companion oddly.

"You are expecting Mrs. Maddison, are you? Who is she?"

Connor took up a half-smoked cigar from an ash tray on the table and lit it.

"A friend of mine," he said. "What have you done with your pal?"

"Who is Mrs. Maddison?" asked the Gunner again.

Connor tried to appear unconcerned. He had heard that steely tone before, and it was rather disconcerting.

"She's the wife of a friend of mine," he said.

"Sit down," said the Gunner, "and let's talk."

Reluctantly Connor pulled up a chair and sat. As he did so, Gunner Haynes walked to the door, closed and locked it.

"Let's talk," he said again, and sat opposite the gangster.

"Look here, Gunner, I don't want any trouble with you," suggested Connor. "If there's anything coming, you can take your corner. I don't know whether Maddison was making up that story he told me or not, but if he wasn't then there's big money in this. Naturally, I didn't take any notice of the yarn he told when we were readying him; but after you got him away Billy—that's the man who's working with me—said he'd seen something in the paper about Maddison's wedding. I had a chat with one of the busies who came to fan this place, and he told me that Maddison's flat was broken into last night by the man who drove the car. That tallied with all Maddison told me—and all I knew. This isn't the first time I've seen a swell playing crook, but I've never had the luck to catch one before. This man will be money for jam."

"You're sure it is he, eh?" asked the Gunner, and deceived by the mild inquiry, Connor went on with greater confidence.

"Sure! I sent a flash fellow up to Maddison's office to see his manager—Stiles, I think his name is. There's a portrait of Maddison hanging up in the private room, which my fellow saw. He got the name of the photographer and tried to buy a copy. He couldn't get that, but he was told where the picture had appeared in one of these illustrated weeklies, and he got a copy of that."

Connor pulled open a drawer of the table and took out a periodical which had been folded over at a page. He pushed the paper to Gunner Haynes.

"That's him all right," said Connor, with a confident smile. "I'd have known him with or without his moustache. Maddison went away the day after he was married. There's a woman in it somewhere———"

"What a brain you've got!" interrupted the Gunner with mock admiration, and Connor scowled. Any reflection on his mentality infuriated him. It was his weakness that he believed himself to be the cleverest of his kind.

"Brain or no brain," he growled, "there's the picture, and that's the man. I could shop him to-day, and he knows it. Naturally, if I have ten minutes' talk with him I shall make him see sense, but if I can't get him I thought I'd send a note to his wife. She's got a bit of money——"

"What sort of a note?" asked the Gunner, and the man hesitated.

"Billy writes a better hand than me—I read in the paper the other day that all clever people write bad——"

"And some of the unclever ones, too," said the Gunner.

He watched the man groping in the drawer, and presently his hand came out with two or three sheets of paper covered with pencilled writing.

"I wrote it down, and Billy copied it and did the spelling," said Connor. "As you're in on this, Gunner, you'd better see what I've said."

He pushed the note across, one hand still in the drawer, a fact which the Gunner did not fail to notice; as he stretched out and took the paper, his own hand came up and an automatic lay flat on the table, the barrel pointing to Connor's diaphragm.

"Take your hand out of the drawer. If there's any murder to be committed, I'd prefer to commit it myself," he said.

Connor's hand came up with great alacrity.

"I'm surprised at you, Gunner—you wouldn't trust your best friend."

"You're no friend of mine," said the Gunner.

He found some difficulty in reading the scrawled words. The note ran:

Dear Mrs. Maddison, I should like to give you some information about your husband. I am afraid he has got into serious trouble, but I can get him out of it. He has fallen into bad hands through no fault of his own——

The Gunner read the last sentence aloud and looked up.

"That's a bit of a smoodge," said Connor coolly. "Naturally I want to wrap it up for him so that it looks as though I'm trying to help him."

"Strategist!" murmured the Gunner, and went on with his reading.

It will be very serious if the police know what I know re robbery at Taffany's, but I think I can get him out of it, though it may cost a bit of money, which I'm sure you will not mind paying.

Haynes smiled sardonically as he came to this line.

Don't take this note to the police but bring it with you. If you go to the police, your husband will be in trouble. Come and see me after dark. . . .

Here followed elaborate directions as to how the wharf was to be reached.

"That's the letter, is it?" The Gunner pushed the paper across the table. "I thought you were a specialist, Connor. I've never known you put the black before."

"This isn't blackmail," said Connor indignantly, "this is compensation for money wasted. Besides, he pretended he was an Australian fellow called Smith——"

"He pretended nothing of the kind. You jumped at the conclusion that he was Smith because he was in Lewing's company the night your crowd knifed him," said the Gunner quietly. "It'll interest you to know that Smith never arrived in England—he was turned back at Plymouth; he is now on his way to Australia."

He took a cigar from his pocket, bit off the end and lit the long brown smoke.

"Suppose Mrs. Maddison goes to the police—they'll catch you for ten years, Connor."

Connor smiled uneasily.

"Is that likely——" he began.

There was a tap at the door.

"Open it," ordered Haynes.

Connor unlocked the door. One of his men was standing outside, and by his agitation he knew something was wrong.

"The Sparrow's here, with a lady," he whispered hoarsely, and watching him the Gunner saw Connor's face go gray.

"Do you hear that?" asked Connor breathlessly. "The Sparrow—she's brought him."

He snatched the letter up from the table, made a ball of it and threw it into the little fire. At that moment they heard the heavy footsteps of Inspector Bird in the passage.

The big man came in, a benevolent smile upon his large face, and behind him a pretty girl whom the Gunner had met before.

"Why, Gunner, this is an unexpected pleasure!" rumbled the Sparrow. "Thirty-eight more of you, and you'd have a regular Ali Baba's cave!"

Haynes saw that the girl recognized him. He was already on his feet, and gave her a friendly little nod.

"How are you, Miss Bolford?" he said, and the sharp-eared Connor heard, as he intended he should hear. The last thing in the world he wanted was for the blackmailer to reveal the fact that he was expecting Margaret Maddison.

He saw the look of bewilderment and relief that came into Connor's face, and knew that he had taken the hint.

"I didn't know you were running with this crowd, Gunner," said the Sparrow. "Old friend of yours, Miss Bolford." His finger shot out. "That's Connor. You ought to know Connor, Miss Bolford." And then, to the discomfited man: "This lady is on a newspaper, and she wants to get acquainted with all the bad and nearly bad men in London. Raided last night, weren't you?"

"They're always raiding me," grinned Connor, "and never finding anything, Mr. Bird."

The Sparrow's eyes roved from one to the other.

"How long have the crow and the hawk been living in the same nest? That's puzzling me," he asked. "Coming down in the world, aren't you, Gunner? What are you doing here?"

"Slumming," said Gunner Haynes coolly. "I like now and again to establish contact with the underworld."

The detective's face was wreathed in a sudden smile.

"Hear him?" he asked admiringly. "Quite a classy line of conversation. There's nobody like him."

This was the Gunner's opportunity. He knew that Bird would keep occupied the discomfited owner of the wharf. He put on his hat carefully and moved toward the door.

"I'll be getting along, Mr. Bird. I presume you don't wish to see me?"

And then he saw a malignant gleam in Connor's eye.

"So long, Gunner!" said the man loudly. "If you take my advice, give up carrying a gat: it will do you no good, and get you a lagging if you're ever caught."

"Carrying a gat, is he?" The Sparrow became instantly alert. "That's a silly thing to do, Gunner. Got a license?"

Haynes smiled.

"I don't carry a license and you can search my clothing for a gat. You've no right to, but you can."

He spread out his arms and Bird's hands passed over him quickly. Mary Bolford watched the deadly byplay and was fascinated.

"No gat there," said the Sparrow. Then, to Connor: "What's the idea?"

"I can tell you what the idea is." The Gunner was at the door. "Our friend was anxious to do a trade in lethal firearms, and I wasn't buying any. The only gun you're likely to see to-day, Mr. Bird, is in that table drawer."

The detective pulled open the drawer near where the man had sat, and Mary Bolford saw Connor's face go

green, for there at the bottom of the drawer was a sil-
ver-plated revolver.

"I'll leave you to it," said the Gunner easily, and
strolled out.

Before he passed through the little wicket gate leading to the street he took off his hat as carefully as he had
put it on, and removed from its interior the automatic
he had cached, and slipped it into his pocket.

CHAPTER XXIII

MARGARET MADDISON had spent a torturing two hours before the shabby messenger had brought her the note which told her at least that Luke was alive. At the bottom of the letter there was scrawled in a different hand—Connor's own—"Come round about eight." The postscript he had not communicated to the Gunner.

The letter confirmed all she had feared. She sat motionless at her desk for half an hour with the copperplate communication before her, trying to formulate a working theory. Luke was in trouble—had trouble. She had accepted this fact as a starting point. In her mind she did not reproach him for the monstrous eccentricity which had brought him to his present position— rather she hated herself that in a moment of crisis she had deserted him and urged him into deeper folly.

A servant came into the room and spoke to her, but she was so absorbed that she did not notice his presence, and he spoke again.

"Mr. Morell?" She came to reality with a start. She had not seen Danty for days, and her first inclination was to send a message that she was not well enough to be seen. And then a thought occurred to her, and she nodded.

"Ask him to come up, please."

Danty came in, a sprucely dressed man about town,

and bore in his smiling face no evidence of his embarrassment.

"Any news of Luke?" he asked, almost jovially. "I was on my way to the City and I thought I'd call in."

She was regarding him curiously. Danton the friend, and Danton the gang leader, were indistinguishable. It came almost as a shock to her to realize that her confidence in him had already evaporated before Gorton had told her the truth about this adventurer. In that moment she realized how complete had been his duplicity, yet in her desk was that fatal message from Rex. That at least must have been true. It was Danty who had arranged to send her the message from Paris which bore Luke's signature.

Yet she felt no indignation, no resentment—Danton was an ugly fact, no less or more a fact because of its ugliness.

"I heard from a friend of mine that Luke's flat was burgled last night. Did they get anything?"

"Nothing of any great consequence," she said.

He saw her fold in some haste a letter that was in front of her, and put it in a little handbag that lay on the table, and he wondered what there was in that epistle which brought the colour into her cheeks.

"I expect Luke's having the time of his life. Have you heard from him?"

She shook her head.

"No, I haven't heard from him." And then, a little awkwardly: "Did you see that curious case in the paper this morning?"

He thought she was trying to turn the conversation into other channels. It seemed a little gauche, but he did not suspect her object in asking the question—her embarrassment saved her from suspicion.

"There are hundreds of cases in the paper: which is the one?"

"About the man who was living a double life: a respectable merchant by day and a—a burglar by night."

Danty smiled. He lived too near the criminal world to harbour any illusions about its romantical character.

"That's the sort of stuff you read in stories," he said, "but I have known such cases. I've read about them, of course," he added hastily. "There was a man in Liverpool who preached in a local chapel on Sundays and ran a forgery plant the rest of the week. I know another man—by hearsay, of course—who was the head of a prosperous shoe company in the Midlands, and one of the cleverest jewel thieves the police have ever had through their hands."

She was looking out of the window, apparently uninterested.

"Why do men do that sort of thing?"

Danty shrugged.

"I don't know. It's a sort of field of adventure—there are precious few fields left. I wanted to talk to you about my South American company, Margaret. I'm in rather serious trouble. I want seventy thousand pounds to finish the deal, to be exact seventy-six thousand pounds, and I've raised sixty-nine. I was thinking this morning that if Luke was here I could get all I wanted. He didn't like me, but he was a very good business man."

She was neither amused nor indignant at the cool request. For a moment she had a wild idea of supplying him with the money he required. He might prove a useful ally, if all Gorton had said was true. Then the danger of making a confidant of this unscrupulous creature became apparent. Danty was a parasite living on society: he would not fail to exact the fullest advantage from his knowledge.

She was confronted with the alternatives of seeking the aid of the society in which Luke had found a discreditable place, or of going to the police, who, she knew, were no respecters of persons, and would as lief send Luke to penal servitude as they would the jailbirds with whom he was in association.

"I'm afraid that is impossible, Danton," she said quietly. "Why don't you see Mr. Stiles? He is a business man."

Danton shrugged his shoulders.

"Stiles! A servant—the man is without any initiative, and a word from you——"

She shook her head.

"That I can't give," she said.

There was a silence after this; then Danton Morell began to speak easily about trivialities, and in a short time took his leave. At least, he thought, as he went down the stairs, he had satisfied himself that she was not definitely antagonistic to him.

That he was on his way to the City was true. There was a little City office where he occasionally met his humble associates. Since Lewing's death the gang which bore his name had lain very quiet. It comprised a not inconsiderable number of men, old and young, who lived on the river and its cargoes. Though Danty took no part in their operations, he had organized their work and reduced their methods to a system. His corner was a small one, for receivers paid badly. The work was dangerous and difficult, and sometimes weeks would pass before the gang could make a good clean-up. Bales of silk, chests of tea, pockets of rubber—nothing came amiss to the thieves; but the commodities they stole were hard to dispose of, and Danty's share hardly paid the rent of his flat.

A proposal put up to him that morning that he should take a more active part in the work was negatived by him.

"It is not my graft," he said. "I'm not a Connor. You don't imagine that I'll come and live in Bermondsey, do you?"

The active leader of the gang—a short, thick-set man who bore the name of Dick and apparently nothing else, did not receive the refusal without protest.

"The boys say that Connor's crowd are making big money, and that they ought to be making the same. Even if you didn't stay in Bermondsey, and only came down occasionally, you might help."

"You're having all the help you'll get from me," said Danty impatiently. "What's the sense of comparing

Connor's crowd with ours? Connor does land work, and that's different. If your people hadn't had my advice they'd spend their time in stir. Who was it made you buy an electric boat—it was I! Who arranged to supply you with lists of cargoes and the lightering contracts? You're doing a small business because it's the only kind of business you know. Do you think Connor would take any one of your crowd and use him?"

"We could go into Connor's trade and make good pickings," insisted Dick doggedly. "Lewing would have been more use to us than you are."

Danty was not easily cowed. He showed his teeth in a mirthless smile.

"And Lewing's dead! Do you know why? It wasn't because he put up a squeal, but because he poached on Connor's territory."

He sent the man away dissatisfied, folded the notes which Dick had brought as his share of a recent haul, and went to a respectable City club to lunch.

Every thief has his failings, and Danty was a gambler. He loved that part of the City which immediately surrounds the Stock Exchange; he would spend hours poring over the rise and fall of prices; he speculated heavily in every kind of share, and had seen the considerable fortune he had achieved by the crooked practice of his profession melt like snow in the sun. Rex Leferre had been a useful lieutenant—he had been the money getter at a period when money was tight. He had served other purposes—paid with real money for blocks of unsalable shares with which Danty was saddled. The time

had come when Danton Morell must find a new source
of revenue, or vanish forever from his usual haunts.

It was his boast that he was the best confidence man
in England; yet he was made to look a child in that place
that has been the ruin of so many confidence men—the
London Stock Exchange.

He stopped long enough in the City to discover many
unpleasant truths. Shares which he held in considerable
quantities were sliding steadily down the list. He met his
broker, a cold-blooded man, who laid before him a statement of account which made Danton Morell go cold.

Danty left the City in a state of desperation, and
arrived at his flat at the same time as the lawyer's clerk
who served him with a writ for £140 from his tailor—
the tenth writ Danty had received in the past month.
Pi Coles, his so-called valet, took his coat and hat.

"Any luck?" asked the little man with the ease and
familiarity of one who was addressing a friend.

"No luck, Pi," said Danty with a twisted smile. "But
every cloud has its silver lining."

He did not realize that the silver lining in this case
radiated from one called Connor. To do him justice,
Mr. Connor was unaware of the fact that he was destined to assist the head of a rival gang.

CHAPTER XXIV

GUNNER HAYNES and his guest sat in conference. Luke was still feeling the effect of the drug: his head throbbed at the slightest noise, and during the day he had consumed uncountable quantities of tea.

"There's the situation," said Haynes. "Connor knows who you are. Naturally, I am not blaming you for telling him, though you could not have expected him to believe you were a man of substance——"

"Not so very substantial," smiled Luke. "You wired to my wife, you say?"

The Gunner nodded.

"I sent a telegram in Connor's name, putting off the appointment," he said. "I should imagine it was not till night, because Connor would not risk detectives seeing Mrs. Maddison go into his wharf. If she doesn't turn up, Connor will naturally make a call on her to-morrow; but a lot of things might happen before then."

"Suppose I saw Bird——" began Luke.

The Gunner shook his head.

"I've no great love for the police, although I've a mighty respect for the Sparrow," he said. "But I can tell you this, that if you were the Duke of Oojah they would have to pinch you for that raid on Taffanny's.

You see, your fatal mistake was to give the shop assistant a punch on the jaw. That made you a willing agent in the matter. If you'd stepped out of the car and given the lady into custody, and then explained your position, there would have been no harm except a few flaring headlines in the evening newspapers. But you didn't. You became an accessory the moment you gave the shop assistant a punch and assisted your lady friend to escape. Anyway, whatever happens, you couldn't escape a lot of unpleasant publicity—or your wife either. That seems to me the one thing you do not wish. No, I've got to find another way of getting you back into society."

His lips curled at the word; he was evidently secretly amused.

"But if Connor sees my wife to-morrow, what then?" asked Luke.

The Gunner considered this question for a little time.

"He mustn't see her. I think that can be managed. It is a pity the Sparow arrived when he did—otherwise, I should have had the solution in both hands. As it is, I don't think we shall have a great deal of difficulty."

He knelt down at the side of Luke's bed, groped beneath and pulled out the case of a portable typewriter. This he unfastened, and, putting the little machine on the table, he took a sheet of paper and began to type laboriously. . . .

Connor, striding impatiently up and down his room, looking from time to time at his watch, heard a knock at the gate and ran eagerly to open the wicket. It was a small boy with a letter. Connor snatched it from the boy, slammed the wicket in his face and went back to his room.

The letter was typewritten and began without preamble.

I'm afraid I can't come to see you to-night. The neighbourhood is so dreadfully squalid that I fear my presence would be noticed by the police. Can you meet me by the edge of the Serpentine at ten o'clock to-night (about a hundred paces from the bridge: there will be nobody there at that time)? But you must supply me proof that my husband is the man about whom you are speaking.

It bore no signature, but there was a postscript.

P. S.   I do hope you have not told a man named Haynes this story about Mr. Maddison. He called to-day, but I would not see him.

Connor smiled. The Gunner was certainly a quick worker.

CHAPTER XXV

MARGARET was dressing in preparation for her interview when the telegram came. It was brief.

Cannot see you to-night. Same time to-morrow night.

CONNOR.

In a sense she was relieved, though she would have been glad to have ended the state of suspense in which she was living. She had a wild idea of taking with her a large sum of money, and with that intention had drawn a thousand pounds from the bank. She had revised this plan, however, and the money was now in her safe. If it was blackmail, and these people wanted paying, they could wait for a few hours. She did not know the neighbourhood into which she was going, but she guessed from its locality that it was not the place where an unprotected woman would carry a large sum of money with impunity.

As she put the money away she caught a glimpse of an envelope which gave her a little heartache. It contained poor Rex's last scrawled message. Several times she had been on the point of putting that envelope into the fire, but something had prevented her. There was a time when she needed the stimulation to her hatred which that pitiable note supplied. But that time had

passed. The boy's dead hand still lay on her, had wrecked
Luke's life and might yet bring her to disaster. Now she
must wait another twenty-four hours before she re-
solved her doubts.

She heard the doorbell ring, and presently came a
tap on the door and her footman came in.

"A man wishes to see you, madam. I think he's been
here before—a Mr. Haynes."

At first she did not grasp who was meant, and then
in a flash she recalled the earlier visit. Here at any rate
was a man who was friendly disposed toward Luke.

"Bring him up, please," she said.

Now she recalled more vividly the previous interview she had had with him. He had told her that Danty
Morell was a man whom no decent woman should know,
and she had rung for the servant and had him shown
out. But he was friendly to Luke, had spoken of some
service which he had rendered to him, and here she
would find an ally.

Haynes was not prepared for the kindness of the
welcome. In a sense it was a little embarrassing. He had
come not to give but to seek information. It was vitally
necessary that he should not betray the fact that he had
any communication with Luke.

"I'm afraid I was very rude to you the last time you
came, Mr. Haynes," she said as she sat down behind her
little desk and signalled to him to sit. "You rather hurt
my feelings about a—" she hesitated—"a friend of
mine, who isn't so much of a friend as he was," she
smiled.

The Gunner nodded.

"That's the best news I've heard for a long time," he said. "I was a little impertinent. I remember I asked you why your husband left you. I wonder you didn't send for the police."

She laughed at this.

"Do you know where my husband is now?" she asked, and when he shook his head her heart sank.

She had had a vague idea that this man might have come into touch with his benefactor.

"I can tell you where Mr. Morell is now," he said, with a twinkle in his eyes, "but that's not going to help you very much. I've come to repeat my impertinence, Mrs. Maddison. At the back of my mind I've got a notion I can help you and your husband, who, I have reason to believe, is in Spain."

He said this deliberately, his eyes challenging hers.

"But——" she began.

"I believe he's in Spain. If a man's in Spain he can't be in London, can he? And if he's a gentleman at large in Spain, taking long hikes through the country, he can't be burgling Taffanny's or getting himself mixed up with Connor."

"You know, then?" she interrupted quickly. "I was seeing that man to-night, but he sent me a wire——"

"I sent you the wire," said Gunner Haynes coolly. "That engagement of yours has got to be put off indefinitely."

"How did you know?" she demanded.

The Gunner smiled cryptically.

"I've got a whole lot of sources of information that I am not making public," he said. "The point I want to make with you is this—your husband is in Spain. You've had letters from him, which unfortunately you've destroyed."

She understood now. Did he come from Luke? There could be no other explanation for his knowledge, and she put the question bluntly.

"I haven't been to Ronda for years," said the Gunner calmly. "And if I had been, and met your husband, he wouldn't know that I was coming to see you. Now, Mrs. Maddison, I'm going to ask you that impertinent question all over again: exactly why did your husband leave you? No, no, I don't mean that. I know why he left you. But why did you suddenly leave him flat? I don't know that; I'll bet your husband doesn't know that. Only you know—and Danty. I guess Danty knows."

She was silent; but she realized at that moment just why she had not destroyed Rex's last note. She had kept it to show Luke some day, and demand from him the explanation she should have asked for when it came to her. It was her justification—the only one she could have for her conduct.

"That is an extraordinary request for a stranger to make, Mr. Haynes, and I don't know whether to enlighten you or not."

She stood for a moment silent, and then, turning abruptly, walked out of the room. Haynes picked up his hat from the floor and rose, thinking the interview was at an end. But in three minutes she was back again with a little envelope in her hand.

"I'm telling you something that nobody knows but me and Mr. Morell," she said. "When my poor brother shot himself, this note was found in his room."

She took from the envelope two telephone slips and passed them to him. Gunner Haynes read:

Margaret darling, I have lost. For months I have been gambling. To-day I took a desperate step on the advice of Luke Maddison. He has led me to ruin—money is his god. I beg of you not to trust him. He has led me from one act of folly to another. God bless you.

REX.

He read it twice and then looked up.

"Is this your brother's handwriting?"

She nodded.

"Could you swear to it?"

"Yes, I'm sure it's his. I've had hundreds of pencilled notes from him, and I couldn't possibly be mistaken."

"Who found it?"

"Mr. Morell found it in Rex's room. Poor, dear Rex had a servant, a very trustworthy man, and he saw the note before Mr. Morell put it in his pocket——"

"He didn't read it, of course?" suggested the Gunner. "The servant, I mean?"

"I don't think so. He only saw the note, and Mr. Morell hide it."

The Gunner had an amazing memory. He could from

that moment have repeated every word in the letter—
there was no need for him to take a copy, and he handed
it back to the girl.

"Naturally, you thought that your husband was responsible for the death of your brother, and that was
why you—acted as you did."

"He told you?" she challenged.

The Gunner neither denied nor agreed. He stood
frowning down at the carpet, his hands pushed into his
pockets, his underlip outthrust.

"Queer bird, Danty," he said after a while, and she
realized that he was speaking as much to himself as to
her. "He used to be a great hoarder of trifles—I wonder if he's got over it. There's something of a miser
about Danty, though he could never keep money and
never will. All crooks die poor."

"Will——" she began, and stopped in natural confusion.

She saw a smile dawn slowly in his face.

"You were going to ask me, shall I? No, Mrs. Maddison, I shall not die poor, unless I go mad. I'll never
have to work again—I'm a reformed character. That
doesn't mean," he said quickly, "that I've got any no-
tions that I have been following the wrong track. I've
known that all my life. Five years ago a brother swindler traded me a block of shares in a copper mine. They
looked to be worth about the value of the paper they
were printed on, but luckily I didn't throw them into the
fire. Copper was found on the property whilst I was on

remand the other day, and I've sold at a big profit. I shall only commit one more crime."

She would have smiled at this, but she saw something in his eyes which froze the smile on her lips.

"Danty Morell has got to be punished one of these days—when I find proof," he said slowly.

He took his watch from his pocket.

"I've got rather an important engagement, so, if you don't mind, Mrs. Maddison, I'll go. Don't ask me to give any messages to your husband, because I don't know where he is. If I did, I shouldn't tell you."

"Is he well?" she asked anxiously.

"Pretty well," said the Gunner.

He made no attempt to move, but stood twiddling his watch guard.

"He'll want money," he said suddenly, "and this sounds like the beginning of the confidence trick. I can let him have all he wants if there's any need, but I think you'd better provide it, just to show your confidence in me." He chuckled at this. "Sounds almost like Danty at his worst! If you have any hesitation, Mrs. Maddison, don't give it to me. I shall want about two hundred pounds, but three hundred would be better."

She went out of the room and returned with a small pad of notes.

"Four hundred will be better still," she said, and he thrust the money into his pocket without counting it.

"Seems a pretty easy game. Pity I didn't start earlier," he said. "Danty's the lad! There isn't a finer tale teller in the world."

He jerked out his hand and she took it.

"I'll be seeing you again, Mrs. Maddison—perhaps some day when you're going to Ronda you'll let me travel on the same train, in case some of the real con men get hold of you!"

CHAPTER XXVI

AT THE appointed hour Mr. Connor arrived, paid off his taxi short of the bridge across the Serpentine, and strolled down toward the water. The night was inclined to be rainy; a high, chill wind was blowing—it was not a night even for the most romantic of couples to spend on the brim of the Serpentine.

Mr. Connor was not romantic; he was very much a realist. He could well understand Margaret Maddison's reluctance to come to his wharf, and he blamed himself for the stupidity of such a suggestion. She might have come accompanied by the police, as the Gunner suggested she would; and that was exactly the way she would have arrived had she intended making a fuss.

He found a wooden chair leaning over upon another, and straightening it, sat down. Here was the promise of an income for life. He could even bless the Gunner that he had interfered in his affairs at the most critical moment in the life of Luke Maddison. He looked right and left; there was nobody in sight. The police, he knew, did not patrol this path except at rare intervals.

Behind him was a stretch of grass which was separated from the pathway by a railing less than a foot from the ground. He was meditating upon all the prospects which his discovery had opened up when a hand dropped on his shoulder and something cold touched the back of his neck.

"Shouting means shooting," said a muffled voice behind him. "Don't look round, kid!"

"What's the idea?" growled Connor, who, to do him justice, was not so much frightened as annoyed.

"Stick 'em up, and let's have a look at you," said the stranger laconically. "Now turn," he said, and Connor obeyed.

His eyes had grown accustomed to the darkness, and had his assailant's face been uncovered, he could have been distinguished; but where the face should be was a black patch.

"Outrage by masked highwayman," murmured the newcomer, as his disengaged hand passed quickly across the outside of Connor's pockets.

"You needn't have covered up your face, Gunner," growled Connor. "I'd know you anywhere."

The other said nothing; his hand went into the inside pocket of Connor's coat and he jerked something free. Connor gripped at his wrist, but the barrel of the automatic hit him gently under the chin—not so gently that his teeth did not rattle.

"You came after the passport, did you? I was a can to fall for your letter. But it's going to make no difference, Gunner, and you can tell the woman who sent you here——"

"You talk too much," said the mask.

He put his hand in Connor's hip pocket, took out the pistol it contained and flung it into the dark pond. Connor heard the splash of the revolver as it hit the surface of the water.

"Probably saved you ten years," said the hold-up man cheerfully. "If there's one thing I like, it is saving people from penal servitude."

He pushed his hand down into the trousers pocket of his victim and pulled out a handful of notes.

"Richness beyond the dreams of avarice," he said, as he transferred the money to his own pocket. "Saving up to buy a car or something?"

"You'll know all about this!" threatened Connor. "You don't think I'm going to take it lying down, do you?"

He heard a faint laugh, but so far removed from amusement did it sound that he shuddered.

"What's to stop me finishing you?" asked the man in the mask. "The answer is—nothing! I'm telling you, Connor, for your own good, not to raise a squeal about this little affair."

"Maddison put you up to this, I suppose—but I'll get him!" said Connor between his teeth. "I'm not kidding you——"

"You talk too much," said the other again, and, gripping his victim by the shoulder, he spun him round, so rapidly that Connor staggered.

Before he could recover his balance the stranger gave him a violent push that sent him sprawling into the water. By the time Connor had recovered, his man had disappeared.

It was not the kind of night to wander about in wet

clothes, but they were nearly dry by the time Connor had made his plans. Now he knew too well why the Gunner had called that day—he had come for the passport, but the arrival of Inspector Bird and the girl reporter had made it impossible to secure the document he wanted.

Connor had half a dozen plans but rejected them all. And then he remembered the one man in London who could be of assistance to him. The fact that he was head of a rival gang made little or no difference to this opportunist. The idea had no sooner settled in his mind than he took up the 'phone and called Danty Morell's flat. Here was one of the widest men in the world, with a brain even more cunning than his own—a man who had mixed with real swells and had reputedly made enough money to retire from the crooked game, though he still maintained nominal direction of the Borough crowd.

Danty was in bed when the call came through and cursing all telephones went into the passage in his bare feet to take the message. He was not sufficiently well acquainted with the gangster to recognize his voice and Connor lost no time in introducing himself.

"What's the game?" asked Danty suspiciously.

He knew there was bad blood between the two gangs, but so far had kept clear of offending either by the lukewarmness of his championship or the vehemence of his enmity.

"It's a big thing with big money in it. Can you see me right away?" asked Connor.

For fully a minute Danty considered the possibilities.

"All right, come up," he said, "but if you start a rough-house here, you'll be pinched."

"Don't make me laugh," smiled Connor. "Why should I call you up to start a rough-house—what's the matter with the streets? You go on 'em, don't you?"

"All right, come along," said Danty at last.

He was not particularly enthusiastic for a meeting, especially as he was aware that his house from time to time was under observation. He woke Pi Coles and revealed the identity of the caller. The dumpy little man shook his head.

"Connor's mustard," he said. "I shouldn't have much to do with him if I were you, guv'nor."

From time to time there had been red war between the two gangs but Danty was so aloof from their operations that he could afford to take a disinterested view. He never went south of the river until the feuds had died down, and it was perfectly understood that he was not to be the object of reprisals.

Danty had dreamed dreams of shaking loose all his old associations and forgetting that he had ever organized river thefts and drawn a small but steady income from the proceeds.

He was dressed by the time Connor called. Pi, his servant, who had spent a quarter of an hour looking out of the window, reported the man's arrival in Half Moon Street.

"He's alone, guv'nor," he said, and most of Danty's uneasiness was removed by this information.

Connor was in a friendly mood—which meant nothing. Friendliness of mood was part of his stock in trade.

"I've got a nerve to call you up, Mr. Morell," he said, "but something has happened and I think you're going to help me. When I say 'help me,' " he added carefully, "I mean help yourself. My crowd and yours are not always matey, but I hope that's going to make no difference."

Danty informed him with the greatest politeness that he was superior to the antagonisms of crowds. With his own hand he pushed forward a box of cigars, and Mr. Connor lit one carefully and thoughtfully.

"I happen to know a lot about you, Morell—everybody agrees you're the widest fellow in London. You know Mr. Maddison, too, don't you—he mentioned your name."

Danty's eyes opened.

"Maddison?" he said slowly. "Why, do you know him?"

Connor grinned.

"I'm not going to tell you any lies. I didn't know him till last night." Then, abruptly: "How much money has he got?"

The question took Morell's breath away.

"What am I, an inquiry agent?" he asked sarcastically. "He's a rich man, that's all I can tell you, and you probably know that yourself."

He might have added that Luke's wealth was a genuine source of grievance at that moment.

He was curious to know why the gangster was interested in Luke, and how he had come to meet him, but for the moment Connor was not prepared to enlighten him.

"The point is this, Morell: if this fellow's rich, and we can get big stuff out of him, are you ready to split two ways?"

Danty did not answer. He certainly had no intention of committing himself to this man, who might be really friendly but as likely as not was preparing a trap for him.

"Well, I'm going to tell you," said Connor, "because you've got to come in, whether you like it or not. If you're in, there's only one way the makings can be split, and that's two ways." He chuckled at his own joke.

"Perhaps you'll be kind enough to tell me just what the graft is?" said Morell.

The other nodded.

"That's fair," he said. "Do you remember Lewing being killed, and a fellow being knifed?"

"I remember," said Morell.

"Do you know Taffanny's was robbed two days ago, and a man with a beard got away with a lot of stuff?"

Danty nodded again.

"Do you know that was the same man—the chap who was in hospital and the fellow who drove the car? And do you know that man was Mr. Luke Maddison?"

Danty stared at him, his mouth wide open.

"Forget it!" he said scornfully. "Maddison's in Spain."

The other chuckled.

"In Spain, is he? I'll tell you where he is. He's hiding up with Gunner Haynes. And what's more, his wife knows he's on the run with the police after him."

Luke Maddison a thief, a man badly wanted by the police? The idea was so fantastical that Danty could not grasp it. And then Connor began to tell his story. He did not explain the circumstances in which Luke had revealed his identity; but after his host had heard of the seeming treachery of Connor's confederate, he had no difficulty in bridging over the gap.

"We were holding him to give him a towelling when Gunner Haynes butted in and got him away. Naturally I didn't take any notice of the yarn he told until one of my men found a passport."

"You wrote to Mrs. Maddison, did you?"

Connor nodded.

"We got a faked letter—I ought to be kicked for not knowing it was a fake. Anyway, the Gunner caught me in the park and got the passport away from me."

Danty began to think quickly. He knew that this story was true, and that in some amazing way Luke had got himself mixed up in a gang war and was now hiding from the police. The reason why the passport was so vital to him he could realize—that had been the real object of his burglarious entrance into his own flat. Once the passport was in his possession it was a simple matter for him to melt away to the Continent, and with his disappearance from London vanished also every hope of bringing home to him his association with the Taffanny robbery. And Margaret knew—if not all, at least the vital part—of Connor's story.

Here in his hand was the lever. To think, with Danton, was to act. He went out into the corridor to the telephone and rang up Margaret. She was certain to be in bed, but he would insist that she answer him.

To his surprise it was her voice which replied.

"Is that Margaret?"

"Who is it speaking?" she asked quickly.

"It's Danton," he said. "Listen, Margaret, this is very important—did a man called Haynes call on you to-night?"

She hesitated.

"Yes," she said, "but I don't think that is any business——"

"Listen, please," he pleaded. "Did you give him any money? This is very important."

Again the hesitation.

"Did you?" he repeated.

"Yes," she said, "I gave him some money—not for himself——"

She realized her error too late.

"For somebody else?" asked Danty eagerly.

He waited, and then heard the click of the instrument as she hung up the receiver. He came quickly back to Connor.

"He's got the passport, and he's got money, and that means he'll leave for the Continent by to-morrow morning's train. I want you to get a couple of your gang down at the station to-morrow morning; they're to watch at the barrier and head back Maddison if he tries to leave England."

He shouted for Pi Coles.

"Bring me my shoes," he said; and, when the man had gone: "I'm going to see Mrs. Maddison and get the first instalment of our pension. How much did you think you'd get from her if she had come over to your wharf?"

"I reckoned on a thousand," said Connor, and Morell laughed thoughtfully.

"If this job is not worth a hundred thousand, it's worth nothing," he said.

CHAPTER XXVII

SOMEHOW Margaret knew that the telephone message she had had from Danton would be followed up by a personal call, and she was not surprised when she heard the bell ring. She went to the landing.

"If that is Mr. Danton Morell will you please bring him up?" she said to the footman who was hurrying to the door.

The first thing she noticed about Danty was a certain unkemptness which she had never observed before. Usually he was a most painfully tidy man: every hair of his glossy head was in place, his clothes were immaculate. But now his hair was unbrushed, he wore an odd coat and vest, and she formed the impression that he had risen hurriedly from his bed.

She sensed his hostility, and the new attitude he had taken to her, within a second of his entering the room.

"Margaret, I am afraid I've got a very unpleasant duty to perform," he said, almost jauntily. "It concerns this lunatic husband of yours. He seems to have got himself into a mess. What on earth made him do it?"

"Do what?" she asked innocently.

He smiled.

"It's no use pretending you don't know, my dear girl.

Luke has got himself mixed up with a gang. I don't know what is the pull they have or who is the woman in it." He added this maliciously, and was disappointed when she smiled.

"Your mind runs on women, Danton. Perhaps it was the same lady whom you discovered in Paris—you remember, your man telegraphed me about it?"

"I swear to you——" he began, but she shook her head.

"It isn't worth while discussing that at all. What do you want now?"

Danton shrugged his shoulders.

"Well, there's a man called Connor, who seems to be pretty sore with you for not turning up to-night after you'd made an appointment. He said you'd promised him a thousand pounds——"

"I promised nothing of the sort, and I shouldn't dream of giving him a thousand pounds," said Margaret, and something made her add: "Or you either."

She saw him wince. She had not known until then how important a part money played in Danton Morell's life.

"There's no sense in getting up in the air about this," he said. "It won't help you or Luke to fight Connor. He's one of the most powerful gangsters in London, and unfortunately he knows that the man who robbed Taffanny's the other day was Luke. What are you going to do about it?"

"I still have no proposal," she said.

"Connor wants money—a couple of thousand pounds. I'm very naturally anxious to save you from the disgrace, and as the man came to me to ask my advice, I thought the best thing I could do would be to act as intermediary. You've been paying the wrong man, Margaret. Haynes cannot help you—by the way, you don't imagine the money you gave him to-night will ever get to Luke, do you?"

When she did not answer, he went on:

"It is nothing to do with me, and if you like to fight Connor that's your business entirely. But——"

She interrupted him.

"Do you suggest I should pay this two thousand pounds blackmail to your friend?"

"He is not my friend," said the man testily, "and it is not blackmail. Apparently Luke borrowed the money from Connor."

She laughed softly at this, her amused eyes on his.

"How terribly unconvincing you can be, Mr. Morell! Well, I'm going to tell you now that I'm not paying either you or Mr. Connor. It will save us a lot of unnecessary argument."

"Haynes advised you not to pay, eh?"

She shook her head.

"No," she said quietly, "Inspector Bird. I got onto him after you telephoned, and put a hypothetical case to him—he is coming here."

There was a sharp rat-tat on the door below.

"I think that is he," she said, and had all the satisfaction she required out of the pallor that came to the face of Danton Morell.

"You're not going to tell him?" he asked agitatedly.

"I mean, about my asking for this money—about Connor. It will all come out—you realize that? About Luke, I mean. His name will be plastered all over London as a friend of murderers and a jewel thief."

He tailed off incoherently, and she went out of the room to meet the Sparrow.

In the early hours of the morning Mr. Bird was always in his most jovial mood. He had been at Scotland Yard engaged upon a case when Margaret had called him, and he seemed in no degree surprised, when he was shown into the drawing room, to find the discomfited Danton Morell, standing guiltily and nervously with his back to the little fire that burned on the hearth.

"Well, well, wonders will never cease. I haven't been asked out to a party for years. Fancy meeting you, Danty!" he chuckled.

His heavy eyes surveyed Margaret.

"If you think I'm going to lecture you about keeping bad company, you've got another guess coming, Mrs. Maddison. I realize you're a social leader, and naturally you do charitable work amongst the criminal classes. What's the trouble, Danty—lost your uncle and want your train fare out of London? This isn't your hypo—what's the word, Mrs. Maddison, hypothetical case? 'What should you do if people asked you for money to keep a secret?' That was the question, wasn't it? Danty wouldn't do such a low thing as that, would you, Danty? He's never done anything except con work, and he's a reformed character now. He's given up thieving and gone into the Stock Exchange."

"I'm not on the Stock Exchange," snapped Danty, stung to an answer.

"Thought you'd gone on to-day," said the Sparrow amiably. "I saw the flags out in the City. Must have been the King of Baluchistan getting the Freedom."

He looked inquiringly at Margaret, and understood the signal in her eyes.

"Well, Danty, we'll not be keeping you much longer. Mrs. Maddison and I have got a few private thoughts to exchange on the subject of blackmail. How's Connor?"

"I haven't seen Connor for months," said Danton loudly.

The detective rubbed his big chin.

"That's queer. Here am I thinking he called at your house to-night and that he's waiting for you to come back. Getting old, I guess—we have these illusions at my time of life—always fancy we're seeing crooks when they're only stockbrokers, and not even that."

It was a very uncomfortable Danton Morell that went down the stairs, too terrified to be angry. There was no cab in sight, but a car that looked suspiciously like a police tender was drawn up near the curb a few houses away, and he hurried past this and was glad when he turned the corner out of the still bright glare of its headlamps.

Connor was playing euchre with Pi Coles when he came in.

"Well, did you have any luck?"

The man was too cheerful for Danty's liking: he

would have preferred a more despondent and unhoping note in his tone.

"I've got no money, if that's what you mean—the Sparrow was there."

Connor sat up, his narrowed eyes fixed upon his host.

"That sounds like a damned lie to me," he said, but Danty took no offense.

"He wasn't at the house when I got there, but I'd hardly started talking before he turned up. She had sent for him."

This time Connor was convinced. His lips pursed as though he were whistling some inaudible tune.

"Did my name come into it?" he asked, after a moment's thought.

"Yes, the Sparrow brought it in. He said he knew you came to this flat to-night and that you were waiting for me."

Connor leaned back in the chair, frowning thoughtfully.

"I wonder if that's a lie, too?" he said, speaking to himself. "It mightn't be—he's been trailing me for a week—not he but one of his bloodhounds. Did she squeal?"

Danty did not reply till he had hung up his coat.

"She didn't and she won't. I know her! She's got a bug in her head that he's an ill-used man, and she's going to try to save him without letting the police know."

Connor took a cigar from his pocket, bit off the end and lit it. He puffed slowly, his eyes on the ceiling, and then he said:

"I'm out of this. I don't go after women who've got the brains to call in the police. You go ahead, Danty, and I'll take my corner. Twenty-five per cent. is good enough for any man."

Danty glared down at him.

"I'm to do the work and you'll take the profit, eh? Is that the idea? When did we float this company?"

Connor smiled broadly.

"I brought the business; that's my answer to you. I can't afford to be mixed up in it now my name's known and they've brought in the Sparrow. You can handle these swells, Danty, and you're wide enough to keep yourself out of trouble."

He rose, reached for his coat and hat, and moved to the door. In the doorway he stood for a little while surveying the other man.

"Twenty-five per cent.," he said. "You'll split that way or I'll do a bit of splitting myself."

Danty followed him to the landing.

"Where does the Gunner live?"

Connor shook his head.

"I'll tail him up and let you know in the morning," he said. "He's got a quiet pitch somewhere."

Danty went back to his flat and closed the door. Usually he did not discuss matters with Pi Coles, but this little man was shrewd and understanding. He had touched most illicit occupations, from larceny to felony, and was a surprisingly well-educated man. He was one of those men, so infrequently met with, who had occupied his many visitations to prison in reading and study;

for though he spoke with the vilest cockney accent and his English was more or less negligible, he could speak French and Spanish fluently—the former accomplishment had served him remarkably well, for he had served a year in a French prison.

For the first time Danton showed his hand. He had not before been very communicative on the subject of Luke Maddison and his wife, but now he opened up. Pi Coles listened with the puckered face which was evidence of his close application. It was when Danton mentioned Gunner Haynes that he shook his head.

"I'd keep clear of him if I were you, guv'nor," he said. "You know what happened?" He nodded significantly.

Danton knew all that had happened; but he flattered himself that he understood the psychology of the criminal mind. Such men as the Gunner forgave even the stealing of their wives. Probably Gunner Haynes, with his philosophical outlook, bore him little or no malice for that incident. Anyway, the girl was dead, and could never tell the story that might bring the Gunner at his throat.

Wasn't there anything he knew about him—something he could hang over the Gunner's head, some old crime in which they had both participated?

Danty was a miser of trifles; he was the sort of man who hoarded even unwanted souvenirs. In his bedroom was a safe where he kept the most precious of these. Letters tied together with bootlaces; old scraps of press cuttings relative to previous exploits; and, in an oblong blotting book, a little square of paper covered with scrawled writing, which he should have destroyed the night it came into his hands. But he hated burning any-thing—otherwise those mad letters of the girl whose heart he had broken would have been ashes years ago.

He found certain records, letters that the Gunner had written to him in the days when they were partners, but nothing that would incriminate him, nothing that he could use to-day. When he had closed the safe with a bang and locked it, he returned to Pi, who in his absence had formulated a brand-new idea.

"You can leave the Gunner alone and get away with it, guv'nor," he said. "Suppose this man Maddison is staying with Haynes, what's to stop you getting at Mad-dison and leaving out Haynes altogether? And what's the use of his wife to you, anyway? You've only to get Maddison away to the Continent with a check book, and you're on Easy Street for the rest of your life."

Danty listened and frowned. That possibility had not occurred to him. He went to bed at three o'clock that morning and did not fall asleep until seven. When he awoke, at midday, he found that Connor had sent a messenger with a letter. It was unaddressed, for that was Connor's way, and tearing open the envelope Danty took out a slip of paper torn from a cheap notebook. It ran:

L. M. staying with G. H. at 974 Pennybody Buildings, Clerken-well.

CHAPTER XXVIII

MARGARET woke that morning with a fixed determination. She had fenced with the detective and once or twice had been badly pinked. He was too shrewd a man, too wise in the artless guile which passes in criminal circles for clever evasion, to be deceived by her. Her hypothetical case he demolished, and revealed with alarming clearness the figure and deeds of Luke. He did not say as much; he did not even connect the missing banker with the Taffanny robbery. All that he knew was that Luke Maddison had made a fool of himself, that somebody had got hold of the fact and was trying to blackmail his wife; but what shape that folly took he regarded as indelicate to inquire.

When she found herself cornered, and the facts which she was trying to conceal coming to light, in sheer desperation Margaret had been forced to accept the suggestion of a woman, though she loathed herself for her new disloyalty. She spoke vaguely of an earlier attachment, but since she was a bad liar she carried no conviction. The very fact that she was not speaking the truth in reality saved her from closer questioning. The Sparrow jumped to a conclusion which was wrong.

"The only thing I can tell you, Mrs. Maddison, is that, whatever happens, you're not to pay anybody any-

thing. If it's Danty or Connor, or whoever it is putting
the black on you, you've only to ring me up to stop 'em!"

He left with the definite assurance that she would
take this step.

She had to force herself to go to bed that night, and
will herself to sleep. She had a heavy day ahead of her
and no plans definitely fixed. The Gunner had told her
nothing except that he was in touch with Luke. Had he
told her that he was trying to get him out of England?
If he hadn't, she had in some occult way received that
impression.

Luke would make for Ronda, whither his check book
had been sent. She must follow him—accompany him if
possible. She went early to the bank and saw Stiles. He
was—for Stiles—in an optimistic frame of mind. Two
or three undertakings in which the bank was interested
had become flourishing.

"One I had written down as a bad debt and it looks
as if it would bring in eighteen thousand a year," he
almost chortled the news. "I wish you'd let Mr. Maddison know that: he'll be delighted. I'd have sent him a
wire to Spain, only I don't know his address."

And then, realizing that her appearance at this hour
was unusual:

"Is there anything you want, Mrs. Maddison?"

"I want to see my husband's private account. You had
it transferred to the bank."

He took her into his private room, brought the pass
book to her, and she ran her finger down the column.
The last check drawn was a few days before his wed-

ding. Since then, Stiles told her, no check had come in.

"I've been expecting some in. Mr. Maddison is rather extravagant at times, and I'm surprised that he hasn't cashed a check—although of course he's got his Spanish account—but I should have thought he would wish to replenish that."

"That is what I've come to see you about, Stiles," she said. "I want you not to honour any check drawn by my husband for any amount over a thousand pounds."

Stiles stared at her over his glasses. This was the resolution she had reached as she lay in bed on the previous night. She had gone over every possibility step by step, had seen the likelihood of the blackmailers transferring their attention from her to Luke. At present Luke was safe under the protection of the Gunner; but something might happen to remove him from this watchful, hawk-faced man.

Somehow, for a reason which she could not understand, she trusted the Gunner implicitly—was sure that whatever his record might be he would do no harm to Luke.

"That's an extraordinary request you're making, Mrs. Maddison," said Stiles, troubled. "It's quite likely that Mr. Maddison may want to make a big purchase—the last time he was in Spain he bought some property in Seville that showed a profit of fifty per cent. the first year."

She nodded.

"I realize that, but I still make this request—in his name."

"Very good, Mrs. Maddison."

Stiles scribbled some instructions on a slip of paper and pinned it to the ledger he had brought in.

"I don't know what's in your mind, but I understood that you had transferred everything back to Mr. Maddison——"

"It isn't that," she explained hastily. "It's the possibility of——"

But here she was at a loss; she could not offer any explanation which an intelligent man would accept unless the whole story were revealed.

Her car was parked in Waterloo Place and she was waiting while the commissionaire brought it, when, turning her head, she saw a man standing at the corner whose attitude had something familiar about it. He was still there when the commissionaire returned with the car, and she had to pass the loiterer. It was then that she saw his face and tapped at the window. He saw her, too, and for once Gunner Haynes's sang-froid deserted him and he looked uncomfortable. The car pulled up with a jerk; she beckoned the man toward her and he came reluctantly.

"Will you drive with me, please?" she asked a little breathlessly. "There are one or two questions I want to settle."

He hesitated.

"It won't do you very much good, Mrs. Maddison, to be seen driving with me."

"Come in, please," she ordered imperiously, and he stepped in and sat down by her side.

Through the microphone she gave an order to the driver.

"I want to see my husband," she said, when this was done.

The Gunner shook his head.

"I don't think that's going to be very useful to you. Too many people have seen him already."

"What do you mean?" she demanded, and she saw Haynes's face harden.

"I tried to get him away this morning by the early mail. Two of Connor's men were there to head him off; I don't know how they did it, but they'd persuaded a couple of dicks—detectives—to watch the barriers, and I didn't dare chance it. I tried again at eleven o'clock and I didn't have any better luck. Of course, Connor guessed, when I took the passport, what I was going to do."

"When you took the passport?" she said in surprise. "When did you take the passport?"

The Gunner deftly slid round the question.

"Your husband's getting a bit on my mind and is interfering with my lawful occasions." There was a faint smile in his eyes as he said this.

"Were you waiting at the bank to see me?"

He smiled again.

"As a matter of fact, Mrs. Maddison, I didn't even know you were there, and didn't realize it was the bank. The truth is—" he seemed more uncomfortable still —"there's a young lady who comes to this part of the world, and I occasionally take tea with her. I think she's more interested in me as a criminal and a source of copy than in anything else." He smiled wryly. "But I'm very grateful to have the opportunity of meeting a decent girl. She's a newspaper woman, as they call 'em in America, and she covers some of these West End functions."

Margaret laughed softly. It was the first time she had laughed for a very long while.

"Poor Mr. Haynes! I'm terribly sorry if I've robbed you of a tête-à-tête."

He shook his head.

"No, there was no possibility of her coming—it's too late. And of course, there's always the chance that that obese Sparrow might be with her."

"You're talking of Mr. Bird—and the girl's name is Bolford."

He started.

"Did you know?" he gasped, and then: "Oh, of course, she has met you. She told me once. No, there's no romance in it, Mrs. Maddison, just a congenial—" he shrugged—"friendship. I am thankful for small mercies."

"Are you married?" she asked.

"I was," was the short reply, and she did not feel encouraged to pursue her inquiries.

"Can I see my husband? I think I should, don't you?"

He looked at her oddly.

"Does it strike you as a possibility that he might not want to see you?" he asked bluntly, and saw the red come into her cheeks.

"I—I have blinded myself wilfully to that possibility," she said.

"But he is in trouble, and a wife's place is by her husband's side," he mocked, and for a moment she hated him.

Then her sense of humour overcame her annoyance.

"Yes, we'll put it like that. It sounds terribly trite, but most trite things are true."

The Gunner was silent for a long time, but presently he sighed.

"I've got an idea that whatever I'm doing is quite wrong, and that I ought to let you help him. Mrs. Maddison, it's going to be a very difficult thing to get this husband of yours away out of England. You're going to say 'aëroplane'—I can see it in your eyes—but you can bet that Connor has got his people at Croydon, too. The only thing to do is to smuggle him away in a motor-car to a seaside place, hire a yacht, and push him across the Channel. It's not going to be easy, especially as he's not terribly keen on your giving him any help at all."

She pondered this as the car went slowly round the park.

"I'll take the risk of a snub," she said, "if you'll take the risk of offending him. Will you let me see him?"

Haynes nodded.

"Yes, but you're not going to take this expensive car, Mrs. Maddison—into my neighbourhood, I mean. We'll stop the car at Hyde Park Corner and get a taxi."

This they did.

"The only thing that's troubling me," he said as they

were driving along Piccadilly, "is whether Connor has tailed me to my home. 'Tail' is slang for 'trail.'"

"You think they followed you there? Didn't they know where you live?"

"They know many places I live," explained the Gunner whimsically, "but this is one they don't know, or didn't until this morning."

They paid off the cab two hundred yards from the model dwelling where Haynes had his home, and at that hour fortunately there were few people about, and certainly none who seemed to evince the slightest curiosity in the presence of this well-dressed woman. They had to pass through a little gateway to reach the asphalt square that formed the quadrangle of the huge block, and she saw the Gunner look back; there was trouble in his face.

"They've tailed me all right," he said grimly. "Did you see that motor-van on the street outside? The man at the wheel was one of Connor's little friends. You won't see him now—he's gone. Connor uses motor-vans a lot."

As he was mounting the few steps which led to the landing from which his flat opened, a slatternly woman came out of a door opposite.

"I suppose it's all right taking your wardrobe away, Mr. What's-your-name?" she said.

The Gunner spun round.

"Took my wardrobe? What do you mean?"

"The men from the furniture place came about an hour ago—two chaps in green aprons. They had the key so I thought it was all right."

The Gunner asked no further questions: he opened the door and ran into the passage. The door of Luke's room was open. He looked at the disorder, saw the bloodstained sheets, and turned to meet the white face of Margaret Maddison.

"I'm afraid your husband's gone," he said, in such a matter-of-fact tone that she was deceived.

He closed the door behind him and led her into the little sitting room.

"He won't be back till late, so I don't think it's worth while your staying."

"How do you know?" she asked. "Why were you so worried when they talked about the wardrobe being taken away?"

"An old wardrobe that I sold," said the Gunner. "It's not worth while keeping stuff that isn't much use to you."

He chatted with her pleasantly before he took her away and, finding another cab, sent her home. She could not guess that he knew in his heart that the wardrobe contained the body of Luke Maddison. Whether he was alive or dead he must find out. After he had left the girl Gunner Haynes went back to his room, rolled up the carpet, took up a floor-board, and, groping, found a box containing two small automatics. One of these he slipped in a specially constructed inside pocket of his coat; the other went into a small holster which buckled to his braces.

"I think there is going to be some trouble to-night," said Gunner Haynes, addressing nobody in particular.

CHAPTER XXIX

LUKE MADDISON had only the most confused memory of what followed his incautious opening of the door. He had been sitting reading when he heard a knock, and saw nothing suspicious in the appearance of two men in green baize aprons and shirt-sleeves.

"Is this Mr. Haynes's flat?" asked one. "We've come to take away the wardrobe."

"You'd better return when Mr. Haynes is here," said Luke, thinking naturally that the Gunner had given instructions for the removal of a piece of furniture.

"If we can't take it away we'd like to measure it," said the man, who carried a notebook obstensibly in his hand.

Luke Maddison hesitated. He knew nothing about wardrobes, or indeed of any of the domestic arrangements of the flat. But there could be no harm in acceding to this request. He turned his back upon the men for a second, and after that he remembered nothing distinctly.

His first conscious impression was of having his face roughly cleaned by a cold, wet sponge. There was a rank smell of tar in the air, and the room in which he was sitting seemed to be in motion. He thought at first that this was one of the many illusions he was experiencing, but when his eyes wandered round the apartment and saw the heavily timbered ribs of the room, the low ceiling, and the black, tar-painted floor, he realized that he was not dreaming.

"Am I on a ship?" he asked huskily, and heard a laugh.

He recognized the man who had the sponge in his hand as the artist who had once before wielded a cosh.

"Was it you in the baize apron? I didn't recognize you."

"It wasn't me this time, guv'nor," said the man, who seemed chronically hoarse. "I wouldn't have drawn blood—you ain't hurt. Drink this."

Luke drank the weak brandy and water that was offered to him, but would have preferred plain water.

"You're a regular nuisance to us, you are, guv'nor," said the man, dropping the sponge into a pail of water and wiping his hands on a grimy-looking handkerchief. "Now you take my advice and keep quiet. There's a proper bed for you here, and you'll find a pail of water in the stern. Nobody's going to hurt you if you behave yourself."

"Am I on a ship?" asked Luke again.

"Barge," was the reply. "There's nothing to be afraid of. The Gunner's looking for you, but he won't find you."

He turned to his silent companion, and only then was Luke aware that there was a second man in the cabin—if such a foul place could be dignified by such a name.

"We oughtn't to have laid him on the bed. That was the give-away, Harry," he said. "It was my fault, but we had to put him somewhere. You're stronger than I thought, Maddison."

Luke chuckled feebly.

"I don't remember that I put up a fight, did I?"

"Put up a fight?" said the other. "I should say you did! It was when we got you in the bedroom that you started scrapping. Don't you remember?"

Luke remembered nothing.

"The guv'nor's coming aboard in a minute—we're moored very near the wharf. If you're a sensible man, Mr. Maddison, you'll do what he asks. There'll be no funny business, now we know who you are."

He looked curiously at Luke.

"A pal of Lewing's, wasn't you? That's a funny game, mixing with a crowd like that. I'm surprised that a gentleman like you should have got yourself into that kind of trouble."

Luke did not reply. The two men went soon after, leaving the smoky lamp to illuminate the gloom.

A short flight of steps led to a heavy hatchway, which was closed. There was a kind of washing-place in the stern of the craft. There was no porthole through which he could see daylight, and a system of ventilation did not exist. Such air as came was admitted through three circular holes cut in the hatchway, and he suspected that over this was a canvas cover, for he could see no light.

Everything of value had been taken from him. His clothes were soiled with blood—he found his sodden collar in a corner of the cabin; and his head ached all the time. Nevertheless he was beginning to feel hungry when the hatchway was pulled back and the legs of a man appeared on the first step of the ladder.

He discovered now why he had seen no light: there was evidently a small deck-house above the hatchway, and he caught a glimpse of this as his visitor was descending. It was Connor, who greeted him with the air of a friend who had been badly treated.

"You've given us a lot of trouble, Mr. Maddison," he said, unconscious of repeating the words of his lieutenant, "and when people give me trouble they have to pay for it. I've come to have a little talk with you. You want to get away to the Continent, don't you?"

Luke did not answer.

"Don't be obstinate," begged Connor, with a friendly grin. "I'm trying to help you. I've fixed up with a boat —the skipper's a friend of mine—to take you to Rotterdam in the morning."

He took something out of his pocket which Luke recognized.

"Here's your passport—my boys found that when they were rummaging at the Gunner's house. You take it from me, Mr. Maddison, I am the best friend you ever had."

Luke smiled wryly.

"I gather that this is the trouble I'm going to pay for, isn't it?" he asked.

"Spoken like a sensible man," said Connor. "Yes, it's going to cost you a bit, but you can afford it."

From his inside pocket he brought out a long envelope, and from this extracted three blank checks.

"I want you to make these out yourself: one for two,
one for three, and one for five thousand. It'll look better that way, and look much better if the checks are in
your handwriting."

"May I see them?"

The man passed the checks to him and Luke chuckled
again.

"My poor conspirator!" he said mockingly. "I
haven't more than a hundred pounds in that account—
or any other."

Connor's eyes narrowed.

"Are you pulling one on me?" he asked.

"I'm telling you the truth," said Luke, "though I can
quite understand it sounds so strange to you that it
seems a lie. This is on my private account, which is down
to nothing—one of the last things I did before I—before
I went away, was to transfer most of the money I had
in this account to my own bank."

"But you always used the Northern & Southern?"
insisted Connor.

He was obviously perturbed by the discovery, as well
he might be, for he had spent that afternoon searching
London for the right "kites." There is quite a brisk
trade in blank check forms, and certain sources from
which they can be obtained. It had taken him some time
to track Luke's bank, a longer time to get the necessary
forms, and his discomfiture was pardonable.

"Anyway, I've got no money," said Luke, "so your labours are all wasted."

"Yes, you have," interrupted Connor. "Your missus transferred all your money back to you after you'd left."

This was news to Luke, but obviously the man was not talking at random.

"Who told you this?"

"A pal of yours," said the other coolly.

"Danton Morell?"

Connor nodded.

"It would not have gone back to this account, anyway," said Luke after a moment's thought. "It would be in my own bank."

Connor understood humanity sufficiently well to realize that his prisoner was speaking the truth.

"But you'll sign the checks when I get them, won't you, Mr. Maddison?"

Luke shook his head.

"I'm not going to threaten you; I want this thing done in a gentlemanly way," said Connor earnestly. "You're a rich man, and a few hundreds more or less isn't going to hurt you. Somebody's got to get you out of the country, and the Gunner can't. If you trust me, I'll see you right, and I'll never come to you for another penny—you know that I can't put the black on you once you get away from England: that's why I'm asking big money now. You're a business man, Mr. Maddison, and you've got enough sense to see that if I blacked you after this I should be cutting my own throat. I've had a cabin made up for you for'ard, and I'll take your word that you won't try to escape—and I don't see why you should either, with the police looking for you. Is it a deal?"

"You'll get not a bean out of me," said Luke defiantly.

Connor looked at him long and thoughtfully.

"All right," he said; "you can stay here and starve till you change your mind."

For a second Luke was tempted to rush at him as he ascended the steps. A low tackle would bring him down; but Luke was still very weak so he sat passively till the hatch was pulled tight. Mr. Connor dropped to the little rowboat which was alongside the barge.

He did not go to his wharf, but rowed to some narrow steps opposite to where the barge was moored; then making his way to the City, he hailed a taxi and was driven to Half Moon Street.

Danty was just going out when his visitor arrived, and Mr. Danton Morell was not in a good mood.

"What was the idea of sending me that address?" he said. "I went down there this afternoon and nearly ran into Gunner Haynes."

"Then why the hell did you go?" demanded Connor.

"To see Maddison. I could have persuaded him to part. Maddison isn't there. A woman in the building told me that the Gunner had locked up his flat and gone away. Where is Maddison?"

Connor lit a cigar before he replied.

"I've got him—I think I was in a quarter here, wasn't

I, Danty? Well, I'm in three quarters now, and I'm being generous. You've had your chance and you've missed it. What is he worth?"

Danty stifled his rising anger which was provoked by the tone of the man. There was no sense in getting on the wrong side of Connor, and the question of distribution might very well wait over for another and more propitious moment.

"Half a million, I should think. Where is he?"

"Half a million, eh?" Connor ignored the question. "Would he stand a hundred thousand?"

The other man thought a moment.

"Yes, he'd stand a hundred thousand if he could get it," he said.

"He said he hadn't got a bean."

"He's got money all right," said Danty savagely. "It's all in his own bank."

Connor pondered this for a long time.

"That'll mean ten kites. Can you get them?"

Danty frowned.

"What do you want checks for?"

Connor closed his eyes wearily.

"You've been so long out of the con game that you've forgotten your business," he said offensively. "I want the checks for him to sign, that's all. Can you get them?"

Danty thought for a moment.

"I've got a check book on that bank," he said. "I had a small account there. But they won't be any good: they'll be able to trace the checks to me. But I can get them."

He went to the telephone and called Margaret's number. The servant who replied told him that she was out, which was just the news he wanted.

"When will she be back? It is Mr. Morell speaking."

He half expected a message to the effect that Mrs. Maddison would not be in to him at any time.

"Not till after lunch, sir."

Danty hung up the 'phone.

"Wait here," he said. "I think I know where I can get all the kites you want."

He knew a great deal about Margaret and her domestic habits—he had been deeper in her confidence than any other man. The butler was surprised to see him, but took him up to Margaret's sitting room without hesitation.

"I didn't make myself clear, sir. Madam will not be back for another hour."

Danty smiled.

"I think you will find she returns a little sooner than that," he said, almost gaily. "Anyway, I'll wait for her."

The door had hardly closed upon the servant before he was at Margaret's desk. It was unlocked, and in one of the side drawers he knew she invariably kept two check books. They were there, as he had expected: one half empty, one unused. From the end of the latter he tore a dozen checks, slipped them in his pocket and closed the desk, before he rang the bell.

"I don't think I will wait: I'll call back in an hour. My business isn't so pressing, and I've just thought of some calls I had to make."

Within half an hour of leaving he was back with
Connor and laid the checks before him. Mr. Connor
asked no questions, nor was there any necessity.

"You're going to make him sign these? Shall I come
along with you?"

Connor grinned.

"I don't think that's a clever idea," he said. "You'll
get your corner, Danty."

He could not approach the barge in broad daylight,
for he knew that he was under police observation. As
soon as it was dark he slipped down the stream and
clambered aboard the craft, carrying with him a basket
of food and a vacuum flask of hot tea. The light which
he had left had burned itself out. Luke was half sleeping on the bed that had been prepared for him, but the
rush of cold, fresh air awakened him.

Connor switched on an electric lamp he was carrying
and put it on the floor, with one or two refills.

"Here's your food," he said. "I'm sorry to have kept
you so long, but I hope you've got more intelligence now
than you had when I left you. And here are the kites:
I'd like you to fill them in in your own hand."

Luke reached for the food and ate ravenously. He
was feeling hungry, and his vitality was at its lowest ebb.
The hot tea probably revived him more than the food,
and he was almost cheerful when he swept the last
crumbs from his knees.

"Now, what are your kites?" he said. "Oh, checks!
You want me to fill them up and sign them—for what
fabulous amount? You can make it a million if you like,

but I can assure you that they will not be honoured. I think I told you before that all my money is in my wife's name."

"In that case we'll have a little joke," said Connor, not taking his eyes from his prisoner. "You'll make each of these checks out for ten thousand, and date 'em a week apart. If you want to stay longer than ten weeks you can date 'em a month apart; or, if you'd like to get away in a few days, you can sign one check for a hundred thousand pounds and you can write a letter to your bank manager telling him the kite's got to be honoured."

Before he had finished, Luke was laughing.

"I've got a very keen sense of humour," he said, "but it doesn't strike me as being a joke for a banker to draw checks on a debit account."

Connor pulled up a stool and sat down.

"Let's have this thing right," he said. "You know me, you know my name; I've put myself in for a ten-year sentence, probably longer. I'd as soon hang as spend my life in Broadmoor, and that's just the risk I'm taking, Mr. Maddison. I'll plug you and drop you over the side, or you'll do as I ask. You're a sensible man and I'm putting the case to you. I can't let you go without the money." He drew the stool a little closer. "I've been battling for years at this river work and gang work, and what do you think I've got to show for it? The lease of an old wharf that's not worth a monkey; about a couple of thousand planted away in country banks, and the certainty that sooner or later one of my rats will squeak on me. I've got a chance now of getting away

with big money—you've got a chance of clearing yourself. I'll make a signed statement, giving the facts about
the Taffanny smash—is it a bet?"

It was not the moment for heroics. Luke realized
this very definitely. He had no doubt in his mind that
in the last extremity Connor would keep his word. There
would lie the end of all things. It was not a monent to
snap fingers in the face of fate. Connor had put the situation on a business basis, and this was not the time to
consider the niceties of business etiquette. If he drew a
check and it were presented, he had no doubt in his
mind that the check would not be met; inquiries would
be set afoot, and possibly he would be traced.

"I think it is foolish to attempt to put in a check for
ten thousand," he said. "The amount is so big that, even
if I had the money, Stiles would be suspicious. I'm willing to make a compromise: I'll give you a check for five
thousand pounds. If that is honoured—which it will not
be—your luck is in, and you had better clear before
there are inquiries. Obviously no bank manager in his
senses would pay out a hundred thousand pounds without communicating with the man who drew the checks."

He saw Connor smile.

"That's the stuff I like to hear," said the man. "That's
intelligent. Where are you supposed to be—in Spain,
aren't you?"

Luke frowned.

"I suppose I am. Why?"

"We'll draw this five thousand, and then you and me
will go to Spain together—I'll get you away to-night."

The scheme did not even seem feasible to Luke, but he made no comment. He wrote and signed the check and handed it to the other.

"And now," said Luke, "I'd like a little fresh air. This place is stifling me."

Connor hesitated.

"Come up on deck, but if there's any monkey business I may have to do something I shall be sorry for."

A few seconds later Luke sat on the edge of the hatchway, sucking in the cool, sweet air. The hatch was on the well of the barge, and this was covered with tarpaulin. He could see this by the light of a flashing electric sign erected on one of the towers that fringed the river. Opposite was a line of lights which stood for the Thames Embankment. A fussy little tug was moving slowly against the tide upstream; he heard the hoot and shriek of a train as it passed across one of the bridges. The lights of the West End painted the low-lying clouds a dull orange. The tide was on the turn; he heard the lap of it against the flat bow of the barge.

For ten minutes he sat in silence, then rose onto the deck and stretched his cramped limbs.

"If I promised not to leave the barge, or attempt to attract attention, would you leave the hatch open, Mr. Connor?"

Connor's laugh was his answer.

"Don't be silly! That word of honour stuff doesn't mean anything to me."

"I'm glad," said Luke. "If you had accepted my word it might have been very embarrassing."

As he spoke, his hand shot out, and Connor went sprawling onto the hatch. Before he could recover, Luke had reached the edge of the barge and without a glance had plunged in and was striking out for midstream.

He heard no sound but the patter of footsteps on the hollow hatches, and then a voice giving urgent instructions. Connor must have a rowboat moored alongside, he decided. The tide had already swept him clear of the barge; it was running strongly, and there was nothing nearer to him than a line of moored lighters in the centre of the river. To make for these, however, would be to invite discovery. He struck back toward the shore.

As he did so, he saw a shape come round the bow of the barge. Connor had come in a motor launch. It moved too quickly to be anything else. There was only one thing to do. He drew a lungful of air and dived toward the launch, swimming hard against the tide. He seemed to be under the water for an eternity; his lungs and head were bursting when he came to the surface, coming up just under the stern of the launch, so close that the whirling little propeller seemed to touch his hair.

Neither of the two men in the launch had seen him. He just caught the silhouette of their heads and shoulders peering over the side, and then he sank again.

He was lamentably weak; his effort could not be long sustained. He had to come again to the surface, and was relieved to see no sign of the launch. As he trod water he saw it, making for the lighters in mid-stream. He was now twenty yards from a barge moored to a wharf, and striking out he caught the mooring chain and recovered his breath before he attempted to reach land.

He was too weak to climb up to the barge; the only thing he could do was to complete his journey to the shore, and with infinite labour he succeeded at last, wading through mud up to his knees until he came to the blank face of a warehouse. There seemed no escape here. Looking back over his shoulder, he saw the launch returning. Somebody was fanning the water with an electric torch, and escape seemed impossible.

It was at that moment he heard a hoarse voice hail him from the barge.

"Give us your hand."

He reached up and found it gripped.

"Catch hold of the top of the pile," whispered the voice cheerfully, and groping upward Luke found a hold, and with a superhuman effort and the assistance of his unknown friend, dragged himself up onto a narrow strip of wharfage running before the warehouse and scarcely wide enough for two people to walk abreast.

"They didn't see you, did they?" whispered the unknown, and before Luke could reply: "Push round to the left. Follow me—there's a watchman here; he's asleep, but don't make a row!"

Luke Maddison found himself picking a way across a yard littered with paving-stones and granite setts. He saw a long shed and the projecting shafts of vans. Somewhere near at hand were horses for he heard one kicking in his stall.

He followed stealthily, past a little lighted hut, wherein the night watchman (as he hoped) was sleeping. After a while they came to a heavy black gate; the wicket door was unfastened, and through this they slipped, Luke's rescuer closing the door softly behind him—apparently he had a key.

"I saw 'em looking for you, but I thought they was out for Connor's lot."

He swore most foully for a few seconds.

"These river busies are worse than the land busies."

By the light of a street lamp Luke took stock of his companion: a sharp, lantern-jawed man of thirty, with a Jewish nose and furtive eyes that never kept still.

"You're wet, ain't you? Come into Connor's yard: he'll give you a change."

"No, thank you," said Luke hastily. "I don't want anything to do with Connor."

"You don't want anything to do with Connor, eh? Well, you're wise. Got any money?"

Luke felt in his pockets.

"No," he said.

The man uttered a grunt of disgust.

"I thought at least I'd get a quid out of it. Where do you live?"

"I don't know where the devil I do live," said Luke irritably, and he heard the thin, whistling laugh of his companion.

"You're a swell—I thought you was when I first heard you speak. Ever busted a safe? There's one in that warehouse and nothing else. They told me there

was a lot of stuff there. I've been three days getting in
and out. The only way you can do it is to go through the
stone yard. But I'll bet there's some stuff in the safe.
Have you ever busted one?"

"Never," said Luke, and added: "It's one of the few
things I haven't done."

"What were the busies after you for? Was you doing
the lighter?"

The man was under the impression that Luke was a
fugitive from the river police, and he did not undeceive
him.

"It's a pretty hard life," said the other agreeably.

They were reaching now a more populous centre, and
the little man, who said his name was Tom, stopped.

"You can't go into the street like this: they'd pinch
you in a minute. You'd better come home with me. But
I can't afford to keep you."

Luke was led through divers byways to the meanest
street he had ever struck. Although the hour was late,
children were playing and screaming, women stood at
the doors gossiping. Nobody took any notice of Luke
and his companion, and presently they passed through
a door, which Tom unlocked, along an evil-smelling
passage and up an uncarpeted flight of stairs.

"Go in there and get your wet clothes off." Tom
opened a door, and striking a match lit a candle.

The windows were heavily screened with an old piece
of horse blanket, and the furniture of the room con-
sisted of a bed with horrible-looking bedding, and
precious little else.

Tom said he was going to see the landlord. He was gone some time and when he returned Luke had overcome his repugnance to the soiled linen, and having stripped and dried himself as well as he could on the one grimy towel that the room possessed, he had crawled into the bed.

Tom threw down on a chair a pair of trousers and an old shirt, which had the advantage of being clean. "That's all I can get for you," he said, and picked up Luke's sodden suit, eying it with approval.

The boots also came under his scrutiny.

"Silk shirt, eh? I thought you was a swell. I'll get these dried for you."

He disappeared and did not return. Ten minutes later, in spite of his unsavoury surroundings, Luke was fast asleep. When he woke the sun was shining through the holes in the blanket. Rising, he put on the shirt and trousers, feeling uncommonly chilly.

There was noise enough downstairs: the howl of a crying child, a woman's strident voice, and the deeper, bullying tone of a man. He opened the door, went out onto the landing and called. Presently the owner of the deep voice appeared.

"What's the matter?"

"Are my clothes dried?" asked Luke politely.

"What clothes?"

The man was interested, and came heavily up the stairs: a big, unshaven brute, puffy-faced.

"Gave Tom your clothes?" He kissed his hand loudly. "Say good-bye to 'em, old man."

Luke stared at him aghast.

"Do you mean he's gone away with them?"

That apparently was what he did mean. He also informed his guest that he needed half a crown for the night's lodging.

"And then there's my trousers and shirt," he said. "What do I get for 'em?"

He took a long time before he consented to add to the loan an old jacket and a pair of worn shoes that were two sizes too small. He could, he thought, "get a bit out of Tom, from which Luke gathered he was going to share the proceeds of the stolen clothing. He added to his other beneficences a cup of tea and a thick slice of bread and margarine, and with this equipment the banker was turned out into the street.

Rain was falling heavily. By the time he had reached Lambeth Bridge he was soaked through. He made for the park, and finding a chair drew it into the shelter of a big, overhanging tree. For a long time he sat there, and then he reached a decision. Disgrace and prison seemed a little less unpleasant prospect than cold and hunger. He decided to go to the bank.

He did not know the time and asked a man who was hurrying past, without, however, eliciting the slightest response. He asked another man, who gruffly told him it was nearly twelve. He would find Stiles in the office, and Stiles meant comfort and food and decent clothing.

As he came out of the park gates somebody caught him by the arm and swung him round, and he looked into the unsympathetic face of a man who was obviously a detective.

"Begging, eh? I saw you speak to those two gentlemen."

"I asked them the time," said Luke.

"I dare say," said the detective, tightening his lips. "Come a little walk with me."

Ten minutes later a door closed on Luke Maddison, and he found himself alone in a clean but very uncomfortable cell of a police station. In this experience he was not entirely unfortunate, for Connor had been trailing him, hoping that he might go to some part of the park where persuasion, peaceful or otherwise, could be attempted.

CHAPTER XXX

No MAN wasted less time or effort than Gunner Haynes. His method represented the very economy of labour. He was satisfied that Connor had carried away his victim, but was wrong when he associated Danty Morell with the abduction.

He called upon Connor but was told vaguely that the man had gone into the country. He did not attempt to seek an interview with Danty Morell, but after a day spent in a vain search of Connor's wharf, made his way to Half Moon Street, watched the house until he saw first Danty and then Pi Coles leave. To get into Danty's flat was a very simple matter—a key blank, a piece of lampblack, a quarter of an hour spent in Green Park filing the soft metal, procured him an entrance.

Once inside the flat he proceeded at his leisure. He was not at all anxious at the thought of Danty's return. His hatred of Morell was in one sense illogical. They had been friends and partners, though he had lost sight of the man and the partnership had broken off. He had no direct proof of the duplicity he suspected. Gunner Haynes had loved that feather-headed little wife of his, and when she had disappeared, never to become more to him than a record in a workhouse register, a tremendous part of his life had been cut away from him. He might suspect Danty as the cause of his agony: he had no clear evidence that the story the man had told was untrue.

Danty had said the girl had disappeared, and that he was as ignorant of her whereabouts as her husband. Yet, for all this, the suspicion in Gunner Haynes's mind amounted to a certainty. He was a just man, and so long as that proof was missing, Danty Morell would come to no harm.

He made a quick but thorough examination of the two rooms. There were letters which had to be scanned, pocketbooks to investigate, drawers to be opened and searched, but in none of these did Haynes find the slightest clue to Luke Maddison's present place of imprisonment. He did find the note which Connor had scribbled, giving the address where Luke was staying, but no more. There remained only the safe, which was not so much a safe as a steel cupboard fastened with a spring lock— the type that is found in most business offices. To open this was a matter of five minutes' patient work.

There were four shelves and each was crowded with letters, bills, and curious souvenirs which Danty had collected—the cupboard was in such disorder as only a man without method could create. On the third shelf he found a wooden box, the lock of which he forced. There were papers here—bundles of letters tied up with shoe-laces, bits of old string—there was nothing romantic in Danty's disposition.

The first bundle did not interest him. At the sight of the writing on the second his face went gray. He brought the box into the dining-room and sat down, read three of the letters, glanced at the others, and very slowly and deliberately tied them up again and put them back in the box. As he did so he caught sight of a scrap of paper exactly the size of that on which Rex had written his last message. He took it out—yes, it was scrawled in the same handwriting. But the message was unintelligible. It ran:

Danty Morell. The man is a common swindler. I was warned against him by——

And then in a flash he realized. He had an extraordinary memory, and could repeat almost word for word the supposedly complete message Rex had left. With these words added it would have read:

Margaret darling, I have lost. For months I have been gambling. To-day I took a desperate step on the advice of Danty Morell. The man is a common swindler. I was warned against him by Luke Maddison. He has led me to ruin—money is his god. I beg of you not to trust him. He has led me from one act of folly to another. . . .

That was it! Danty had found that the first and last of those scraps made a complete message; he had put the second in his pocket (it still bore marks of being screwed up).

It took him quite a long time to realize all this. His mind was numbed from reading the letters; he was almost stupid in his horror and hate. Mechanically he put the tell-tale slip of paper into his pocketbook, closed the lid. . . . His wife's letters must be burned. He opened the box again, took them out, threw them into the fireplace and put a match to them. He stood watching and stirring them until they were black ashes, then he put the box back where he had found it and closed the steel cupboard.

For the moment Luke Maddison and his safety were subsidiary considerations. The only thing that mattered was Danty. The agony and appeal in those letters! Gunner Haynes caught a glimpse of his face in a mirror over the mantelpiece and for a moment was shocked. He had become suddenly old.

Danty did not return—he was glad. He turned out all the lights, closed the door behind him, and went out into the street. He had hardly crossed to the other sidewalk before a cab drew up to the pavement and a man alighted. It was Danty.

The gunman watched but made no effort to intercept him. That would come later; there would be a great accounting.

He strolled into Piccadilly, moving like a man in a dream, and heard his name spoken twice before he turned with a start to look into the pretty face of Mary Bolford.

"I wondered if it was you," she said, "and if you were contemplating some nefarious act. Of course you're not!"

The Gunner drew a long breath.

"To tell you the truth, I was," he said gently. "I haven't had the good fortune to meet you in this last week, Miss Bolford."

She shook her head.

"I've been very busy. I've accepted a job on an Australian newspaper, and I'm leaving London next week." Her tone was jaunty, but he could detect a strain in the voice that was very flattering to him.

"Well, I've given you enough to write about," he said. "Enough material, I mean."

She sighed.

"Yes." A little pause. "I shall miss you. I suppose if I told Mr. Bird that he would be annoyed."

"He'd be furious," said the Gunner, a slow smile displacing the pained look she had seen in his eyes.

"You won't come to Australia, of course, ever? I shall be there for seven years."

"By what boat do you travel?" he asked, and when she told him: "There's another mail leaving a week or so after. Do you sail from London?"

She nodded.

"They wanted me to pick up the boat at Naples—we call there; but I rather want the sea journey. I've got what is called a lung—not a bad one: that is why I have taken work in Australia."

They had coffee together, and in that flying time he thought neither of Luke Maddison nor of Danty Morell nor of the letters which were ash in the grate. When he left her at eleven o'clock, he said:

"If I can get my business through I may join your ship at Naples."

She looked at him very gravely.

"Do you really mean that?" she said. "And is Australia to be the scene of your next——" She hesitated for a word, but he anticipated her.

"I am going to be the rarest of phenomena—the reformed crook," he said.

She sipped her coffee in silence.

"Would anything help you to that end?" she asked, and Haynes nodded.

He did not put into words the thought that was in his mind and hers, but she understood. It was then that he gave her his first confidence, and she listened open eyed, stricken dumb with amazement, to the true story of Luke Maddison.

"I've been searching for him all day," he said, "and I haven't even got a thread of a clue."

"He isn't dead?"

Haynes shook his head.

"That is most unlikely," he said. "The trouble is that the police cannot be told—I suppose the press shouldn't be either," he smiled, "but things are—different now, aren't they?"

"Have you got the little piece of paper you found in Morell's flat?" (He had omitted nothing from his narrative.)

He passed it across the table to her. She read and nodded.

"What was the rest of it?"

He recited the full message almost word for word.

"I have seen Rex—in fact I know a great deal about him," she said. "Mr. Bird was very confidential and told me about the forgery. I could have given him a lot of

information, because I was standing in the doorway of
the bank the day the forged check was cashed. It was
the day Mr. Maddison gave me a hundred pounds—
I've still got it."

They were talking of the Sparrow as they came out
of the restaurant, and at the corner of Bury Street they
met him. He looked disapprovingly at Gunner Haynes
and frowned at the girl.

"Getting a first-hand crime story? What's doing,
Gunner? Are you giving evidence before the select com-
mission?" he asked with a sneer.

Gunner Haynes chuckled. There had been one of
those periodical police scandals; somebody had been
arrested who ought not to have been arrested, and there
was the inevitable inquiry on foot into police methods.

"We've got to go so carefully nowadays that I
wouldn't arrest a man if I found him cutting his wife's
throat, without making a few inquiries," said the Sparrow. "I'll tell you how bad it is: they've just turned a
tramp out of a police station, charged with begging,
but only one witness—a policeman. So they hoofed him
out. When we've got to consider the feelings of tramps
you might as well turn Scotland Yard into a home for
lost dogs. I mention the tramp because I was down at
the police station just after they pushed him out. I suppose it's happening all over London. You're going to
Australia, they tell me, Miss Bolford?"

His keen eyes searched the Gunner's face.

"You're not going too, are you, Gunner? You'll miss
those little tea-table talks, won't you?"

Mary Bolford turned red. She had never dreamed that those unrehearsed and informal meetings with Gunner Haynes had attracted the attention of this stout man.

"Both of you ought to be warned," said Sparrow soberly, "and I'm warning you! There never was a crook who could be anything but a crook. There never was a girl who married a man to reform him who didn't finish by bolting with somebody better."

"You're in your most prophetic mood to-night, Mr. Bird," said the Gunner coolly. "Now tell us what's going to win the Derby?"

The Sparrow grunted and went on with a little chuck of his head—a gesture of farewell. Haynes and the girl walked along Piccadilly till they came within sight of the Circus, and here they parted. As they lingered, her hand in his, he said:

"You've saved a man's life to-night, Mary," and wisely she did not question him.

CHAPTER XXXI

IT CAME as something in the nature of a shock to Margaret Maddison to discover how completely changed were her feelings toward the man with whom she had passed through stages of toleration to liking, and from liking to a sort of passive affection, and from that again, in the cataclysmic revolution of feeling that her brother's death had brought about, to the bitterest loathing.

For the first time in her life Margaret was in love, and in love with something which was neither a memory nor an idea, but something which was to her as real as her own hand. She had gained that sense of possession which is the wife's own sense—an understanding of her obligations. She could not afford to waste time in regrets at the amazing follies and wicked errors of the past: in the days that followed her mind was occupied with schemes for helping him out of the morass in which he struggled.

She did not hear from Gunner Haynes, although she stayed up until nearly two o'clock the next morning, having the telephone switched through to her bedside. Nor did the next day bring news. She was out when Danty called, and having no occasion to go to her check book, she did not discover his theft.

The following morning brought the Sparrow—professionally.

"Did you give orders that none of your husband's checks over a thousand pounds were to be cashed at the bank?" he asked.

She nodded.

"A young man brought one in for two thousand this morning. Very foolishly, Mr. Stiles didn't call me up, and he got away before I arrived."

"Was it in Luke's handwriting?" she asked eagerly. "Where is he?"

The Sparrow could not supply information.

"I thought he was abroad—is it usual for your husband to send people to the bank with checks to cash? It seems queer to me."

"The money was not paid?" she asked.

"No—Stiles said if it had been for a thousand he'd have cashed it."

She was purposely evasive, and after the detective had gone she telephoned through to Stiles. He had little to add.

"The man who brought the check seemed very respectable."

"But did you ask him where he got the check?" she demanded impatiently. "Surely, Mr. Stiles, you weren't satisfied——"

"I thought that you expected him to send checks," said Mr. Stiles.

She had never realized how dense a man this middle-aged manager was.

After she had rung off she sat down to think. Luke had broken into his flat to secure his passport and clothes. The passport was now in the Gunner's possession—she must see that he had a change in case he arrived unexpectedly. She went herself to his flat, made a careful collection, packed such toilet articles as she thought he might require, including a case of razors, and had them taken down to her car. It was the first wifely duty she had performed, and it brought her a pleasing sense of novelty. Even that faint pleasure brought to her a realization of the strain under which she was living, and the ever increasing anxiety concerning Luke's fate.

If she could have got into touch with Gunner Haynes she would have done so. She would almost have welcomed the arrival of Danty Morell. She had a reminder of his earlier visit when she went to her bureau to make out household checks. She took out the wrong check book and saw that some were missing. Putting through a call to the bank, she learned that the check presented that day was one of these. Then Danton Morell was in the conspiracy!

Her first inclination was to send for Inspector Bird. But at all costs the police must not be called in. She turned the leaves of the telephone directory to search for Danton's number, and was on the point of calling him when she came to a decision to see him herself.

She did not wait for her car, but hailing a taxi and leaving certain very definite instructions behind her, drove to Half Moon Street. Pi Coles, who opened the door to her, stared in amazement at this unexpected vision.

"Come in, miss," he said awkwardly. "The guv'nor's inside."

Danton heard her voice and was coming across the hall to meet her before the door was closed.

"This is an unexpected pleasure, Margaret," he said. "Is anything wrong?"

She did not answer until she was in his room.

"Before I tell you why I've come," she said, "I think it is only fair that you should know I have left instructions that unless I am back in my house in three quarters of an hour my butler will ring up Mr. Bird and tell him where I have gone."

He frowned at this.

"What's the idea?" he asked harshly. "That's an extraordinary way to behave—why the dickens shouldn't you be back in three quarters of an hour?"

"Where are the remainder of those checks that you stole from my check book when you called the other day?" she asked.

She saw his face go red.

"I don't know what you mean," he said loudly. "I steal checks? What nonsense you're talking——"

"You came into my house and you were in my sitting room long enough to extract ten checks. One of them was brought to the bank to-day, made out in Luke's name and signed by him. On my instructions the check was not honoured."

The colour left his face.

"Not honoured?" he stammered, and in his embarrassment he betrayed his share of the guilt.

"I'm less interested in the check than in my husband," she said quietly. "Where is he?"

He strove vainly to recover his self-possession and forced a smile.

"Really, my dear girl——" he began.

"You'll address me as Mrs. Maddison, if you have to address me as anything," she said. "I want you to return those checks; I want you also to tell me exactly where Luke is."

"As far as I know, he's staying with a convicted thief named Haynes," the man answered roughly, and to his surprise she nodded.

"I thought so, too. I went down to see him—but he had gone. I think Mr. Haynes was surprised to find that he had gone, and I'm only now understanding that Luke did not go of his own free will. Then I thought he may have wandered out by himself in order to escape association with Mr. Haynes. But the check explains a great deal. Where is Luke?"

He shook his head.

"I don't know."

"In that case I am going to do what I was trying to avoid," she said. "I am going to the police, and I shall charge you with stealing the blank checks, and leave it to Mr. Bird to connect you with Luke's disappearance."

She half turned to the door, but he caught her by the arm.

"For God's sake, Margaret, consider what you're doing!"

She saw he was really alarmed; his voice was tremulous, his whole air suggested panic.

"I swear to you I don't know where Luke is—he was on a barge, where Connor was keeping him. The swine didn't tell me that Maddison had signed a check. All he told me was that he jumped into the river and got away or was drowned—I don't know which. That's the truth. I knew nothing about it till Connor had found him. I swear to you this is the truth!"

"Where is Connor?" she asked.

"I don't know. He was here this morning, and told me about Luke getting away. That is all the information I have. I didn't believe him, and probably it's a lie he told me."

He saw she was undecided and eagerly sought to turn her from her intention. He had no doubt that she meant what she had said.

She did not know what to do.

"Could you find Haynes for me?"

"Find Haynes?" he almost shouted. "You don't imagine I would communicate with that felow, do you? He's a dangerous man, Margaret——"

"Mrs. Maddison," she said coldly.

"He's dangerous—you oughtn't to have any dealings with him."

He did not attempt to deny the theft of the checks.

"You don't know where Mr. Maddison is at all?"

He accepted the corrected relationship without demur.

"No, Mrs. Maddison, I've no idea. Connor's been looking for him all night."

When she returned home she found the Sparrow waiting for her on the doorstep. The sight of a large kitbag at his feet surprised her, and when he carried it into the house and into the little study on the ground floor, she was to have a shock. She did not recognize the crumpled clothes he took from the bag.

"These clothes were found in the possession of a river thief, who was trying to sell them this morning," he said. "He didn't know that your husband's name was stitched in the inside pocket."

"My husband's name?" she gasped, turning pale. "Where did he get them?"

"That's what I want to know. The yarn he tells is that last night he picked up a man who was wet through and who had come out of the river, and took him to a house. We've since verified that—though from the description I've had it couldn't possibly be Mr. Maddison, who is still abroad, I presume?"

Was there a note of sarcasm in his voice? She thought she detected it, and very wisely did not answer.

"The man said the clothes were given to him, but that of course is the usual yarn. I have reason to believe that they were stolen while the owner was in bed. Can you throw any light upon them."

She shook her head. It was a pitiable confession, but she knew she could not even recognize an old suit of clothes worn by her husband. It was the suit into which he had changed when he broke into his flat.

"What do you make of that, Mrs. Maddison?"

She shook her head helplessly.

"It couldn't be a suit your husband gave away, because the date it was delivered is written on the tab, and it must have been new a month ago."

He looked at her keenly.

"There's a lot of mystery about this husband of yours, Mrs. Maddison, and I think you're in some kind of trouble. I'd like to help you if I could."

She was going to speak, but he held up his hand to stop her.

"Don't tell me anything until I have told you just how much I know." He ticked off the facts on the fingers of his hand. "I know your husband disappeared the day after your marriage. I know that there was a burglary at his flat, and that when the police arrived they recognized the man who had been concerned in a robbery that afternoon. I know that among the things stolen from his flat was a passport—I interviewed his servant subsequently, and he told me there was a passport in one of the drawers of the desk. Now, if there were any chance —and it seems one of those fantastic theories that writers make a lot of money from—that this man is Mr. Maddison, the best people to help him are the police. I know him well enough to be sure he wouldn't hold up Taffanny's. If it's a question of impersonation—we can be more than useful. Won't you tell me, Mrs. Maddison?"

She was silent. With a shake of his head the detective took his departure, carrying with him the suit of clothes and a very deep-seated conviction.

It was a curious coincidence that he should have brought those crumpled garments to the house when, neatly packed away in a new suitcase in her bedroom, was the change of garments she had arranged for Luke.

She was puzzled as to the arrangements she could make that would be most convenient. She decided ultimately upon leaving the suitcase at a railway cloak-room. The ticket could be sent to Luke as soon as he was discovered. She waited for the night to come to carry this plan into effect.

The night brought its problems for Danty Morell. That afternoon, after Margaret Maddison had left him, he made a discovery which turned him sick with apprehension. He had lost his hold on Margaret; at any moment she might go to the police, and just then he was most anxious not to renew acquaintance with Scotland Yard. Things had gone badly with him; he owed a very large sum of money which had to be paid in the City on the following day; and now, with the added possibility of police intervention, his position was perilous.

Danton Morell was in some ways a careful man. However extravagant he might be, he had reserved for himself a fat nest egg in cash which, in spite of all temptation, he had never touched. He had collected the money that day from two or three accounts which he ran in an assumed name. Nothing was needed now but to follow the line of retreat he had planned. There was a small aërodrome on the outskirts of London, from which exhibition flights were given. Danty had found it expedient to finance the small company which owned the airplanes, and by telephone he arranged his flight. This was facilitated by the fact that the company had recently acquired a big rebuilt monoplane which was capable of a long flight. Danty, who had decided upon Switzerland for his first hop, gave orders for the storage of petrol and necessities for the journey. He certainly did not anticipate taking a companion with him, but he was not the only panic-stricken man in London.

Danty made a very quick search for papers which, left behind, might have awkward consequences, and his first attention was directed to the little box in which he kept the most dangerous of his correspondence. He brought this into the dining room before he discovered that the lock had been forced. With an exclamation he threw up the lid, shook out the contents—— The one packet of letters that he had been mad to keep was gone! And the little telephone slip—that also had disappeared.

His hands were shaking so that he could hardly hold the papers he was examining. There was no need to speculate upon the identity of the man who had forced that box. The Gunner had been seen in the neighbourhood: Pi Coles had told him that, and it had been the Gunner who had made this search and found the documents. Danty Morell saw death grinning at him; hypnotized into sheer inaction. When there came a knock at the outer door, he leaped up from his chair, a shivering wreck of a man, not daring to open to the visitor.

He calmed himself sufficiently to go to the door and demand who was there, and when he heard Connor's voice he could have cried aloud for joy.

"What's the matter with you?" asked Connor, when they were back in the room.

"I've had a bit of a shock, and I'm not particularly well. You know they're after those kites?"

Connor himself was not particularly happy-looking.

"I know. They've stopped a check I sent to the bank and half the busies in London are looking for him. They know who it is, too—that's the worst of it. You're in this, Danty."

"We're both in it, aren't we?" snarled the other. "I'm getting out of London to-night."

Connor laughed raucously.

"You've got a fine chance of getting out of London, unless you take a rattler." And then, suddenly: "How are you going?"

It was on the tip of Danty's tongue to invent a method of escape, but just now he needed the association of Connor. Connor was not above using a gun at a pinch, and, moreover, hated Gunner Haynes.

"I'm going by airplane from Elford," he said. "We've got the Gunner to thank for this. He squealed."

"He's never stopped squealing," said Connor without heat. "Where do you land in your flying machine?"

Danty told him his destination.

"That'll do for me," said Connor.

He looked at the papers on the table.

"Having a burn-up?" he asked pleasantly. And then: "How much stuff have you got?"

Here Danty lied. He could not tell the truth about money.

The conference was a brief one. They agreed to visit the aërodrome that evening and make final preparations for their jorney. The journey through the suburbs into outer London was a silent one; now and again Danty lifted the flap at the back of the hired car in which they were travelling, and peered along the darkening road.

"What's the matter with you?" growled Connor.

"There's a car, a two-seater, following us."

"Why shouldn't it?" demanded the other sarcastically. "Do you want the road to yourself?"

A few minutes later, when Danty looked back, the little car had disappeared.

The preparations for the night's journey were not easily made. The pilot had only just been communicated with. He was on a holiday in the Midlands.

"It's a good job we came, or we might have been in Queer Street," said Connor as they were driving back. "What time did you say you'd be here?"

"About midnight."

"What are you looking for?" asked Connor ten minutes later. "The little car?"

He pushed his companion aside and peered.

"There's a motor lorry: has that got anything on us?" he demanded.

Danty said nothing. No man could know the terror that was in his heart. Behind him stalked the grim

shadow of vengeance, and every second he expected to
see the hawklike face of the Gunner peering into his
from the darkness.

Danty did not go near his flat. He telephoned to Pi
Coles and they met in the park, Pi bringing with him an
overcoat and wrap which were to be Danty's sole luggage. His servitor he rewarded liberally. There was
nothing to do now but to pass the few hours which inter-
vened before he left England forever.

He telephoned to the hangar and learned to his satisfaction that the pilot had arrived. He would have
liked to advance the hour of his departure, but he knew
that for once he must keep faith—Connor was a dangerous man, and he had no desire to let two enemies
grow in the place of one.

Once or twice, as he loafed about the less frequented
streets of Pimlico, he had the impression that he was being shadowed; but when once he walked back in desperate boldness to interview the man who was following
him, he found it was a perfectly inoffensive stranger to
the neighbourhood who was trying to find a street and a
number.

He had work to do—vengeful work—and he com-
pleted this in a teashop near Vauxhall Bridge. Making
a wide detour, he reached the central post office and
handed in the telegram addressed to Inspector Bird. It
ran:

The man who was concerned in the Taffanny robbery was Luke
Maddison. He is attempting to leave London to-night. His wife and
Gunner Haynes are aware of the double life he has been living.

He signed it with his own name.

Late as was the hour, he knew that the telegram would be delivered. He went back to meet his companion in misfortune, feeling more cheerful than he had felt all day.

CHAPTER XXXII

IT WAS nearly eleven o'clock that night when Margaret had the car brought to the door and Luke's suitcase deposited. Her intention was to drive the car to the lower part of Villiers Street and send the chauffeur with the suitcase to the cloakroom. She came into the south end of the Strand and the car had some difficulty in making its way through the returning theatre traffic, but after a long wait it turned down the steep street toward the Embankment, and at a signal from Margaret the chauffeur stopped the machine.

It was raining heavily; there were few pedestrians in sight, and those were hurrying to reach the shelter of the Underground station. She pulled at the catch of the door to open it, that the chauffeur might more easily take the suitcase at her feet, when, out of the shadows, came a shabby-looking figure. He must have seen her difficulty, for he turned the handle and pulled open the door before the chauffeur could descend.

"Thank you," said Margaret, and handed him the piece of silver she had ready to pay the luggage-room attendant.

As she did so she switched on the light. For a second she stared into the unshaven face and the grimy figure.

"Luke!" she gasped.

He was stricken dumb with amazement, was unable to speak or move.

"Luke!" she said again.

Then, as he shrank back, her hand shot out and gripped him by the coat.

"Come in, for God's sake!" she said breathlessly, and half dragged him to her side.

At that moment the chauffeur arrived.

"Drive on," she said hurriedly. "This is a—a friend of mine."

She only hoped that the man could not see the scarecrow who was seated at her side.

"Where shall I go, madam?"

"To—to the house," she said.

As the chauffeur climbed back into his seat, a third figure appeared. He came running down the street like a man pursued, and gripping the handle of the door, leaped onto the running board as the car moved. She thought at first it was a policeman, but then a passing street lamp revealed the dark face of Gunner Haynes.

"Don't make a fuss," he said, as he blundered in, slamming the door behind him. "I've chased your car from the Haymarket. Who's this?"

He peered forward and she heard him whistle.

"Is that Mr. Maddison?"

"Yes, it's me," said Luke, speaking for the first time.

His voice sounded pitiably weak. He had been turned out of the police station in the early part of the afternoon and had not eaten since the morning. He made no attempt to explain his need, he was too tired and weary to care very much. The soft luxury of the padded seats dulled him into lethargy: he was nodding almost before the car reached the Embankment.

"All right, don't wake him," said Gunner Haynes in a low voice. "He was arrested this morning, I've only just found out; one of my—friends told me. The police are looking for him. Somebody sent a wire to the Sparrow—I suspect it was friend Danty. Where are you taking him?"

"Home," she said.

She was wrapping a rug about the chilled figure in the corner of the car.

"You'll have a policeman waiting on the mat. No, you'll take him to Elford. What's this?"

He kicked against the suitcase and she explained, and heard him chuckle.

"You must be a thought reader. That's the very thing he'll require—not to-night perhaps, but in the morning. We're going to Elford. Do you know it? It's three quarters of an hour's run, and if we're lucky we'll reach there before two of the biggest rats that ever climbed out of Thames mud."

She leaned out of the window and gave directions to the chauffeur.

"Couldn't we drive on to Dover and get on board the boat?" she asked urgently.

Gunner Haynes shook his head.

"No, that won't work. The Sparrow's a good fellow, but he'd shop his own mother. And if, as I believe, Mr.

Morell, or whatever his present name is, has blown—
has told the story of Taffanny's—every boat will be
watched. Besides, there isn't one till daylight that we
could possibly catch. There's only one chance, and that
is for Mr. Maddison to appear in Spain, where he is
supposed to be. I think that can be worked—unless Mr.
Danty Morell has got too far ahead of us."

He peered forward again.

"You've got a fur coat on—that's good. You can lend
it to your husband. It'll look rather silly, but nobody will
see him."

"What are you going to do?" she asked.

"I'm going on an airplane ride to-night, and he's going with me," he said. "As for you, Mrs. Maddison,
your work is very simple. You'll return to London;
you'll lie a little—I hope it won't hurt you very much—
and leave for Spain to-morrow. If I can't get him there
after I've landed him in France, I'm a Dutchman."

There was a silence, and then:

"I know a better way," she said quietly. "I can go
with him."

To her surprise, the Gunner did not combat that suggestion.

"Perhaps you're wise," was his comment.

They came at last to a dark and bumpy road, and here
the car was stopped by the Gunner's instructions. He
got down and pointed into the darkness.

"Pull your car over there and shut off all your lights,"
he said, and when this was done and with great trouble

the car had been manœuvred over the rough ground and the engine had been shut off, he came back to the girl. "We're here first," he said. "I'm banking on Danty being cautious—look!"

Lights were coming along the road from the direction of London. It was a car, which stopped a hundred yards away, and then after a while turned round.

"They're walking the rest of the journey," murmured the Gunner with grim satisfaction. "Wait here."

He walked back to the entrance of the untidy little aërodrome and slipped something from his pocket. He had not long to wait: Danty and Connor turned out of the road again.

"Is that you, Higgins?" asked Danty. "Is the pilot here——?"

"Everybody's here including me," said the Gunner. "Don't try any funny business, Connor; I've got you covered, and there's a silencer on my gun. You'll hear no more than a 'plop' and you'll be in hell!"

Danty said nothing. Haynes could almost hear him shivering with fear.

"Well, what next?" asked Connor.

"The next is a long walk back to the nearest town, unless you've had the intelligence to keep your car. If you're clever you'll run—I'm afraid you haven't a chance," he added, as he saw the red tail light of the car moving rapidly away. "The police are controlling this aërodrome, and you've a snowflake's chance of getting away."

"You're being a friendly little fellow and helping us:

is that what you're telling us to believe?" sneered Connor.

"Don't talk—walk," said the Gunner sternly. "I'm not in my best temper to-night. I've practically promised I wouldn't kill you, but it won't take a hell of a lot to make me change my mind."

"All right, Gunner, we'll go." Danty found his quaking voice. "Come on, Connor. The Gunner wouldn't put us in bad——"

"I found the letters, Danty," said Haynes softly. "You know just how near you are to eternal rest, don't you?"

Danty said nothing: he grabbed the arm of his reluctant friend and almost dragged him back to the roadway. They walked rapidly back the way they had come, and must have gone a hundred yards before Connor stopped.

"I'm not going to stand for this bird——" he began, when a voice behind him said: "Walk!" and he obeyed.

When he had seen them well on their way, the Gunner sped back to the car. Luke was awake; they were talking together in a low tone, he and this strange bride of his, and Gunner Haynes thought it delicate to leave them and interview the pilot.

He found the machine waiting, with two weary mechanics and an impatient pilot, and to the latter he gave new instructions. The other argument he employed was a very effective one, for the airman agreed cheerfully to all conditions.

"I can carry three or ten," he said. "There'll be no

difficulty about getting up. I've done this night trip hundreds of times."

Satisfied on this score, Gunner Haynes went back to the car and interrupted the more than usually intimate conversation.

"I've a little scrap of paper to give you when it's light enough to read it, Mrs. Maddison. It concerns the death of your brother—I'm sorry to be so brutal, but I think you ought to know that the man who ruined him was Danty, and——"

"I guessed that," she said quietly.

It was still drizzling and the clouds were low, but neither of the three passengers evinced the slightest anxiety as, with a roar of the engines, the big monoplane swept into the darkness, up and up, through the thick mist of clouds, until they emerged with the moon riding in a clear sky above them and billowing white clouds beneath.

Less than a week later, three people dined at the Café Ritz in Madrid, and the dinner was in the nature of a farewell banquet to Gunner Haynes, who was going to Naples to join the Australian mail boat.

"I shan't be comfortable till I get on board the Barcelona express," he said. "I've done many things in my life, but this is the first time I've played third to a honeymoon couple."

THE END

TO THE READER

If you have enjoyed Gunman's Bluff, *perhaps the following sample of Mr. Wallace's next book,* We Shall See, *will whet your appetite sufficiently to make you want to finish it.*

WE SHALL SEE

By Edgar Wallace

Chapter I

A SHOT IN THE DARK

I HAVE often wondered whether Dawkes was sincere when he told us that his sole desire, so far as the girl was concerned, was to get hold of her secret. He was a rich man, but that, of course, made little difference, for there are very few rich men of his calibre who do not wish to be a little richer or who are ever satisfied with their worldly possessions. There is, too, something of a kudos attaching to the working of a system, and a man who consistently wins at Monte Carlo gets a pleasure beyond the actual possession of easy money. He is courted by the women and made much of by the envious men, and to a fellow like Dawkes that sort of thing was as incense to the nostrils of the devout.

Perhaps he was genuine. I am inclined to think that he was, and that it was the girl's beauty and the sense of having her in his power that aroused the brutal passion of the man and brought about such a tragic ending to the interview.

I did not go straight to Billy's room the next morning. I wanted to see Levy Jones. He was rather more cheerful than I had expected, because he had got together the loose strings of the insurance case and had that morning placed the regular police in possession of a number of very important facts which led to certain wholesale arrests, which the reader may remember.

"Billy's got it bad," he said, shaking his head. "Do you realize that we've been in these darned offices for a fortnight and that Billy has never sat down once to his desk to do a bit of honest work?"

"What is he doing now?" I asked.

"He's stalking up and down the new carpet, taking years of wear out of it," said Levy sadly, "and I rather think from the ferocity of his countenance that he is rehearsing the nasty things that he is going to say to brother Dawkes."

"Did he tell you?" I asked quickly.

"He told me as much as it was good for me to know," said Levy with a sigh. "But, my dear Mr. Mont, I am so used to these exalted moments of Billy's that I have ceased to worry about them."

Nevertheless, he sighed again.

"Why couldn't she have been a plain woman?" he began, but shook his head. "It wouldn't have made any difference to Billy," he said bitterly. "So long as she was a good weeper and could turn on the sob music Billy was certain to fall."

"She is a very charming girl," said I in defence, and he looked at me in cold wonder.

"Have you got it, too?" he said sadly. "Well, it will be all over soon, and I've got a lovely case for Billy. To see him at his best you've got to put him on the track of a red-nosed bucket-shop keeper with a passion for onions."

Billington Stabbat was at a loose end. I saw that the moment I went into his office. He was standing staring gloomily out of the window, and taking an interest in little, inconsiderable things which only a distracted man could take. For example, there was a small panel in the recess of the window with which he fidgeted. I didn't discover the fact that it was a panel until he fidgeted to such purpose that it swung open on hinges, revealing a tiny dark cavity and the rough edges of the brickwork beyond.

"What's that?" said Billy, eager for distraction.

He peered down what seemed to be an interminable shaft and then remembered.

"Oh, yes, they had central heating in the building, but it wouldn't work. The pipes came up here from the basement, I think," he said, and closed the panel.

He was staring at it for quite a while, then he pulled

it open again—he had to use the paper-knife to get a grip on the edge.

"That would be a fine place to hide anything, wouldn't it?" he said.

"Yes," I replied. "If you wanted to go down into the basement to find it again."

He slammed the panel hard, threw the paper-knife on the table with a crash, and stalked up to the marble fireplace, with its lions sejeant and regardent. On the grinning head of one of them, he leaned an elbow and dropped his head on his hands.

"Good Lord!" he groaned. "Suppose she is! But it is absurd!"

"Suppose she is what? And what is absurd?" I asked.

"Don't be a fool, Mont," he snapped. "You know what I'm talking about. Suppose this dear girl has borrowed the money from the bank to help some rascally brother——"

"Or lover," I murmured.

"Don't be a brute," he almost shouted. "And for God's sake be decent, Mont. She has no lover."

"She has no brother, either, so far as you know," said I, lighting one of his cigars.

"Well, suppose all this has happened and she has borrowed the money from the bank?"

He was silent for a while, then:

"It would be tragic," he said.

I sat down in the chair and regarded him wonderingly.

"Honestly," said I, "do you always get like this over a woman case?"

I expected an outburst, but it did not come.

"I am always sorry for women," he said quietly, "but I have never loved a woman before."

And the simplicity of that confession silenced me. He walked across to the desk and stood towering over me, resting his palms on the edge.

"Mont," he said, "If Thomson Dawkes is offensive to this girl to-night I shall shoot him."

It was in the most matter-of-fact tone that he made this threat.

"Oh, rubbish!" said I. "In the first place he isn't going to be offensive, and in the second place you are not to shoot him."

"He has been on the 'phone to me this morning," he went on. "He says he wants to see the girl alone."

"Well," said I, "that isn't extraordinary. If he intends demanding something from the girl on the threat of exposing her, he is hardly likely to want a detective sergeant and an ex-detective officer as witnesses."

"I don't like it," said Billy.

"Did you agree to the private interview?"

He nodded.

"It doesn't matter very much. I shall be in Levy's room, and I shall come in at the first cry from the girl. And I tell you, Mont"—he smashed his fist on the desk —"if that blackguard insults her I'll—— Do you want me, Levy?"

This latter to Levy, standing in the doorway, his

hands in his pockets, his head bent on his chest, and looking straight at Billy.

"Whom are you killing, Billy?" he asked softly, and Billy smiled.

"Come in, Levy. Don't stand in the doorway."

"Whom are you killing, Billy?" asked Levy as he came forward.

"Dawkes," said Billy.

"Fine," said the sarcastic Levy. "I'll send lilies and Mont can send roses, and we'll come along and see you the day before you're hung. I want to tell you a story, Billy."

He sat down on the edge of the desk, and Billy, leaning against the wall, looked at him with a twinkle in his eyes.

"Go on. It's about a Hebrew."

"A young Hebrew," corrected Levy. "He was in a Sunday school at Glasgow, and the teacher asked the class who would like to go to heaven, and every hand shot up except one. 'Why, Izzy Isaacs,' said the teacher in surprise, 'don't you want to go to heaven?' 'No, miss,' said Izzy; "I want to go to hell, where our business is going.'"

Billy chuckled.

"*Verbum sapienti*," said Levy significantly.

"Meaning that there's where our business is going?" Billy clapped him on the shoulder. "We'll be through with this case to-day, Levy, and then I can devote my mind whole-heartedly to your outside brokers."

"If you were through with the case to-day I wouldn't

mind," said Levy, shaking his head, "but you're not going to be, Billy. I've got a feeling in my old bones that this job is going to last for a year and there's going to be trouble at the end of it, and maybe at the beginning of it," and he stalked gloomily forth.

"Do you remember that third-class ticket they found in Miss Ferrera's bag?" asked Billy when Levy had gone.

"To Brixton?" I said. "Yes."

"She has a cousin she stays with on her way from London to Monte Carlo," said Billy. "That's all."

I tried to get him on to some other topic, but only partially succeeded, for every now and again he would come back to the girl and his problem.

In the midst of a perfectly thrilling description I gave of the struggle we had had with our murderer on Wanstead Marshes he broke in:

"She carries a revolver in her bag. You see, she takes so much money about with her that she cannot afford to run risks. I knew that at Monte Carlo that night I talked with her on the terrace, because, swinging round, the bag struck my hand."

"She is a very capable young person," I said patiently, for no man likes to have the story of his own perils broken in upon. I refused his invitation to lunch and promised to come up at half-past seven that night. As a matter of fact, I did not get there until a quarter of eight, and Miss Ferrera had already arrived.

I could see that even the skeptical and hard-hearted Levy Jones was somewhat under her spell. As for Billy, his face was flushed and his eyes, which never left her face, were bright and sparkling. The girl was, as I expected, wholly self-possessed. Once again I saw that beautiful face in its loving-kindly aspect. I know it is a ridiculous word to apply, but there was something motherly about her, a certain soft tenderness in her voice which was not designed for Billy any more than it was designed for me, but was just the natural woman in her.

"He will insist upon the explanation," Billy was saying as I went in, and after shaking hands with me she went straight on to where he had left off.

"Then he must insist," she said calmly.

"Could you tell him the system?"

She smiled.

"It would be quite impossible to tell him the system," she said. "In the first place, it is not my system to give, and in the second place it would be impossible to give it offhand if it were. It is like asking me to explain the differential calculus to somebody who imagines it is a recent addition to the Zoo!"

Billy chuckled.

Further conversation was arrested by the arrival of Mr. Thomson Dawkes. To my surprise, he came alone. I had fully expected to see his shadow—for Inspector Jennings had become little else of late—following him into the room.

"I'm early," he said with a genial smile all round, "but I think we might get this business over as we are all here."

He looked from Mary Ferrera to Billy.

"I wish to speak alone with Miss Ferrera," he said, and Billy nodded and turned to the girl.

"If you want anything, Miss Ferrera, don't hesitate to call for me," he said pointedly. "Just ring that bell" —he indicated the push by the side of the desk—"and I will be with you before the bell stops ringing."

She nodded gravely, and we three left the room together.

Did Thomson Dawkes take Billington's implied threat seriously? I fancy not. He was a man who had a most inordinate faith in the power of money and in the authority which the possession of great wealth could impose. There was always something of good-natured contempt in his attitude toward Billy, and indeed toward the whole of the world. He gave me the impression that he was just humouring a capricious and inconsiderable man, and that also was the view which Billy took of his attitude.

I knew Billington Stabbat perhaps better than any living man, for we had been together in moments of supreme danger, when the very souls of men were bared by the sheer terror of their circumstances. And I knew that what in another person might be regarded as an idle piece of bluster had a deadly significance when it was uttered by my friend. Billy would not hesitate to destroy this big, smiling creature any more than he would hesitate to crush a beetle under his foot; and at the moment we left the room I uttered a prayer, a silent prayer, that that evening might end well. It was a prayer, unhappily, that was destined for rejection.

We gathered together, a curiously tense party, in Levy's office, which opened from the bigger room.

"I hope this interview is not going to last long," said Billy irritably. "If he dares——" He did not finish his words.

I could find nothing to say, and we sat there in silence and watched the slow minute hand of the clock move from ten minutes to eight to five, and still there came no sound from the room. Another five minutes passed, and then Billy, with a snarl, slipped from the table on which he was sitting, and began:

"I'm not going to stand this any longer. I——"

And then the interruption came.

It was the sound of a shot from the next room!

Billy leaped at the door and flung it open. The room was in darkness, but there was a switch near the doorway, and his hand found it and turned it down. I shall never forget the sight which met my eyes. Near the door leading into the corridor stood the girl, white-faced and staring like a thing demented. In her hand was a tiny revolver, and as the lights went on she lifted it from her side and looked at it with a kind of fascinated horror. It was Levy who broke the silence.

"We've lost a client," he said in a shaky voice.

Even in that awful moment his queer sense of humour did not desert him. And lost a client we undoubtedly had; for sprawling over the desk lay Thomson Dawkes, with a hideous wound in his head, and his blood lay in a pool upon the writing table.